No Sweeter Madness

SAGE RIDGE: BOOK THREE

DEVIN SLOANE

Contents

Sage Ridge

Hailey's Falls

Sage Ridge Resort

Downtown Sage Ridge

Silver Lake

Wildflower Bluffs

The Beaver Dam

BAR

Little River

Crystal Beach

Carousel Island

Hope Harbour

Hawk's Place

Dedication

For every woman who lost herself to motherhood.
And was brave enough to find herself again.

Playlist

Lansdowne – Used To Be

Camylio – I'm Sorry

Blu Eyes – Healing Hurts

Benson Boone – Beautiful Things

Diamante – Unlovable

Blake Shelton, Gwen Stefani – Nobody But You

Rachel Grae – Outsider

Seether – The Gift

Ashes Remain – On My Own

Live – The Dolphin's Cry

Live – I Alone

Halestorm, Amy Lee – Break In

Flights Over Phoenix – Hypnotize

Art Of Dying – Best I Can

Pink Floyd – Wish You Were Here

Nickelback – I'd Come For You

Fancy Cars, SVRCINA – I'll Follow

Jamestown Story – Barefoot and Bruised

Ashes Remain – Right Here

Kelly Clarkson – Breakaway

Camylio – Leaving Home

Ashes Remain – Everything Good

Failure Anthem – Here For Good

Christina Perri – A Thousand Years

https://open.spotify.com/playlist/1kCRl2pitJwbrTKOZaDsxq?si=
9937e7ac29ba47a1

1

The Edge of Indecision

On the outside, I wasn't much to look at.

My once hourglass figure had settled into that of a rather juicy pear. Chronic stress shadowed my eyes and aged me beyond my 39 years. Thankfully, my round cheeks saved me from premature wrinkles.

Score two points for cheesecake and mashed potatoes.

And yet, even with the increase in weight over the years, I was somehow half the woman I used to be. Sometimes I wondered if anyone saw me at all or if I'd simply shrunk into obscurity.

Inside told a different story.

Inside, I was swelling exponentially, my irritation growing to the point I feared my skin would split and spill out all my secrets and lies.

And I couldn't afford to fall apart.

"Renata," my mom cut into my thoughts impatiently. Picking up the teapot on the table between us, she topped up my cup. "Did you hear anything I said?"

Renata.

Only my parents called me by my full name, everyone else called me Wren. A very few special souls called me Wrennie. 'Renata' made me cringe as if I was in trouble.

She tutted in dismay at my purposefully blank stare. Annoyed, she continued, "I said, my friend's grandson who had autism was cured. You know how?"

I shook my head minutely, pressing my tongue against the roof of my mouth so hard I felt it in my ears.

Sitting in my usual spot at the kitchen table, I grazed the tip of my index finger over the deep scratch marring the otherwise pristine surface. Every year, my mother sanded the scratches and imperfections from the surface and revarnished it. Only this one tiny scratch, one I accidentally etched while working on an art project, defied her efforts.

Leaning forward, she leveled me with a hopeful gaze. "Prayer." She nodded excitedly. "It turned out he didn't truly have autism."

What did they do? Pray it away? Perform a quick, easy, run-of-the-mill exorcism in the Sunday school room between services?

"Mom," I interjected patiently despite the blood simmering in my veins.

She raised her palms. "Hear me out. Isn't it worth a shot? What if it works?"

Some days it was all too much. "Mom, we have to accept reality."

She leaned toward me, hope in her eyes. "The pastor's wife thinks it's worth a shot."

I quietly inhaled deeply through my nose and gritted my teeth together at the Pastor's wife backing advice most likely offered by the same good Christian women who got Audrey tossed from the Sunday school room for being too disruptive.

In retrospect, I should have thanked them for giving me the excuse to leave my parents' church without shouldering more of my father's disappointment. Evidently, they could still reach me.

Anger prickled uncomfortably underneath my skin, and it was all I could do to keep it there. "What exactly would we be praying for?"

For the first time, she began to look uncomfortable.

I tilted my head to the side. With my gaze steady and a polite smile on my face, I forced her to continue.

"Well," she twisted her hands in her lap, "the way they explained it was like," she swallowed, "like a... a... demon was on his back."

Though it was exactly as I expected, I still flinched. It wasn't the first time a loving sister in the church wondered aloud if there wasn't 'a demon on Audrey's back.'

Fucking lunatics.

My eyebrows rose. "So, like an exorcism."

Her face crumpled as I knew it would. Even she, wrapped as thickly as she was in denial, could not escape the insanity of this latest suggestion. "I wouldn't call it that."

"What would you call it?" I challenged briskly.

I was not opposed to prayer. I believed in it strongly. But I prayed for strength. Mercy. Patience. Perseverance. And humility. Not miracles.

And this was far from the first miracle cure my mom had touted.

First there were the specialized diets that claimed to calm gastro issues, which they did, and decrease inflammation in the brain, thereby curing autism, which they did not.

Raw milk, from a camel if possible, came next.

To my knowledge, there were no camels in Sage Ridge. I was positive, even if there were, I would not be trotting over with my trusty bucket to milk it.

But I wouldn't have put it past my mom.

Then came the cures touting the benefits of drawing out toxins followed by a nutrient regime that would put an Olympic athlete to shame. Both of which I forbade.

Her heart was in the right place.

Mostly.

If grossly misled.

As for my father, he claimed I desperately needed parenting classes. The type that might make me a stricter parent and give Audrey a more secure foundation that would eliminate her need to rely on those pesky autism behaviors to get what she wanted.

I looked at Audrey bathed in the weak winter sunlight streaming through the front window. She held up a crystal prism dangling from a string. Mesmerized, she twisted it in the light, throwing rainbows on the walls.

She was radiant, her pleasure evidenced by the small smile on her pale face.

There was no doubt Audrey needed assistance, but fly-by-night cures were an energy-sucking waste of time.

Behavior therapy, while effective if done correctly, required the finely tuned balance of a tightrope walker to toe the line between teaching and manipulating. There were not too many so adept.

Thank God for Brooklyn, her sunny shadow. She reclined behind Audrey even now, her furry butt pressed up against Audrey's, ever ready to pop up the moment Audrey needed her.

That dog was my saving grace and I loved her like a third child. She was the closest thing to a cure we'd found. And the only one we needed.

People meant well, but advice from those who did not have the first clue what it was to raise an autistic child grated against my ears like nails on a chalkboard.

Luckily, I learned the benefits of keeping my head down in my teens. It was a lesson I drew upon almost daily to quell my impatience and stem the retorts that more and more often sat ready to be expelled from the tip of my increasingly acerbic tongue.

My mom, who should have known better but refused to accept reality, pissed me off the most.

I'd lost count of the hours and energy I spent explaining autism to my mom, researching her miracle cures to show her the holes in the logic, then dealing with the disappointment, fear, and uncertainty that resulted from her lost hope. I spent so much time soothing her worries, I could ill afford the time to work through my own.

"Mom, all of these 'cures' are a waste of time. We need to focus on the things that do work, the things that give her a bigger, happier, life."

She furrowed her brow. "I just don't see much progress."

Her words hit me like a jackhammer, drilling deep into the ever-present fear that I wasn't doing enough. I didn't fool myself into believing she was pleased with Audrey's progress, but she'd never stated her opinion quite so baldly before.

Nor had she ever undermined my efforts quite so harshly.

Some small part of me, the part that understood intuitively that I deserved better, rose up and thundered in my ears.

She shrugged apologetically then hit me again. "I don't think what you're doing is working."

My hands trembled in my lap as I slowly inhaled a supposedly calming breath.

Every atom in my body vibrated with the urge to split.

Exhaling just as cautiously, I fought the storm threatening to suck all of us under.

Because as much as my mom irritated me, undermined me, and constantly questioned my parenting, she was the only person Audrey would stay with other than Aaron.

Aaron, the sweet result of the unplanned pregnancy that compelled my father to kick me out of the house while my mother did nothing to stop him.

Thank God for Max and his extended family.

Max.

I gave my head a small shake. It did not bear well to dwell on thoughts of Max.

My heart, desperate for a reprieve, latched on to the one subject sure to distract her. "Aaron said you called him yesterday?"

Her face brightened.

Despite my father's 'vast embarrassment' over the 'disgrace' I brought to our family, he fell in love with his grandson the moment he finally deigned to lay eyes on him. Aaron's existence and my sin sat in mutually exclusive boxes in my father's head. He thanked God for Aaron, his pride and joy, with one breath, and berated me for my foolishness with the next.

"Yes! I wanted to ask him how he's doing with school," her expression tightened, "and remind him to take care not to ruin his life."

For fuck's sake.

"I didn't ruin my life, Mom. Aaron is a blessing. Always has been." I abruptly pushed back from the table. "Aren't all children blessings from the Lord? Or is it just Aaron who's exempt?"

She twisted her hands in her lap while her mouth flapped like a fish out of water. Did she even know where my father ended, and she began? Away from him, she was fun and loving just as she was when I was growing up.

Around him she faded like an old photograph.

And every now and then, his words spewed from her mouth.

"I didn't mean it like that. There's no need to get upset. I'm simply disappointed—"

I cringed at the word then steeled my spine and cut her off. Smiling tightly, I gave my excuses. "Audrey and I have things we need to do."

Frowning, she looked up at me and opened her mouth to speak.

I shook my head in warning.

She offered me a small, hopeful smile. "I can keep her here, give you some free time. There's no need to take her with you."

I teetered on the edge of indecision. Because while it would be faster and easier for me to complete my errands on my own, Audrey needed more in her life than the four walls of our home, my parents' house, and school.

But leaving her would add at least another half an hour to my day as my parents lived on the outskirts of town beyond Hope Harbour. And I'd reached my maximum level of exposure to my mother for one day. Never mind the increased possibility of running into my father the later it got in the day.

I swallowed the ball of anxiety crowding my windpipe and quelled my internal shudder. "Audrey, let's go see Anita at Mary Lou's Candy Shoppe," I called cheerfully.

Audrey's head snapped up. She and Anita had a long-standing tradition of sneaking a small treat bag into Audrey's pocket. The last time I went back and tried to pay for them, Anita threatened to spank my bum.

It had been so long since I'd had any action, I almost took her up on it.

Audrey tilted her head to the side. "Brooklyn is coming with us."

"Of course," I agreed as she slowly rose to her feet.

She looked longingly at the crystal spinning in her fingers, her inner debate fierce. Watch the light bounce off the walls or Anita and candy?

Mom raised her voice. "Are you sure, Audrey? You can stay—"

"Mom," I interrupted sharply. "Don't."

She pressed her lips together and beseeched me with her gaze.

But I didn't have the energy to ease her anxiety.

"Don't," I simply repeated quietly. "We will see you one day next week."

2

Decadent

"**M**om?" Aaron bellowed.

Aaron never simply spoke, or called, or yelled, he bellowed. But then, that kid never did anything by halves.

"In the kitchen!" I called back.

He loped through the kitchen doorway. With a wide smile on his face, he dipped his knees to kiss my cheek. "Did Grandma tell you about our impromptu sex ed class?"

Tension radiated up my spine to prickle under the collar of my shirt. "Yes. She mentioned it when I was there yesterday."

He snickered and wagged his eyebrows. "Don't worry, Mom. I always make sure to ask a few questions."

My mouth dropped open. "You do?"

"Of course," he laughed as he nabbed an apple from the bowl on the counter. He took an enormous bite that didn't deter him one bit from continuing. "I give her back some of the crap she gives you."

Humiliation stung my eyes. I was essentially powerless to shield him from the infection of their attitudes. Grabbing the dishcloth, I turned away and swiped furiously at the already pristine counter.

"Don't think I don't see," he confided, resting a lean hip against the counter beside me.

That's the fucking problem. You shouldn't have to.

Gathering myself, I tossed the cloth into the sink and turned to him with a forced smile. I didn't care what she said to me but intimating to him that his existence rested on a mistake, or worse, a sin, added kindling to the fire growing steadily inside me.

He shrugged. "She's old and completely out of touch with reality."

I shook my head. "There's no excuse. Old doesn't mean you can't offer kindness and respect."

Old doesn't equal ignorance.

"It doesn't matter, Mom."

I forced a smile into my eyes and gave him my truth. "You do know you're the best thing that's ever happened to me?"

He swept an arm down the length of his body with a cheeky grin. "I'm perfect."

I barked out a short laugh. "You are. Now tell me, what kind of questions did you ask?"

A sly smile curved his lips. "Oh, you know, would a baby really ruin my life? Is pregnancy out of wedlock the worst thing that can happen to a family? Doesn't God say a baby is a blessing? Is it only some babies who are a blessing? Is adoption the best solution?" He shrugged. "Stuff like that."

I snorted out a laugh, half amused at his antics, more furious that he might secretly harbour those same questions. "And what does she say?"

"She stutters a bit then changes the subject."

"Does my father ever say anything to you?"

He snorted out a laugh. "Never. My conception is the family secret that everybody knows but no one talks about."

Asshole.

I wrapped my arms around his slim waist, my heart bleeding. "You are not now, nor have you ever been, a mistake."

He looped his arms around me and rested his cheek on top of my head. At nineteen, he towered over me. And he wasn't done growing yet.

"I was kind of a mistake," he murmured.

I smiled and answered the way he'd come to expect. "Only the best one I ever made."

"I love you, Momma." He squeezed me tightly for a moment then released me to toss his apple core into the garbage. Scrunching his nose, he rubbed a rough hand over his head nervously before blurting, "I picked up two extra shifts a couple of weeks ago. I just got paid and put the extra money in your account."

My stomach dropped. "You don't have to do that."

Regaining his equilibrium, he snagged a freshly baked roll off the cooling rack, stuffed half of it into his mouth, then proceeded to talk through that as well. "I'd much rather it come from me than you asking Grandma and Grandpa when we fall short." His eyes narrowed. "As good as they are to me and Audrey, they're kind of dicks to you. Especially Grandpa. It's fucked up because it's not like he's hurting for money."

I covered my eyes with my hand to hide my amusement and reprimanded him. "Aaron."

He wasn't wrong, but I appreciated the car they bought for him when he turned 18, and even more so, the account they continued to top up to cover his education. When he finished school, he wouldn't have a single loan to pay back.

Unlike me.

I suspected Aaron was my father's do-over. More likely he was simply the son he always wanted rather than the daughter he got.

It pained me to the depths of my soul that I wasn't able to give those things to Aaron, but that was my reality. And Aaron deserved every good thing. So, I held my tongue.

If I pissed them off, there was a real possibility Mom would curl up with her fragile feelings, which would infuriate my father. Only God knew what he would do. I scoffed to myself. And me. I knew very well what he might do. And I didn't want Aaron or Audrey to suffer through that rejection because of me.

My lip curled in self-disgust. There was also the part of me that still cringed away from the threat of his icy disapproval.

"What?" He played innocent. "Was it that I said fucked up or called them dicks?"

I huffed out another laugh, this one genuine. "Both."

He grinned. "It'll be our little secret."

"You're a menace." I smiled.

He grinned unrepentantly. "Anyway, my afternoon class was canceled. Why don't you leave now for work and take a couple of hours to yourself?"

I cocked my head to the side. "A couple hours to myself?"

Monday to Thursday, I worked the breakfast and lunch shifts at Susie Q's. It made for an early morning to school for Audrey, but she loved the before-school program, and I was able to pick her up as soon as school let out for the day.

On Fridays, I worked the lunch shift, ran out to pick up Audrey from school, and then went back to cover the Friday night dinner rush as soon as Aaron got home from school. Friday's dinner rush provided fantastic tips.

With Audrey off school for the day, I didn't make my lunch shift. Now that Aaron was home early, I suddenly had two free hours.

"Yeah," he reiterated. "Take some time for yourself. Me and the bean have plans. Bean!" he hollered.

Thank God our closest neighbor was hard-of-hearing.

"What?" she yelled back from her bedroom.

"Are we gonna do this or what?" He turned to me and offered a crooked smile. "Grab your stuff, say goodbye to the bean, and go, Momma. I got this."

I swallowed my objection. "Thank you, Sweetheart."

The Beanery boasted a sign with a dancing coffee bean wearing a beret for some unknown reason. Every day on the way home from school, we walked past that sign. When Audrey was a toddler, she'd point up at it excitedly. Finally, at the age of four, she said her first words, 'That me!' Aaron busted a gut laughing, and from that day onward, she became, for Aaron at least, 'the bean'.

Feeling like I won the lottery, I settled at a corner table with a hot cup of coffee, one I'd actually get to drink while it was still hot, and a jumbo chocolate croissant.

I closed my eyes as the rich, flaky pastry melted in my mouth. Unwilling to risk any distraction from the almost illicit pleasure, I didn't open my reader.

Two hours alone?

Decadent.

"You enjoying that, Wren?"

Speaking of decadent, my eyes snapped open as the deep voice that starred in my dreams skated up my spine and sent a shot of longing straight through my heart. I barely suppressed my shiver.

I think I just orgasmed.

"Max," I replied, my voice embarrassingly breathy. I touched my napkin to my mouth to buy a second to compose myself. Clearing my throat, I continued in my normal voice. "It's good. Very. Highly recommend."

Me. Cavewoman.

He smiled easily, that damned singular dimple winking at me just as it did on those summer nights so long ago.

Back then, it captivated me. Now, it tempted me beyond reason. Considering how I'd deteriorated over the years, and the fact I now had two children in tow, I assumed my born-again virtue was safe enough from his charms.

He held up the plate I hadn't noticed. "Already a fan." Jerking his chin toward the empty chair beside me, he asked, "May I sit?"

I blinked in surprise. *Sit? With me?*

"Sure!" I chirped like a maladjusted bird. This was the third time in as many months that Max had singled me out, and I was beginning to entertain dangerous ideas.

First, he sat with me and Audrey almost the entire length of the movie they played for the kids at the Sage Ridge Halloween Howler event.

Then at Susie Q's, he came in during my break and sat down with me while he waited for Hawkley and Daire.

Those two handsome devils gave off daddy vibes like nobody's business, and both were very much taken. Hawkley had married Max's younger sister, Noelle, while Harley and Daire tied the knot two short weeks ago. Those two were couple goals if I'd ever seen them.

Not that I was looking for a 'daddy'. Although I wouldn't say I'd turn one away.

I glanced at Max then quickly looked away.

Max? Max was not like them. Max was 6'3" of boy-next-door sweetness wrapped up in a man's strong, drool-worthy body.

Sitting there with him reminded me of the girl I once was.

The dreams I once held.

And the opportunities that slipped through my fingers.

"I wasn't expecting to see you here," he murmured as he settled onto the chair beside me, his elbow very nearly brushing mine. "Aren't you usually at Susie Q's at this time of day?"

My face flushed at his proximity. And his voice, God, I loved his voice.

I shrugged and tamped down my reaction to him. "Normally, yes, but Aaron's afternoon classes were canceled. He sent me out for a couple of hours of me-time."

Max's eyes smiled. "He's a great kid. You've done an incredible job with him."

My hand dropped onto the table.

I stared at him mutely, internally squirming with pleasure and pride.

He continued, not seeming to notice the effect his words had on me. "He works part-time at the resort?"

I nodded jerkily. "He works there on weekends mostly. Have you seen him there?" I asked, greedy to hear more about my sweet son.

"A few times. Harley adores him."

I brightened. Nothing made me happier than other people enjoying my kids.

"Really?"

"Oh, yeah." He laughed. "She said whenever she needs muscle, she looks for Aaron. Says he's always willing to kick in if needed somewhere else." He smiled. "Says he's funny as hell, too."

I could not fight my smile. "That's so good to hear."

"You're lucky to have him."

Reveling in his words, my gaze snapped to meet his and I unconsciously leaned toward him. "Yes. I am," I stated forcibly.

He cocked a quizzical brow and leaned in, his face mere inches from mine. "You'll get no argument from me."

I jerked back and tried to dismiss my overreaction with a polite smile. "Oh, you know…" My smile faltered as I petered off because he did know.

He was the first person I called when I found out I was pregnant. The only person I apologized to. I stared down at the table, the space between us heavy with transgressions from the past.

"Wren."

I closed my eyes briefly.

God, what I wouldn't give to be his.

I raised my chin and met his warm, brown eyes.

"It's ancient history. We were kids."

He picked my hand up off the table, touching me for the first time in twenty years, and curled his fingers around mine. His touch burned away the years as he continued quietly. "We probably would have torn each other apart back then. And we weren't committed to each other. You have nothing to feel bad about."

His touch was firm, his gaze steady.

The butterflies in my stomach settled. He'd always had a calming effect on me, as if by his very proximity, his nervous system regulated mine. He was so sure of himself. Steady. Unshakeable.

"I don't regret my actions," I confessed, bracing myself for what I was about to say next. "I can't because that would mean regretting Aaron. I never have." For once I forced myself to swallow my trepidation instead of my words. I took a breath and released them all at once. "But I have often regretted ruining my chance with you."

He shook his head, his grip on my hand tightening as his dark, serious, gaze locked on mine. "I wasn't ready for you back then. Nowhere close to ready for you. If I had been, Aaron wouldn't have been an obstacle."

The guilt I'd carried for almost two decades shrunk a fraction of an inch. "Really?"

"Truly."

That damned dimple winked at me again. This time the zing of awareness hit me much lower.

We'd never, not ever, ventured down this road since I came back from school pregnant with Aaron.

I narrowed my gaze on his face. What was he playing at?

Abruptly, he glanced at his watch, released my hand, and stood. "Are you working tonight?"

"Yes." My eyebrows flew up at the sudden change. Did he regret this trip down memory lane?

He pressed his lips together as his eyes wandered over my face, and he nodded briefly. "I have an appointment in a few minutes so I've gotta run, but I'll see you later."

I stared up at him, wondering how we'd gotten to this in-between place. Wishing things were such that we could go further even as I berated myself for my foolishness.

I nodded like a dashboard dolly. "Sure."

At the door, he turned back. "Make sure you seat me in your section."

Before I could gather my wits to answer, the door swung shut behind him.

3

Currency

Susie Q's boasted a tiny entranceway that immediately opened up to a large, square-shaped, homestyle eatery. Booths lined three walls, two of which were mostly windows. Each window boasted quintessential café curtains in a cheery, slightly faded, coastal blue.

The tables were uniform, but the wood chairs boasted a mishmash of muted greens and blues in several different styles. Framed pictures and sea-themed décor covered almost every inch of the exposed brick wall. Susie often switched pictures and challenged Audrey to guess what she changed.

It was a test Audrey never failed to pass. She loved that game.

Susie Q's wasn't large but boasted a steady stream of customers. An hour and a half into my shift, thankfully, I was running my feet off. More people equaled more orders equaled more tips which equaled more shoes and clothes and books for the kids.

And fifty-dollar antlers for Brooklyn whenever they went on sale.

It was a good thing the people of Sage Ridge were generous with their tips because they barely had an ounce of my attention all night.

Whenever the damn door opened, I spun to look. And each time the absence of Max's large frame hit me with a blast of relief along with a sharp stab of disappointment. I gave myself a good, mental shake. Dwelling on unattainable dreams would only lead to despair. I'd already traveled down that road once. I didn't relish a return trip.

Max was a harmless fantasy when he had held himself at a distance. Talking to him and spending time with him fueled it with hope, and that was dangerous. Whatever this was would sputter out, now or later, with the same result. Better for it to end now before my impulsive, jump-first, think-later, heart got involved.

That perfectly sound advice didn't stop me from scanning the room, the doorway, and even the sidewalk outside for him.

Distracted, I swung through the wrong door to the kitchen and slammed into Susie.

"Oof," she grunted, staggering back.

My eyes widened at the cranberry juice splattering her near head-to-toe. "Susie! I'm so sorry!" I grabbed a roll of paper towels and began to blot the front of her uniform.

Shit, shit, shit.

My heart pounded.

Was she angry?

I kept my head down.

"Whew! That's one way to cool me off!" Susie grabbed the paper towels from my hand. "Don't be feeling up an old lady, now. John will take offense." She winked. "Either that or he'd want to watch," she hooted at her own joke.

My face split into a grin and I shook my head as relief washed over me. "I'm so sorry, Susie. I don't think there's any getting that stain out. I'll pay for its replacement."

"Bah! Don't worry about it, doll. Anita is a laundry whiz. She'll have no problem getting this out for me." She laughed and waved away my concern. "We get by with a little help from our friends, right?"

She looked into my dubious face and squeezed my shoulder. "It really is okay, Wren. You're allowed to screw up. Perfection is over-rated." She chucked me under my chin with a gentle finger. "Good enough is good enough, yeah?"

I offered her a tight smile as I fought to hide the anger that momentarily flashed hot and bright.

Good enough didn't provide Aaron the means to get to school. Sage Ridge had no bussing, and Aaron refused to stay in the student residence.

Good enough meant Audrey fell through the cracks.

I could not afford a single misstep. Because when I screwed up, everybody suffered.

"You don't believe me. That's okay, someday you will." She smiled softly. "I have faith in you."

Her words rolled around in my head for the rest of my shift. The longer I turned them over in my mind, the greater my sense of hopelessness.

The parameters of my life were tight, the margin for error almost non-existent. I would never be perfect- that ship had sailed long ago but my definition of good enough meant everybody got what they needed. And I wasn't even close to meeting that.

Audrey needed an awful lot. So far I was the only one who could give it to her.

Teachers at school were great, but their understanding of her needs was limited by the boundaries of their education, their experience, and most importantly, their time that was necessarily divvied out amongst too many students.

My parents stepped in here and there, but their brand of support came with a boatload of anxiety from my mom and not-so-subtle reprimands from my father. And they could not support what they would not accept.

The Sage Ridge community, other than the churchy people my parents hung out with, were mostly accepting. Susie and Anita were wonderful with Audrey and Aaron, always had been. Rachel from Artitude was one of Audrey's favorite people, and she'd stepped in to look after Aaron on more than one occasion when he was small. Harley's parents, Dan and Lou, gave me a job and a home when I had neither. They fed me more times than I could count, and offered to keep me on even after my father ordered me to return home.

I should have stayed with them.

But I couldn't in good conscience burden them further. I'd already wracked up a debt I could never hope to repay. And as my father said, I was not their burden to carry.

There were plenty of good people in our lives.

It seemed Harley had taken Aaron under her wing at work. That warmed me to no end.

If it wasn't for Harley, we wouldn't have Brooklyn. I owed that girl more than she would ever understand. After what she did for us, my love for her was unconditional. If she called me and confessed to murdering somebody, I'd show up with a plastic tarp, a canister of gasoline, and a shovel.

When Brooklyn came, she brought peace to our home. Audrey's tantrums, which had been legendary, drastically decreased in both intensity and number with her furry friend to ground her. And in the space of that newfound peace, Aaron blossomed.

With Brooklyn by her side, Audrey could go out in public and take in new experiences without melting down. School became a pleasure for her rather than the torture it was previously. At home, Brooklyn provided the companionship Audrey was not yet ready to pursue with her peers.

Brooklyn was her touchstone. Her lucky charm. Her friend. Her rock. Her center. And her guide.

And when Audrey went to bed? Brooklyn divvied up her attention between Aaron and me, often curling up on the couch between us. When she wasn't working, she was an adorable bubblehead. And we loved her. All of us.

So, it wasn't like I had no support. My community had done a lot for us, and I loved them all the more for it.

But it barely scratched the surface of the stresses and demands of our everyday reality.

When the school called me on those occasions Audrey was having one of her bad days, I had to decide whether or not I could afford to lose that day's pay. If I couldn't, it meant calling my parents. Which inevitably led to a discussion of autism cures, parenting skills, lamentations over my lost potential and low-paying job, and concern over Audrey's lack of progress.

Either way, I paid. The only difference was currency.

At home, we had three separate locks and an alarm on our front door. It hadn't happened since Brooklyn came home, but Audrey had been prone to wandering.

If something scared her? She ran and hid.

If something caught her attention? She followed it. Didn't matter where or how far. Once I followed her a hundred yards into a cornfield, my heart in my throat, wondering if she'd even once turn around.

She didn't.

Homework was a nightly battle.

Toilet training took years.

And Aaron. I'd let him down more times than I could even remember. Countless times he'd requested my presence, and my attention, and I failed to show up because Audrey's needs were greater, or at least, louder.

It broke my heart.

I couldn't even hope to be good enough for Aaron because Audrey's needs always took precedence over his. By necessity. Still, I would have loved to have been able to divide my attention more evenly.

A frigid breeze swept through the restaurant. My gaze swung back to the door only to be disappointed yet again.

It was almost time to close. I had to accept he wasn't coming. With the direction my thoughts had taken, it was just as well.

I swallowed my disappointment, quashed my hope, and served my final customers for the night.

I came with far too much baggage. What man would want to take us on?

To me, Audrey was every good thing. But I wasn't ignorant to her challenges. I couldn't deny my fear for her future or the fact I would have spared her the struggle if I had the choice.

Susie cashed me out and topped up my tips.

"Susie…" I protested.

She raised a palm. "Nope."

"But—" I tried again.

She dipped her chin and leveled me with her 'mom' stare. "Goodnight, Wren. Thank you for all your hard work tonight. You make Fridays tolerable for me. These legs aren't what they used to be."

I ducked my head, fighting tears yet again. I was turning into a veritable faucet. I blinked them away impatiently and nodded briefly. "Thank you."

As usual, she pressed a large takeaway container into my hands, the consequences of which had contributed greatly to my juicy figure. "There's enough in there for the three of you for dinner tomorrow." She gave me a second, smaller one. "This one is for you when you get home. You didn't have time to eat tonight. And if you can make it in tomorrow for the lunch rush, I won't turn you away."

I trudged home, my pockets, and my conscience, just a little bit heavier.

4

Trajectory

I eased the front door open and shut it just as quietly.

"She's sleeping, Mom," Aaron stated quietly. Aaron had been trained at a young age never to disrupt Audrey's sleep. It was perhaps the only time he was quiet.

Sprawled across our wide leather couch, he was watching some reality tv show that was slowly but surely rotting his brain. One hand lazily scratched Brooklyn behind her ears, the other kept tabs on the messages coming through on his cell phone.

He grinned at me. "She's sleeping like the dead."

I scowled, my superstitious mind gasping at the audacity of tempting fate. "Don't say that."

He laughed.

He laughed all the time. That, I'd gotten exactly right.

I held up the take-away containers. "Are you hungry?"

"Nah, I ate my dinner and half of Audrey's." He smiled sheepishly.

"If you're still hungry, I have this small one."

"You eat it, Momma."

I didn't argue. Now that I was home, my stomach was making itself heard.

I looked around our place as if with new eyes. Our apartment, located over a business just a few doors down from The Beanery, was small but comfortable.

Not just physically comfortable, but emotionally comfortable.

I could be myself here.

So could Aaron.

And Audrey, God bless her, was herself without a single care for who she might offend everywhere. But she was her happiest self here at home.

Our couch, bracketed by two large, equally inviting reading chairs, faced a wall equipped with a large TV, a stereo system complete with a turntable, Aaron's guitars, our collection of vintage vinyl, and our books.

Brooklyn's enormous bed nestled in the corner between the couch and one of the chairs, but more often than not, she claimed space on the couch beside one of us.

The wall behind the couch hosted a collage of frames, some of which displayed pictures of us, others showcased Aaron's photographs, and the rest boasted an ever-changing array of Audrey's artwork.

The adjacent wall, little more than a massive window, faced the street. Hand-blown glass hearts, a bittersweet souvenir from my youth, cascaded down from their mobile and caught the light from the streetlights outside.

Some days I reveled in their delicate beauty, other days I couldn't stand the sight of them.

The galley kitchen emptied into a tiny dining room with just enough room for four to sit and eat comfortably which was one more than we ever had. Its tiny size was never a problem. The scratch and dent surface of our table offered a visible testimony to the Lego, wood-burning kits, sports equipment, and science projects that had abused it over the years.

One day, I'd refinish it.

The bathroom separated my bedroom from Audrey's, while Aaron occupied the tiny den off the family room. It didn't have a closet and the window was small, but he plastered the walls with posters as well as his own photography and made it his own. He had outgrown the futon some time ago but didn't want a bigger bed as it might interfere with his gaming set-up.

When Audrey's father, David, and I were married we had a house with a backyard.

Moving to this apartment broke my heart in so many ways. It took a while, but we grew to be happy again here. And here is where we became a family so tightly knit nothing could unravel us.

Thank God, David didn't take anything with him other than his half of the house or we'd be sitting on the floor.

"Are you working tomorrow?"

Aaron stretched and stuck his hand under his shirt to scratch his flat tummy. "First thing. I'll be gone before you even wake up, lazybones."

"Ha," I scoffed, though it was more than likely true.

Audrey tended to catch up on her sleep on Saturday mornings. Sometimes I slept in, other times I caught up on laundry and prepared our meals for the week.

"Want to watch a movie?" I offered.

Looking stricken, he faced me. "I was going to head out for a bit."

I quickly shook my head. "No problem. Go have fun."

His eyes narrowed and his brows scrunched together. "Are you sure?"

"Pass over the remote, son, and nobody gets hurt."

The worry on his face dissipated. He chuckled as he stood up and looped his arm around my neck. Turning momentarily serious, he bent low to tuck his face into my neck.

No matter how big he got, he was still my baby.

"You're the best, Momma."

My throat tightened.

I closed my eyes.

Wrapped one arm around his slender waist and squeezed. "You're pretty okay too, kid."

From the window, I watched him lope down the street and whispered a prayer over his retreating form. Checking on Audrey, I carefully eased her door open and tiptoed inside. She did sleep like a rock but I still didn't dare sit on the edge of her bed.

Asleep, she looked like any other twelve-year-old girl. It was her mind that was so utterly complicated.

Sensitive.

I loved her with everything I had. When David left, I promised to love her enough for both of us. The pain in my heart when I looked at her told me like nothing else did that I'd succeeded.

The memory of Aaron's face when David left flashed into my mind making me flinch. Aaron was only three when I met David, and he was the only father Aaron had ever known. It made no difference. David left when Aaron was ten, and never looked back.

I would never forgive him for that.

I closed my eyes. *Forgive me Father, I know it's wrong, but I am but dust.*

Dropping my clothes in the hamper inside my bathroom, I changed into pajamas and retrieved the dinner Susie packaged up for me then settled into the corner of the couch.

Unfurling the edges of the foil, the smell of shepherd's pie hit me.

Thank you, Susie.

I breathed it in, my mouth watering. Thoughts of Max and home and girlhood dreams as fleeting as wisps of moonlight wrapped around me.

I opened my email while I ate. Most of it was junk, subscriptions I signed up for on a whim. Most centered around some kind of self-improvement, but I never read or followed up on any of them. When I had spare time, I turned to my books for company.

Foregoing the tv, I finished my latest read, *The Realm of You* by Amanda Richardson, and mulled over the wonder that a single decision could change the entire trajectory of a life.

Was there an alternate reality where I was happily married to Max? One where we had children together?

I mentally drew back from the idea. Not for anything or anyone would I give up my children. But what if I could have had both?

What decisions had I made, or not made, after having my kids that might have changed the trajectory of my life?

The education I couldn't finish.

The jobs I didn't apply for.

The boundaries I didn't set.

The risks I didn't take.

And the excuses I made for each and every one of them.

I rested my head on the back of the couch. Brooklyn, her intuition on point as always, climbed up beside me and laid her head in my lap.

I was so damn lonely, starved for adult company.

Yearning to be touched.

Loved.

Tired, but in mind, not body. Tired of myself. Tired of my excuses. Tired of living in survival mode with constant vigilance my default setting.

Tired of the monotony of my routine, the struggle to keep everything going, monitoring Audrey's mood to stay one step ahead of her while keeping my finger on Aaron's pulse to ensure he, too, was okay.

Brooklyn jumped off the couch and sniffed around her toy basket until she put her mouth on the stuffed elephant we bought her for Christmas which Audrey named, quite appropriately, Elephant.

With her sad, droopy eyes trained on my face, she stepped back up on the couch and dropped Elephant in my lap. Her chin followed a moment later.

I scratched her ears. "I love you, Brooklyn."

Her thick coat was smooth under my palm.

"I should be happy," I murmured. "I feel bad that I'm not but sometimes a girl wants more, you know? Is that wrong?"

You're talking to a dog. It's safe to say you could use some adult company.

"I don't have the best track record with men, yet I still want a good man to call my own."

There's nothing wrong with that. People say love makes the world go around for a reason.

"I don't have very much to offer."

We all know you're a freak in the sheets just waiting to happen.

I chuckled at my imaginary conversation with Brooklyn, then admitted my greatest shame in a whisper. "I'm so angry, Brooklyn. I'm so angry and I don't know why."

Then it's well past time you figured it out.

5

Excuses

Contrary to expectations, Audrey woke up bright and far too freaking early on Saturday morning. And she was ready to boogie.

I supposed that was my penance for my two hours of freedom the day before. Any change in my routine knocked her off hers.

"Let's go see Anita," she suggested sprightly.

"What are you after, Bean?"

"I want a waffle cone."

My stomach fell. "Anita doesn't make waffle cones in the wintertime."

Her brow furrowed for a moment, then she smiled. "She'll make one for me."

I knew for a fact the waffle maker wasn't set up. "How about a candy apple? Anita makes candy apples in the winter. Do you want one of those? Or maybe a giant cookie?"

"I want a waffle cone," she reiterated, growing frustrated with my seeming inability to understand her.

"You want a waffle cone."

"Yes," she replied, relieved.

"Me, too. Where can we get one?"

She looked at me suspiciously. "Anita."

I shook my head no. "Anita doesn't make them in the wintertime."

She scowled, the bad news sinking in. "Can we at least go see her?"

That we could do. Relieved her disappointment didn't escalate into a full-fledged meltdown, I would have taken her anywhere. We bundled up to brave the short walk from our place to Mary Lou's, Brooklyn padding along in her service vest beside Audrey.

When the vest went on, Brooklyn slipped into working mode. She was quiet, took up as little space as possible when at rest, and remained alert to Audrey at all times. Take it off and she was just as goofy and loveable as any other Labrador.

It was barely past 9:00 am when we pulled open the door to Mary Lou's and walked in.

"Hi, girls!" Anita greeted us with a smile before turning her attention to Audrey. "My first customers of the day! What can I get for my favorite girl today?"

Audrey marched up to the counter. "I'd like a waffle cone."

Anita's face fell. "I don't have any waffle cones, sweetheart." She thought for a minute. "However, I do have a waffle cookie you might like?"

"Can you show me?" Audrey asked, heading toward the display case.

As soon as she made her choice, she began yanking at the zipper of her coat. "I'm overheating."

"Take off your coat," I replied, settling Brooklyn under a table in the back corner where we wouldn't be a bother to other customers.

Her voice rose. "I'm overheating!"

Brooklyn immediately trotted over and leaned against Audrey's legs.

Audrey frowned fiercely, her face rapidly turning red. "I can't get my zipper down! It's stuck and I'm overheating!"

I reached for her zipper, but she slapped my hand away. "I'm overheating!"

"Would you like me to help you with your coat?"

"It's stuck!"

"May I try?"

"It's stuck," she said louder.

"It's stuck. And you're overheating. Do you think I might be able to help you get it off?"

"I don't know. Maybe. I'm too hot."

I reached for her again. "I'll just give it a try."

As quickly as possible, I pulled her zipper down and slipped her coat off her shoulders. "Better?"

She took a deep breath and twisted her wrists around in concentric circles. "Better."

Anita came out from behind the counter. "Audrey, do you want to come into the back and help me make some waffle cookies?"

Her hands stilled as she considered Anita's offer. "Can Brooklyn come?"

Anita shook her head solemnly, well used to the routine. "No. No dogs allowed in the kitchen. We can't have Labrador fairy dust in the food."

Audrey shook her head and moved toward Anita. "It's not fairy dust, it's just fur." She slipped her hand into Anita's. Eye contact was off the table, but Audrey loved to hold the hands of people she loved. "Labradors shed a lot in the spring and summer. Once the weather turns colder, they begin to grow in their winter coat. Brooklyn is wearing her winter coat but soon it will be spring, and she will shed like a beast."

I snorted at hearing her use the same expression I did to describe Brooklyn's shedding.

The door to the kitchen swung closed behind them only to open again almost immediately, a stunningly pretty woman about my age coming out from the back with a huge smile on her face. "My aunt just kicked me out of the kitchen. Said it's her special time with her apprentice and I needed to give them some space."

"Oh, I'm sorry," I explained. "Audrey is autistic, and it takes her time to warm up to strangers."

She waved away my apology. "No need to apologize. I'm the intruder here, not her." She busied herself at the glass for a moment before looking back at me. "I'm Bridget. My friends call me Bridge."

"Hi Bridget, I'm Renata. My friends call me Wren."

"Bridge and Wren it is then." She winked.

My head filled with so many questions I didn't know what to ask first. "Are you visiting?"

She cocked her head to the side and pressed her lips together before grabbing a plate and ducking back behind the glass. "Not sure. This might be a stop along my way, or it could be my end point. It depends how it goes."

"What are you looking for?"

Her face blanked of all expression. "Peace."

Peace.

She wanted peace, and I craved excitement.

She shimmied slightly and smiled once more. "I'm a chocolatier. There's not a huge demand for my profession, and I'm not interested in leaving it behind for something practical, so I'll have to find a place that suits."

"That's admirable."

She cocked her head to the side. "How do you figure?"

"Well," I began, flames of anger cooking up an uncomfortable serving of jealousy. "I'm a server at Susie Q's. Susie is great, the job pays well, but I wouldn't say it's my calling."

"What is your calling and why can't you follow it?" Grabbing two glasses off the shelf, she turned to the sink.

A waste of time.

I laughed but didn't sound happy. Why was I ripping open my chest to this stranger? I looked into her eyes and found a reflection of my own.

She wasn't untouched by pain. But could she be trusted? It didn't matter, it wasn't like she'd be staying. How much demand could there be for a chocolatier in Sage Ridge?

"I have so many reasons, I'm just not sure how many of them are simply excuses."

"Ah, you're scared."

"Oh, definitely," I agreed, a sense of relief as gentle as a summer rain settling over me at the admission. Offloading a little honesty tasted surprisingly sweet.

Carrying a tray with a plate of cookies and two ice waters, she rounded the counter to my table.

My spine straightened. Few people understood service dog etiquette. Fewer still accepted correction with grace.

"Don't worry, I'll ignore your doggo when she's wearing her vest."
She set the tray down and seated herself across from me. "Have a
cookie. It's on me."

"Thank you," I answered politely. Gingerly, I reached out and took
a cookie. It would be rude not to take one, but I couldn't just not pay.
Anita already gave Audrey way too many freebies.

I nibbled on the edge, then relaxed. I'd simply pay Anita when
Bridget went back into the kitchen.

My anxiety dissipated, and I took a larger bite. "This is so good! Is
this a new recipe?"

"It's one of my recipes, more chocolate than cookie," she replied
with her mouth full. She pushed the last bite into her mouth and rolled
her eyes. "Mm, chocolate."

I agreed with a sigh. "There's just something about chocolate that
does it for me."

She smirked. "It does it for most of us. Do you have any other
children?"

"A boy." I smiled warmly. "Aaron is 19. He goes to college and
works part-time at the Sage Ridge Resort. He's a great kid."

"He's lucky he has a momma who loves him so much."

I shook my head firmly. "It's not hard."

"Married? Engaged? Slumming with the town bad boy?"

I snorted out a laugh. *In love with the town's good boy, maybe.*

Where I hesitated with my questions, Bridget had no such compunction. I wasn't sure how I felt about it. Impressed? Envious? I'd
love to be so forward instead of biting my tongue all the damn time.

I took a sip of water and answered, "Divorced."

She nodded and wiped her mouth with a napkin. "Me too. Well,
at least I'm headed in that direction. It's all signed, sealed, and in two
more weeks, it will be delivered."

"I'm sorry."

She shook her head, her face grim. "Don't be. I'm not."

Walking back home, with a much happier Audrey, my cell phone rang. As serendipity would have it, Grandma and Grandpa planned to pick Audrey up to take her to the movies. Which meant I could work the lunch shift at Susie Q's.

By the time it was over, I wished I hadn't.

6

Different Worlds

The relief on Susie's face when I walked through the door made me doubly glad I made it in.

"I'm so glad you're here. I have an idea I'd like to pitch to you. Can we meet next week?"

"Sure," I answered slowly. "What kind of idea?"

She waved me away. "Something that could increase your hours and decrease your stress." She paused. "And mine."

Increased hours and decreased stress sounded good; I just didn't see how it would be possible.

"Where's Audrey today?"

"With my parents."

Her eyebrow rose leading me to believe she understood more about my family situation than I let on. "You called them?"

"No, honestly, I didn't plan on coming in." I studied her expression warily, hoping she didn't take that to mean I didn't value my job.

"They wanted to take her to a movie, so I ran over as soon as they picked her up."

Her face softened. "You need some time to yourself, too. I would have understood if you decided not to come in, but I'm really glad you're here."

I smiled back. It felt good to be wanted, but it felt even better to be appreciated.

Working Saturdays was a rare event for me but after two hours it was more than evident Susie needed the help. There were three of us on the floor, and not one of us had managed to sneak in a break.

I barely had time to think, but when I did, I thought about Bridget. *Bridge.*

She possessed romance novel heroine level of gumption. I bet she didn't hold her tongue for anybody. She was bold, direct, and un-flinching about her hopes and dreams for herself.

She didn't hesitate to put herself in my space. She just assumed she'd be welcome and marched right over with her tray of chocolate cookies while I'd approached everyone with caution even as a child and learned to keep my distance as an adult.

Not one of the moms I connected with when Audrey was a baby had maintained contact with me after her diagnosis. There were only so many times I could cancel or leave abruptly when Audrey couldn't cope before people stopped making plans with me. I understood, but it hurt.

As for my old high school friends, we lost touch when I got pregnant with Aaron.

The door swung open just as I passed, the cold air skating around my ankles. Noelle Bennett breezed in, her handsome husband half a step behind her carrying baby Hunter who was snugly tucked into his car seat.

Hawkley and Noelle had always belonged together though they took their sweet time getting there. Around eight months old now, Hunter was one of those deliciously plush babies you couldn't help but squeeze.

Hunter was named after Hawkley and Harley's brother. It still hurt me to think about him.

There wasn't a person in town who hadn't been touched by that family's kindness in one shape or another, and losing Hunter ripped every single one of them apart. Ripped the whole town apart, including me. He'd been kind to me when my world fell apart.

"Hi, Noelle." I smiled warmly. Noelle was a year or two behind me in school, but I'd hung out with her a bit that sweet summer I spent with Max. "Hunter's getting so big!"

"Heavy, too!" she quipped. "How are you doing, Wren? How's Audrey? I see Aaron at the resort. He's practically a man now!"

"He is!" I beamed. "Audrey's doing well and Aaron, honestly, that kid is my saving grace. Table for two plus a highchair?"

"No, actually more of us are coming." She turned to Hawkley. "How many are we, Hawk?"

A photograph of Hawkley Bennett featured beside the definition of grumpy and slightly feral alpha male in the dictionary, but when he looked down at his pretty wife, his face almost softened into a smile.

Turning to me he gave a polite nod. "Eight including Hunter's highchair."

I nodded. "No problem. Give me a minute to set you up."

Susie wandered past as I fixed the tables. "I know they're in my section, but it's starting to slow down. Do you think you can manage?"

"Sure!" It would give me an opportunity to ogle that beautiful baby, though the sight of the happy family sparked a flame of shameful jealousy in my heart.

Fifteen minutes later, when the newlyweds, Harley and Daire rolled in with Shae, another girl I used to go to school with, I was happier still. Harley was, and would always be, one of my favorite people.

Bridge walked in shortly afterwards and exclaimed with pleasure when she saw me, surprising me with an exuberant hug before joining the rest of them at their table.

One seat left. My heart squeezed in my chest because I suspected I knew whose it was.

I would be serving Max and his friends. Two of whom were attractive single women. Was he seeing one of them?

And what does it matter if he is? You should never have entertained even the idea of him.

I closed my eyes momentarily.

Bridge would be perfect for him.

Who was I kidding?

Shae would also be an excellent choice.

They were a lot alike. Both beautiful, effervescent, outgoing, confident women who would match perfectly with his tall, dark, and drop-dead fucking gorgeous.

They were everything I wasn't and carried less baggage.

I marched resolutely over to the table, calling on my inner Susie. "Can I start you off with something to drink while you look at the menu?"

Shae, her long blond ponytail swinging, looked up at me. Her eyes narrowed for a moment, then she brightened. "Wren?"

I smiled warmly, as I would with any customer. "Hi, Shae. It's been a long time. How've you been keeping?"

Small talk came easy to me, it was the deeper stuff I struggled with. After the expected back and forth, she recited the same old tired line, "We should get together."

Oh, God. The big smile, the enthusiastic offer to make plans that never came to fruition. No matter how I warned myself not to have hope, my stupid heart didn't listen.

Making things worse, she turned to Harley. "Harley, let's pull Wren into our next get-together."

"Oh, that's okay," I began, my face flushing.

Shae's eyebrows flew up. "Nonsense. I've been wasting away in Mistlevale. I need to get out and reconnect with everyone."

"It's just that, I've got Audrey and it's difficult to make plans due to her needs."

Harley perked up. "We can be flexible, Wren. It's no problem."

"Sure, I'd love that," I replied statically. It was the standard, expected response, and the only way to call a halt to the conversation. I forced an excited lilt to my voice even as I dealt with the surety it wouldn't go anywhere.

The door opened.

I stiffened as both Shae and Bridge looked up to see who had come in. And I knew by the light of appreciation in their eyes it was Max.

Tall and dark, his body lashed with lean muscle, his gorgeous face blessed with the deepest of dimples. Anyone with eyes couldn't help but appreciate the view.

I excused myself quickly and scurried back to the kitchen with my gaze trained on my notepad to avoid meeting Max's eyes. As if he'd even notice me with those two beauties eyeing him like he was a thick wedge of chocolate.

I threw my apron up on a hook. "Be right back, Susie. Just going to the ladies' room."

I'd never been so grateful as I was at that moment that Susie Q's had family-style bathrooms. No one would come in and see me, my face pale, lips stark white, eyes wide with pain I had no business feeling after all these years.

Was it him? Or was it just everything he represented?

I ran the cold water, rolling my hands under the icy spray, a trick I picked up to help stave off my overwrought emotions when they threatened to upend me. I held them under the tap until they stung, then continued to hold them there until my skin numbed. Turning off the water, I pressed my icy, wet hands to my face and breathed through the memories.

It was the summer before my third year of university, when my favorite place was nestled snug in Max's strong arms, laughing at something he said, his cheeky dimple winking at me, dark eyes warm on my face.

The night before I left for school, he came to my house and told me he thought we should take a break.

The first month in student residence, nursing a broken heart, crying for a solid month. When the pain became too much to bear, I boomeranged, reveling in being out from under my father's thumb after commuting for the first two years.

I soaked up the sudden deluge of male attention like a dry sponge, went to parties at the neighboring university with the girls from my small dormitory, drank just enough to lower my inhibitions, and finally, woke up in someone else's bed, my v-card punched, a sickeningly sticky residue between my thighs.

I remembered *him* asking to take me out to breakfast.

Wanting my phone number so he could see me again.

Me fleeing as if my life depended on it.

My late period.

Those two pink lines.

The horror I felt calling Max even though he was the one to break things off before I left, telling me we'd catch up at Christmas.

I gave no excuse for my actions. I couldn't. Everything that happened was on me. My decisions led me to the place where I lived without a hope for us.

The brutal pallor of the father-to-be when I informed him I was pregnant. It took me a week to find him. Just as I'd been about to give up, he walked out of his university library.

His pleasure at seeing me faded fast. I stoically let him off the hook because I preferred to do it on my own rather than be tied to someone who would view us as a burden.

I covered my eyes, the icy chill of my hands distracting me from the shame of Harley's parents taking me in.

And Max's certain hand in all of that.

I couldn't even think about the day my dad threw me out without getting dizzy.

My breath shuddered in and out.

Once.

Twice.

Then once more before evening out.

I conjured up my cozy home in my head and my heart rate slowed. My record albums and my reading chair, Brooklyn's bed in the corner, Aaron's feet hanging off the end of his bed, Audrey singing at the top of her lungs with her headphones clamped over her ears.

"You have a good life," I murmured against the coolness of my palms, picturing Aaron's laughing face and Audrey's hard-won smile. "It's small, but it's good. You love and you are loved. It's enough."

Facing the mirror once more, I admitted I didn't look much better. But my heart was no longer bursting out of my chest, and the roiling dread in my stomach had at least congealed in one spot.

Either way, I couldn't hide any longer; Susie needed me on the floor. I huffed out a small laugh. And she was not above picking the lock if she thought something was wrong.

I swept into the kitchen, tied my apron back around my waist, and put the drinks they ordered on a tray. Taking another deep, calming breath, I backed out of the swinging doors into the dining room.

Everything I wanted, everything I would never have, sat around that table.

Even had I known that dream would forever be out of reach, I'd make every mistake just the same to have my kids. But that didn't mean I didn't grieve the loss of the dream. A good man. Friends. Vacations. Going out without worrying. Being able to go out at all.

I couldn't remember the last time I went out with a group of friends.

Their laughter filled the whole restaurant. Even Hawkley's shoulders shook, his wide smile splitting his handsome face. Daire, a wonderful teacher at the school whom Audrey idolized, sat back with a lazy smile, his arm resting along the back of Harley's chair. His fingers tangled in her hair as if he couldn't bear not to touch her.

To be wanted like that, how would that *feel*?

I hovered around the perimeter, like a ship with no place to dock.

If ever there was a dividing line between me and everyone else, this was the perfect illustration.

"Well, someone's having a good time," I quipped, avoiding Max's eyes.

Harley waved a hand. "Sorry, Wren. This crowd is rowdy when they're hungry."

"No problem," I smiled. "Laughter is never a bad thing. Are you ready to order?"

I went around the table, noting Max's position beside Bridge and directly across from Shae.

I swallowed when I got to him. "Max?"

His warm gaze rested steadily on my face. "Wren."

I shuffled from one foot to the other in the silence between us. "What can I get you?"

He tilted his head to the side. "You know what? You decide. I'll take whatever you give me."

I blinked in surprise. "You want me to surprise you?"

His lips quirked. "I'd love you to surprise me."

The table quieted during our exchange. I chewed the inside of my lip as I glanced quickly around at them.

Shae's eyebrows rose as she smiled at Bridge. Noelle leaned forward, her eyes wide.

I met Harley's curious gaze. Heat blistered my cheeks.

Was there a subtext I was missing?

Was there some message I would deliver if I brought him steak and eggs rather than chicken fingers, or God forbid, sausage on a bun?

"Okay," I answered weakly and turned my attention to Bridge for her order.

In the kitchen, I snatched up the menu I knew by heart and perused the options for Max. It hadn't changed in all the years I'd worked there. I had so many ideas, but I hesitated to approach Susie for fear of offending her.

Especially now that I couldn't even finish what I'd started.

Finally, I chose what I would make him for dinner if he was mine. Food that tasted like home. A dish that just happened to be his regular order during those few precious weeks when we were us.

Back and forth between their table and the kitchen, I refilled water glasses, topped up coffees, brought extra napkins, and cooed at baby Hunter when he reached out and latched onto my apron.

Max chatted with Bridge and Shae, his dimple making regularly scheduled appearances, as I was forced to bear witness.

He had changed in the past few months.

Gone was the stoic, hard-faced, workaholic he'd become. In its place was the old Max, the one who smiled and laughed and didn't bring a pile of work to the diner when he came in to eat.

But now he directed his smiles at someone else.

The initial pleasure of waiting on Noelle and Hawkley and their new baby died a slow, painful death under the nightmare of watching Max interact with those beautiful, vivacious women.

Surely one of them would fall under his spell.

God knows it wasn't difficult.

I brought out their food, placing each plate down carefully.

Max took one look at his plate and jerked upright.

I didn't know whether to be thrilled or mortified that he caught the reference.

My eyes darted around the table, looking at anyone but him. "Is there anything else I can get you?"

Max cleared his throat. "I'll take a shandy."

My eyes flew to meet his. "A shandy?"

"What the hell is a shandy?" Hawk grumbled.

"It's half beer, half soda," Max answered easily.

"Are you twelve?" Daire joked.

Max chuckled, his gaze never wavering from mine. "Something like that."

I backed away from the table, a stiff, polite, smile on my face. Because shandy was my drink, the only thing I could handle back then. Frig, it was the only thing I could handle now.

In the kitchen, I poured the beer and soda into a glass, added a couple of ice cubes, and topped it with a slice of lemon before carrying it to the table.

Standing slightly behind him, I reached past his shoulder to set it down.

My hand trembled, the clink of the ice cubes betraying my nerves.

Max raised his hand, but instead of taking the glass, he cupped my elbow, steadying me as I placed it down. "Thank you, Wren."

I snatched back my arm, my entire body electrified by his touch.

I replied, my voice thin but easily heard over the heavy silence at the table, "You're welcome."

As I served my other customers, my eyes strayed to their table over and over again.

Laughter and smiles punctuated an ever-flowing conversation.

When Hunter began to cry, the entire table vied for the privilege of calming him.

God, that stung.

The fact my children never had that made me want to drive my fist through the nearest wall. I sucked in a breath through my nose and carefully blew it back out.

When they called for the bill, Max took care of it, treating everybody. A pleasure I would never afford on my salary.

Shae and Bridge hugged Max and thanked him for lunch which turned my stomach into a boiling cauldron of bitter jealousy.

On their way out, Shae made plans with Harley and Noelle to get their nails done.

I ducked back into the kitchen.

The size of the tip Max left me filled me with chagrin.

There was no denying the truth.

We lived in two different worlds.

I knew that. I'd always known it.

But I hadn't realized until that moment just how far apart they were.

7

Overwhelmed

I t couldn't have happened at a worse time: halfway through the lunch rush.

"Susie," I smiled nervously. "I have to go. I just got a call from the school. Audrey needs to go home."

It had been almost two weeks since the Saturday I served Max and his friends.

All that night I had tossed and turned, wondering if I could somehow bridge the gap between his world and mine. But everywhere I turned, I encountered obstacles. And two of those obstacles were the best things that ever happened to me.

They came first. Always.

So, the first time Max came into Susie Q's afterward, I took my break to avoid serving him and kept our interactions down to a brief hello. The second time, I made sure he got seated in Susie's section. He was back again but at least this time I had a legitimate excuse to avoid him.

Because until my heart caught up with my head? I needed to keep my distance. There was never going to come a time when proximity with Max wouldn't lead to intensifying feelings for me.

Susie's face dropped momentarily before she slapped her customary smile back on. "No problem. You go, but we need to have that meeting."

My face paled. "Is everything okay?" Oh, God! I couldn't lose this job.

I understood how difficult it must have been for Susie, having me running out without notice, of course, I did. I closed my eyes.

I should call my parents to pick Audrey up.

The thought filled me with dismay.

It wasn't as bad before my dad retired. My mom would gladly spend the day with Audrey. But now that he was home more, there was always the risk of encountering his disdain. Not only that, but he would insist I drop Audrey off. By the time I got her there and made it back to work, the lunch rush would be over.

My stomach twisted.

I can't. Not this time. I can't handle my father on top of my turmoil over Max.

I'd just have to pray this time was not the straw that broke the camel's back.

Her face softened. "Everything's fine. I just had an idea I wanted to discuss with you."

It couldn't be that bad, I soothed myself. "When?"

She frowned and drummed her fingers on her hip. "Tomorrow morning, once the breakfast rush is over, we'll sit down."

I nodded and pressed my lips together. "Sounds good."

Though it sounded anything but.

As soon as I got Audrey home, she closed herself up in her closet. Her hidey-hole. Her safe place. Most kids kept clothes in their closet. Audrey's was lined with pillows, blankets, and fairy lights.

One of the kids had pulled the fire alarm on a dare. The assault on her senses sent her into a tailspin. Usually during fire drills, Audrey's Educational Assistant took her outside before it went off. Without that warning, Audrey retreated inside herself, covered her ears, and curled up under her desk.

With Brooklyn laying half on top of her, the teacher couldn't coax her out without making things worse.

Protocol had to be followed which meant things got worse. By the time they got her outside and away from the noise, she'd far surpassed her capacity for the day.

Cuddled up in her cozy closet nest, locked away from the rest of the world, her overwrought senses got the break they needed.

The next morning, Audrey went to school as usual, and I went to work with my heart in my throat. When the breakfast rush was over, Susie waved me over to sit down with her.

"Okay, doll. I can see you're stressed, so I'm just going to cut to the chase. My knees aren't getting any younger and my hips aren't too far behind."

"I'm sorry, Susie," I interrupted. "I'll call my parents next time."

Her face twisted. "No, God, no. Don't do that. Hear me out." She tilted her head to the side. "First of all, you know Audrey can come here anytime. She's no trouble. We'll set her up at the corner table with her loot and she'll be fine."

I grimaced at the uncertainty, but it was true Audrey loved hanging out at Susie Q's.

"She usually is," I admitted. I didn't bring her in often, but the few times Susie asked me to come in for a meeting or to help her with inventory, she'd been more than fine. "But what if she's not?"

Susie spread out her hands. "You tell me. What if she's not?"

"I'd have to take her home."

"Exactly. You'd have to take her home. But you won't know that until you try. In any case, I have a proposal for you."

I swallowed. "I'm listening."

She leaned forward. "First, did you finish the small business diploma you've been taking?"

My cheeks blazed. "I've got one course left to do but I'm not sure if I'm going to do it."

Susie's eyebrows hit her hairline as she demanded, "Whyever not?"

Anger and frustration collided. Had I known the last course would require me to attend in-class, I never would have started the program in the first place. All that money wasted. Money I couldn't afford to spend on myself, but I justified it based on the hope of a better-paying job.

"It has an in-class component."

"So?"

"So, I'd need to go there three days a week for three weeks in a row. And it's two hours north."

"What's stopping you from going?"

She waved her hand at my incredulous look. "I know there are obvious obstacles. Humor me."

I blinked at her. Obstacles? More like roadblocks.

I ticked them off on my fingers. "Audrey's never been without me for more than one night. I'd need to stay in a hotel which would cost money I don't have. I'd lose pay for missing work. And I'd have to borrow Aaron's car which would leave him with no way to commute to school."

She sat back. "Would Audrey be comfortable with your parents?"

I nodded and added a fifth finger tick. "Yes, but they don't know about the program."

She smiled grimly. "This is the last course?"

"Yes."

"Were you planning on telling them after you graduated?"

I shrugged. "Not really. You know them. If it's not a university degree, it doesn't count."

She frowned. "If Audrey is good to stay with your parents, the main obstacles are the car, not wanting to tell your parents about the program, and the money for the hotel."

I nodded. "And the fact I'd be missing work."

Susie slapped her hand down on the table lightly. "You've worked too hard to give up now, doll. Leave it with me. When do you have to confirm?"

"I already enrolled and paid before I realized. It's non-refundable."

With a sharp nod of approval, she said, "You're not going to miss this. I can solve two of those problems right now. You're going to tell your parents that I'm sending you on some business training. This way they won't question anything, and they can take Audrey. If you're comfortable with them taking her."

I answered slowly, wondering where she would go with the rest of it. "It would be worth it to finish the program. And they're very good with her."

Even my father treated her with a softness he'd never extended to me.

And, God, what if I finished and got a higher-paying job? Something that enabled me to get out from under his thumb?

I wouldn't have to ask anybody for anything.

"Attagirl. As for the car and hotel, I have a few ideas for that too. But we've gotten off-track. I have a proposal for you. Something that will help both of us, but if it's not something you want, I don't want you to feel pressured."

"Okay."

She drummed her fingers on the table and bit her lip then sighed. "I need to work less hours, you need more. I want you to start working my hours."

I sat back, ready to object.

She raised her hand. "Hold on. Hear me out. It comes with a raise."

A raise would be good, so good, but with Audrey needing constant supervision, I'd have to turn it down.

My eyes stung.

"And I'd like to offer to look after Audrey every day after school. If she needs to come home from school, you'll stay here, and I'll look after her at your place or mine. I could also bring her here so she could be close to you."

My jaw dropped. I sat forward as my eyes skittered back and forth. More money and more hours? Could it possibly be this easy? To be able to stay at Susie's? But how much would be left after paying Susie? And how long would it take for Audrey to adjust to the changes?

My breath quickened; my heart pounded. There were too many variables.

She continued, almost nervously, "We could set ourselves up in the break room, or at the staff table in the corner. I could take her down to the beach for a walk or to visit Anita. Does she like the carousel?"

"She loves the carousel," I murmured, swallowing my anxiety.

The carousel was one of her favorite places when she was younger. I took Aaron all the time until Hunter passed. Pregnant with Audrey,

I walked up one morning with Aaron and ran into Max. I stopped going for a while after that.

The Bennetts and Brevards were the best of friends, their two families did everything together. The five kids, Max, Hawkley, Hunter, Noelle, and Harley, had been inseparable. Their childhood antics, often led by Hunter, were the stuff of Sage Ridge legends. And the carousel had been their place. I knew this because I'd been part of their circle for that short, golden, summer. Going to the carousel, for Max, was tantamount to going to the cemetery.

And I would not impose on his grief.

I swallowed as Susie continued enthusiastically. Would it be worth it? "How much would you charge?"

She scowled. "I'm not going to charge you anything."

Shock rolled through me at her kindness only to be ploughed over by a deep sense of unworthiness and shame. "What?" I whispered. "You can't do that."

Her eyebrows lowered indignantly. "The hell I can't! Listen, doll. You'd be doing me a favor. I'd be doing you a favor. It's that simple. You're saving my knees and I'm looking after Audrey."

Tempted, so tempted, but it wasn't right. "I can't. I can't take advantage of you like that."

"You wouldn't be. With you working more, I can keep my restaurant. And most of my income. Without you, I'm going to have to think about retirement. I'm not ready for that. Besides," Susie crossed her arms on the table. "How long have you worked here?"

I thought back. "Ten years."

"Ten years," she repeated. "And in those ten years, I've watched you do everything yourself, and more than you should for other people. More often than I can count, I've wished I could give you a hand. Now I'm in a position where I can. And you're not going to deny me."

I scoffed and crossed my arms on the table in front of me. "Susie, I don't do anything for anybody. And I can't just keep taking and taking and taking. I'd feel so guilty. My kids are my responsibility, not yours."

Her eyebrows rose. "You think they're not still going to be your responsibility if you accept help?"

"Well, no..."

"Furthermore, who does all the baking for the women's shelter? Organizes the school bake sale? Made my business cards? Designs ads for the newspaper? Redesigned the menu for the resort?"

My jaw dropped.

She laughed. "You think I don't know about these things? My only question is why you haven't updated my menu!"

My mouth flapped ineffectually for a moment before I stuttered, "I can do that."

Reaching across the table, she wrapped her hand around my forearm. "Let me give you a hand. Everybody needs help. Everybody." She squeezed my arm gently and continued. "You're like my second daughter. And with Quinn so far away, I need to love on you. Let me help. Let me love on you."

I dropped my forehead onto my arms.

Her kindness overwhelmed me.

I didn't know what I was feeling but whatever it was, it was too much.

She sat quietly with her hand cupped around the back of my head until I composed myself.

Then sent me home with the admonition to prepare to attend my course.

Great, fat, tears, swollen with shame, grief, and for the first time in a long time, hope, rolled down my face the whole way home.

8

Buffer

I froze in my tracks, one boot off, one still dangling from my toes in Susie's front hall. I'd come willingly, even a little excited, to hear Susie's plan. She'd neatly removed two of the obstacles and I was curious how she might manage the others.

But now I stood unmoving, my ear cocked to the voices coming from Susie's living room. One voice in particular stood out from the others.

Audrey stepped closer, her eyes widening as she sought out the threat that paralyzed me. She picked up on emotions easily; she just didn't always understand what elicited them.

Forcing myself to relax, I looked at Susie, hoping my shock at her betrayal didn't show on my face. "Why is Max here?"

Because it was his voice, clear as day, I heard coming from Susie's living room.

Susie's brow furrowed. "Is that bad?"

I swallowed, hoping to ease the constriction in my throat. "Just surprised you didn't tell me it wasn't just going to be us for dinner. Like usual."

Immediately, her face creased with regret. "I'm sorry, doll. I know you need to prepare Audrey. I didn't think..."

"It's okay," I forced my feelings down and rushed to appease her distress. She was only trying to help, and I was making her uncomfortable. And in her own home. "It's fine. Truly."

I dipped down, using the curtain of my hair to shield my expression as I removed Brooklyn's service vest and booties before directing her to shadow Audrey who had nervously slipped her hand back into mine.

Glancing down at my attire with distaste, I admitted even if Susie had told me Max was coming, I wouldn't have been able to do much better. At the very least, I would have fixed my hair and stroked on some lip gloss. I had some in my purse, but with Susie hovering beside me, I couldn't very well whip it out without giving myself away.

When I rose, Susie smiled at me ruefully. "Would it be a good time to tell you Dan and Lou are here as well?"

Audrey perked up.

I huffed out a laugh. "Well, I didn't think Max was in there talking to himself. I love Dan and Lou, and Audrey does too."

Dan and Lou had been there for me when no one else was, and they'd never entirely let us go. Christmas, Easter, Aaron's birthday, Audrey's birthday, and even mine, they showed up with arms overflowing with gifts.

They invited us to use the pool during off hours, knowing Audrey loved the water but hated the community center with its constantly rotating doors and echoes of children's shrill voices bouncing off the walls.

We didn't take them up on the offer often, but when we did, it was wonderful.

I dipped my chin down.

It was Harley who taught her to swim the summer she turned ten. She wouldn't take no for an answer.

And how did I repay them?

By enforcing a polite distance between us, never allowing them to enfold me into their lives, and refusing them entry into mine, for fear I was an obligation, a burden, when I could have found some way to contribute to their lives instead.

Well, that and the fact they were too closely connected to Max.

A booming voice sounded from the other room. "Is my girl Audrey here?"

Audrey dropped my hand like a hot potato and bolted.

Susie worked to quell her smile. "I'm thinking you needed the warning more than Audrey."

I huffed out a laugh. "In this case, you're right."

Serious, she asked, "Is it okay that I asked them to help? I know they care about you, Aaron, and Audrey. I was so bent on working things out for you to attend your course that I didn't think to clear things with you ahead of time."

"It's okay." I smiled ruefully. "I probably would have said no."

She grimaced. "That might have played a little into my reasoning."

I snorted out a small laugh.

Susie grinned, threw her arm around me, and led me into the fray while I braced myself for the confrontation ahead.

I pushed away my chagrin. One day I would cease being Sage Ridge's most prominent charity case. And when that day came, I'd hold my head up.

Susie's hold on me tightened. "It'll be all right."

Lou's face lit up when she saw me. She stood and crossed the room immediately, her arms open. "Wren! It's so good to see you, honey!"

Being enfolded in Lou's arms was what coming home was supposed to feel like.

Warm and soft and inviting.

Safe.

A place where you could drop your sword and shield at the front door.

I closed my eyes and cut off all my other senses to revel in the warmth of her embrace. I let it fill me like a hollow vase. Lou. It was Lou who set the standard for how I wanted to be with my kids.

She reminded me of the hugs my mom used to give me.

Before I disappointed them.

Before she took my dad's side.

Some small part of me understood. She was completely dependent on him, and he was a force to be reckoned with. They were from a different era. His word was law, and she obeyed. But to allow him to toss me out of the house?

Unwittingly, I clung tighter to Lou. It had been almost two decades, and that night still cleaved me in two.

Lou's hold loosened. Embarrassed, I released her abruptly. But she didn't go far. Grasping my hands, she only leaned back far enough to look into my eyes. "How are you, Wrennie?"

"I'm good." I smiled warmly to lend credence to my words.

She narrowed her eyes on mine.

I blinked in surprise and drew back. It was rare anyone looked deeper.

"Hm," she hummed. "We have some ideas for this program of yours. I didn't know you were doing all this on top of everything else." She squeezed my fingers. "I'm so damn proud of you."

My chin dipped as I stared back at her.

I didn't know what to do with that type of praise.

"Oh, it's nothing," I murmured, shaking me head to dismiss her words.

"It's most definitely not nothing," she stated firmly. "You're like superwoman doing everything you do."

I huffed out a laugh. "Without the cape, the fantastic figure, or the ability to fly."

She laughed and drew me deeper into Susie's living room.

My eyes flitted first to Dan, deep in conversation with Audrey.

He waved at me with a smile, his big hand sending Brooklyn into the stratosphere as he rubbed her ears.

Susie's husband John gave me a brief hug then went outside to attend to the roast he was cooking on his new smoker and 'give us a chance to talk.'

"You don't have to go, John," I protested.

He replied with a barely intelligible grunt.

Susie laughed. "You know John, Wren. He doesn't do emotion."

He growled in response then dropped a kiss on the top of Susie's head and delivered a swat to her arse before escaping to his garage.

I couldn't avoid Max any longer without being outright rude. My smile trembled as I sought him out. Everything in me longed to cover the tiny, frayed hole, not the fashionable kind, marring the front pocket of my jeans.

Sitting in John's armchair with his long legs stretched out in front of him, Max's dark eyes met mine almost lazily, and my breath caught in my throat.

"Hi, Max," I breathed, my cheeks coloring at the sound of my voice.

He rolled his full lips between his teeth, his dimple deepening, before wrapping his tongue around my name. "Hello, Wren."

My gaze dropped to his mouth. This was a most inopportune time to remember how his lips felt on mine.

I forced my gaze back up to his eyes and remembered how they had looked up close from the shelter of his arms. Drawn to him, I stepped closer, then stopped abruptly.

Where was I planning to sit? On his lap? The mental picture left me momentarily speechless.

My eyes strayed to his hips. The urge to straddle his lap and take his face in my hands hit me hard.

Would he fill his hands with my ass?

Whoa.

I gave my head a small shake. "Uh, how are you?"

I'd never been an extrovert, but what little social skills I mastered when I was younger had further deteriorated due to years of social isolation. Audrey's sensitivities did not lend themselves to social outings.

I could do diner small talk just fine.

One-on-one with Susie? All good.

At my parents' house, the conversations had run along the same script for two decades, and we all knew our lines.

"I'm good," he replied easily. He cocked a brow. "I haven't seen you in a while."

I pressed my lips together.

That's because I've been avoiding you.

"Busy!" I blurted. "Working. Audrey. Aaron. Home."

My eyes dropped to the floor as I twisted my mouth to the side.

Me, Wren.

You, Max.

Cave.

Fuck.

I'd heard women hit their sexual prime in their mid-30s to 40s, but I hadn't honestly noticed any change until the past couple of months. My hormones had turned me into a cavewoman capable only of grunting out solitary words.

I blew out an unsteady breath. "Um…"

When I looked back up, his gaze had sharpened on my face, but his voice was soft, so soft I was sure it only reached my ears. "Sit down, Wren. Nothing to be nervous about. Relax, Tweet."

Tweet.

The nickname he christened me with right before he kissed me the first time. Tears prickled behind my lids.

Ducking my head to hide my face once again behind the curtain of my hair, I turned and tucked myself into the corner of the loveseat across from the couch, one end of which was occupied by Dan's tremendous frame wedged in place by Audrey's small one.

Lou bustled over and took the other side of the couch beside Audrey, directly across from me just as Susie set down a tray with cookies, coffee, and chocolate milk for Audrey.

Susie settled in beside me and handed me a mug.

I wrapped my cold hands around it immediately.

"I hope you don't feel bulldozed," Lou began with an apologetic smile.

Dan cut her off with a snort, side-eying me with a wide smile. "Oh, you're being bulldozed, Wrennie," he assured me. "Just know it's all done with love."

"Hush, Dan," Lou admonished, her widening smile taking the sting out of the reprimand, before turning back to me. "Susie told us about your program. I can't tell you how excited I was for you. Then she told us you might not be able to finish." She took a breath, shaking her head. "Well sweet girl, we just can't have that. We have company trucks. We'll loan you one. Gladly."

I opened my mouth to protest, but Dan intervened. "Everything's insured. Nothing will happen, and if it gets a scratch or dent, we won't even be able to identify it amongst the rest from being driven down the old forest roads."

"We have a cabin in Moose Lake. It's about 20 minutes from your college. You can stay there so you won't incur hotel costs," Lou added.

Car.

Cabin.

20 minutes.

Every ounce of self-preservation urged me to decline. I owed these people too much already, and nothing came without strings.

What if I failed the course in the end?

What if Audrey couldn't handle the change and I had to pull out?

What if my parents withdrew their support?

If I let them down, after everything they were doing for me, I wouldn't be able to bear their disappointment.

I latched onto the most obvious issue. "I can't pay you back."

Dan's head swiveled away from Audrey's iPad. "Nobody wants that."

Thinking of Max footing the bill for his entire table at lunch, my face flamed as I admitted, "It's too much work to miss. I can't afford it."

Spilling my personal business wasn't usually my modus operandi, but their surprise attack had breached my normal barriers.

"We'll work it out," Susie promised. "First of all, if you take me up on my offer, you'll be working longer hours when you are there. And you'll work the dinner rush which will pad your pocketbook nicely."

I nodded as my eyes skittered back and forth, my mind whirring. That was a lot of change to force on Audrey in a very short amount of time.

And I'd never been on my own. Not since I was pregnant with Aaron, living in one of Dan and Lou's cabins.

What the hell would I do with myself?

This time there would be no teenage Hunter dropping by to check on me and bring me treats from the resort's kitchen before heading out with his friends. At only one year younger than me, I hadn't expected the richness of his compassion. But it only made me treasure it all the more.

I nibbled my bottom lip. "I'm not great with directions. I've never driven that far by myself."

And definitely not that far up north into the boonies.

Other than the times I borrowed Aaron's car, I barely drove at all.

Could I do it?

Could I actually leave Audrey for that many days and finish this thing?

How isolated was this cabin?

"I'll take a test run with you," Susie soothed.

My eyes darted between Lou and Susie.

Was the cabin secure? Did it have a good lock?

Oh, God! Did it have a woodstove? I didn't know how to operate one of those.

What if it caught on fire?

"I'm n-n-not sure about the cabin," I stuttered. "Does it have a woodstove? What if it snows?"

Max leaned forward and braced his elbows on his spread knees. His expression had settled into the one I'd grown accustomed to seeing before he began to smile again.

Intense, focused, and serious, the brackets around his mouth etched deep.

"Wren," he stated firmly. "I'll take you up tomorrow. I'll show you everything you need to know." He nodded toward Audrey. "Audrey will love it, or she can stay here with Dan and Lou if you prefer. Harley said she'd take her swimming while we're gone, and Daire will be there, too."

His sudden and unexpected grin sent my heart into flight. "He assures me Audrey loves him. Also, Aaron's working tomorrow. He can check in on her throughout the day."

Harley and Daire knew about this as well?

"Seems like you've got it all figured out," I snapped then clapped my hand over my mouth.

Ungrateful.

Selfish.

"I'm sorry," I blurted.

I hated being railroaded, no matter how well-intentioned.

I needed to make my own decisions.

I needed to control my own life. My hands began to shake. I tucked them under my thighs.

I could not be beholden to anyone else.

"You're fine," he answered quietly.

Mortification burned my cheeks hotter.

I'd never be able to repay their kindness, and instead of thanking them, I'd lashed out.

I was just so *sick* of being so damned needy. But even that discomfort paled in comparison to two hours in the car alone with Max.

I swallowed.

Not to mention another two hours back.

Why would he even offer? There was a time when we'd been just friends. For two years, I watched him date other women, convinced it would never be me. Then it was me, and I screwed it up.

I could not be his friend again. That was a torture I refused to submit myself to.

But who else could show me how to handle the cabin? I stared down at the floor. Could I ask Harley? No. That would be the height of selfishness. She was practically a newlywed. She didn't need to spend her day off driving me up to the cabin.

Dan?

Maybe Dan could take me up?

I glanced up to find Dan and Max locked into some kind of staring contest until Dan finally gave Max a small nod, his lips tight.

Dan turned to me. "I'd love to take you myself, Wrennie, but I've got a few pressing issues I have to take care of tomorrow."

"No, no," I assured him with a shake of my head. "That's okay."

I swept my overgrown bangs out of my eyes.

I was a practical woman.

This was an opportunity to do better for my family. I'd be a fool not to lean on these kind people for a few weeks.

My fingertips danced over my forehead once again.

There was no help for it. I was trapped with few options. Only this time the lash of excitement curling around my womb told me like nothing else that this trap was dangerous.

Max was dangerous.

But the lure of being self-sufficient and independent was too shiny to ignore.

"Max? Are you sure it's no trouble?" My mouth twisted to the side. "I mean, of course it's trouble. It's a complete waste of your day."

"No, Tweet. I'll enjoy every minute of it. It's been ages since I've gotten out of town."

He'll enjoy every minute!

"What about Audrey?" he asked.

I met his eyes in question. "What about her?"

His dimple winked at me. "Would you like to leave her to spend the day with Dan and Lou? Harley and Daire will be there—"

I squeaked, "She can come."

Audrey lifted her chin. "I want to swim with Harley."

I turned to Audrey, my voice shrill. "You'll love the cabin, Audrey. It'll be an adventure!"

"No, thank you. I'll swim with Harley."

Max's eyes crinkled slightly, a hint of a smile playing at the corners of his beautiful lips. "It'll be a long day in the car for her."

I nodded briskly, tucking my hands between my thighs to keep them steady. "I'm sure she'll be fine. Thank you for taking us."

If I couldn't avoid him, I would need a good buffer.

9

Warmer

Aaron wagged his eyebrows and offered a crooked grin. "Is it kind of a date?"

"No!" I exclaimed. "It's not a date. Max is just being kind, showing me the cabin so I can stay there and finish my course. For goodness' sake, Audrey is coming with us!"

He side-eyed me. "Isn't Max the guy?"

Aaron stood in front of the open fridge shoving whatever he could grab into his backpack before going to work.

I sighed and sat down with my breakfast at our small table. This was what happened when a child had a child. You grew up together and that kid became your ride or die.

Fortunately, or unfortunately.

In this case, it was unfortunate I blabbed my mouth and told him about my first love a couple of years ago when he was caught in the painful throes of his.

Lucky for him, he and Nadine had been together ever since. I didn't see her often. Even Aaron struggled to see her. Nadine's parents were older, and like mine, they were strict. Strictly speaking, they weren't enamored with the idea of Nadine dating anyone.

Aaron didn't know the exact timeline of my first love, only that it was before him.

"That was a long time ago," I answered quietly.

He paused then asked just as quietly. "Is he my father?"

My chin jerked up. "No! God no, Aaron. If he was, he would have claimed you. You'd be part of his family. So would I. Max is a good man."

"So, my father was not a good man?"

I sighed. *Kian*. The truth was I barely knew his father. "I've told you everything I know about your father. Which isn't much. When you want his name, I'll give it to you. I'll even help you track him down. I'll contact him for you myself to ask if he wants to meet you. He can't contact you, son. He doesn't even know our last name."

"Do you regret it?"

"Never." I shook my head vehemently. "Not once. If I had to go back and relive my life, I wouldn't change a thing if it meant I wouldn't have you. I promise."

At that moment, Audrey walked out of her bedroom dressed in her swimsuit and a pair of shorts.

"Oh!" I exclaimed, the pit in my stomach sinking. "Audrey, honey, it's cold at the cabin. Far too cold for swimming."

"I'm not going to the cabin," she informed me. "I'm going swimming with Harley and Mr. Newman."

Aaron huffed out a laugh as he walked past, bumping me lightly with his shoulder. Spinning around to look at me, he continued to walk backwards and teased, "Now is it a date?"

"Get to work, brat!" I answered, working hard to quell my smile.

The front door closed on his laughter, and I prepared to face off against my daughter.

Her mutinous expression stopped me in my tracks.

Was it fair to deny her this little bit of independence? This opportunity to forge new relationships because I was scared?

I sighed. "I'll call Lou and tell her you're coming. Go put warm clothes on and put your towel and swimsuit in a bag."

She walked over and held open the bag in her hands. Inside was a pair of underwear and socks.

"Good start, Audrey." I stood. "I'll help you pack the rest of what you'll need. You'll need to put something warm on over your swimsuit. And remember, Brooklyn can't go with you. Harley and Mr. Newman aren't trained to manage her."

Audrey's lips tightened. Part of me hoped she'd change her mind and come with me, the better half of me silently urged her to be brave and try something new.

"I want to swim. If I get sad, Harley can bring me home to Brooklyn."

A tingle of wary excitement warmed my chest.

Two hours later, that tingle had spread to all four limbs and had me fairly trembling.

Sitting beside Max in his SUV, nothing behind us but road, the same in front, was a dream I didn't know I had.

Snow-capped trees stretched as far as the eye could see, the weak winter sunlight turning those white-washed domes to polished marble.

What would it have been like to live this life with him? To pack Audrey, Brooklyn, and Aaron up in the car and take off for a family vacation?

To go out for dinner, hold his hand, sleep in his bed, wake in his arms?

His car, warm and comfortable, embraced me as my mind wandered.

What would it be like to be his, to have the right to rest my palm on his thigh as he drove? My hand twitched in my lap with the urge to do just that. I could almost feel the soft rasp of denim under my fingertips.

His deep voice wrested me from my daydreams. "Tell me about this program you're taking."

"I'm sorry, what?"

He glanced at me and flashed his dimple. "Your program. Tell me about it."

I blushed and tucked my fingers under the outside of my thighs. "It's just a diploma in small business management."

"Why do you say 'just'?"

I raised my chin defensively. "Well, it's not like it's a PhD in psychology."

He frowned. "It doesn't make it less valuable if it's what you want to do."

My brows lowered.

Was it?

Was it what I wanted to do?

Or was it simply what made the most sense?

I shrugged and stole a look at him. "It makes sense."

One hand wrapped around the steering wheel, the other curled loosely on his thigh. "That sounds practical."

His knees spread, the denim of his jeans hugged his thick thighs. I tore my attention away from the enticing sight to answer. "You make it sound like being practical is a deficit."

"Not if it makes you happy."

My eyes returned to follow the line of stitching up the inside of his thigh. When I realized where my eyes were headed, I yanked my errant gaze away. "Does being a psychologist make you happy?"

He tipped his head back and forth. "Most of the time? I'm not sure happy is the right word. I'm satisfied, like I'm fulfilling my purpose when I'm able to help someone heal." He grimaced. "But when I can't reach someone, it's devastating."

I lapped up every little bit of information he gave me. The thought of Max distressed over a patient wrapped around my heart like a barbed wire and squeezed.

Heat billowed through the vents. I loosened my scarf and unbuttoned my coat.

Outside the window, the trees whipped past in a blur. Every now and then, the wind stirred up the snow in a glittering whirlwind before dropping it back down onto the road.

It was bitterly cold, but locked in this bubble with Max, hanging on his every word, I was warmer than I'd been in a long time.

I studied his strong profile. Dark hair swept back off his forehead, sharply defined jaw liberally peppered with scruff, high cheekbones, and deliciously firm, full lips.

He was beautiful.

And his devotion to his patients made him more so.

Stop digging into his life. You're only going to fall deeper.

I failed to heed my own warning. "What made you go into psychology?"

"My mom."

I raised my eyebrows. "Your mom?"

"Yeah. From the time I was a little guy, it bothered me when someone was hurting. I always wanted to fix it." He huffed out a sad little laugh. "She used to cup my face in her hands and say, 'you can't save everyone.' It made me crazy."

"She's right, though," I murmured.

He slanted a curious look my way. "We used to have these long talks well into the early hours of the morning. I can't tell you how often she explained how important it was to respect people's boundaries; to not push people to change before they were ready. Finally, in high school, she suggested I go into psychology so I could exercise that part of me that so desperately wanted to reach people. To set myself up so that the people who wanted help came to me."

"That's beautiful." I swallowed my trepidation. "I know it was you who spoke to Dan and Lou about helping me. I never thanked you."

He shook his head, his relaxed expression fleeing. "I just asked them to keep an eye out for you because I was worried about how your dad would react. They told me they would look after you. I didn't want your thanks. I just wanted you safe."

My heart slammed against my ribcage; my voice squeaked. "Were you angry?"

A muscle in his jaw tightened. "Not with you. Never with you."

My fingertips dug into my thighs. Why was I doing this to myself? "Who were you angry with?"

Without looking at me, he reached out and cupped his big hand around the back of my neck.

My breath ceased in my lungs.

"My feelings for you scared me. I wasn't ready, so I broke things off. I told myself it was temporary, that I'd give myself until Christmas to see if the feelings went away. But leaving you that night...the look on your face...I should have known--" He released me abruptly and cleared his throat, his knuckles turning white on the steering wheel. "I'm sorry I hurt you."

Panic fluttered in my chest. Almost twenty years had passed, and I still couldn't think about that night.

There were three events in my life I never revisited. First, the night Max broke things off with me. Second, the night my dad threw me out of the house. And third, the night David left.

I swallowed the pain and shook away the chill of those memories while I longed for the return of the warmth of his hand on my neck. "It's okay," I rasped.

He continued drily. "Would now be a good time to tell you I came home looking for you after I graduated and found you engaged?"

"You came home looking for me?" I repeated weakly. My heart thudded in my chest; I could barely hear my own words over the rush of blood in my ears.

I blinked at my lap. I missed my chance with him *twice*?

He shook his head. "My timing with you was always off."

I cleared my throat. "What—" The air was sharper, colors brighter, but the world passed by in a blur.

I stared unseeing out the windshield, afraid to voice my next question, yet perversely determined for the reality check I so desperately needed to guard my wayward heart.

"You can ask me anything and everything," he murmured.

My voice was gruff. "What do you mean your timing was always off?"

"First, we were young, and I wasn't ready. When I was ready, you were engaged. In retrospect, I should have whisked you away. But then you wouldn't have had Audrey.

"The next few years were brutal. We lost Hunter who was the very best of all of us." Max's eyes glazed as he sank back into the painful memory. "Full of fun and mischief." He looked at me and smiled, his eyes sad even now. "There was nothing he wouldn't do to make us laugh, and he was generous to a fault. I swear his heart was made of gold." He sighed. "Noelle packed up her car shortly afterward and moved away. Hawkley withdrew from everyone. My whole family fell apart. It was like, without Hunter, we lost sight of each other."

He blew out a breath, his brow furrowing. "Then my mom was diagnosed with cancer. For two years, she fought. Her passing completely decimated what was left of us.

"My entire family was locked in a prison of suffering, and there wasn't a single thing I could do about it. So, I threw myself into my work, the one place I felt I could make a difference.

"By the time your douchebag husband left you, I'd lost too much. I thought about you, but I didn't think I could afford to lose anything else. I told myself I was over you."

Everything in me wanted to see his face when I asked this next question, but I couldn't risk it. Eyes fixed on the scene outside my window, I rasped, "Were you?"

"Not sure I'll ever be over you, Wren."

10

Fucking Finally

.

My breath froze in my lungs.

Not sure I'll ever be over you, Wren.

"You—" I snapped my mouth shut as I blinked, wide-eyed, out the window. "You—"

"Anything and everything, Tweet. There's nothing we can't talk about. I'm an open book."

I swallowed. Quashed the tiny sprout of burgeoning hope. He could not possibly have thought this through.

After all this time? "Why?" I blurted. "Why now?"

My eyes skittered back and forth between the passenger side window and the windshield, barely registering the view beyond the glass as something akin to panic bloomed in my chest.

The brass ring brushed the very tips of my fingers, but experience told me I'd never grasp it.

He hesitated. "There are a few factors, one day I'll share, but mostly it's because I finally figured out that we're just going to keep missing each other until we get this right."

Could this be happening?

He wanted me? Me?

I didn't believe it.

Couldn't allow myself to believe it.

Look at him.

"What would make it right?" I whispered, twisting slightly to face him.

He was so beautiful it hurt my heart. Every single one of my dreams featured his face, his hands, his voice, his smile.

His beautiful heart.

I fisted my hands in my lap as they began to shake.

What would it be like to live this life with him?

To go out for dinner, hold his hand, sleep in his bed, wake in his arms?

To be his, to have the right to rest my palm on his thigh in the car?

It was like my thoughts had manifested themselves into truth.

He flipped the indicator up, came to a stop at the lights, and his eyes met mine.

Dark. Warm. Steady.

I took a breath, the icy panic in my chest melting under the warmth of his attention. My heart fluttered with apprehension, longing, and disbelief.

If I fell into him again, I'd never willingly come back up for air.

My brow furrowed. If he left me again, I wouldn't want to come back up for air.

He glanced at me; his jaw clenched with determination. "Finally getting to see what we could be to each other."

I couldn't hold his gaze.

What we could be to each other.

Could I make him happy? What did I have to offer? The parameters of my life barely allowed me to eat.

I looked down at my short, chipped nails. "I'm not like Shae or Bridge."

A sound of disbelief huffed out. "Why would I want you to be like Shae or Bridge? If I wanted you to be like Shae or Bridge, I'd pursue Shae or Bridge."

"What I mean is, I have kids."

His deep chuckle filled the space between us. "I've noticed. And you're a wonderful mother."

My gaze snapped to his. "I am?"

His brow furrowed. "Surely you know that, Tweet. How can you not know that?"

I shrugged slowly; my mind still caught on *'finally getting to see what we could be together.'*

"You want to, like, date?"

He jerked his chin down briefly in a nod. "I do, but I'll take whatever you'll give me. I want to spend time together. Get to know one another again. I want to get to know Audrey and Aaron when you're ready for that. Introduce you to my dad. You already know my sister, but she's going to want to know you better."

He pulled the steering wheel around and brought the car to a stop. Pocketing the keys, he opened his door.

My brain lagged thirty seconds behind like a 1990s desktop with too many tabs open.

Introduce me to his dad?

I didn't even notice what road he turned down to get here, but the cabin sat just a few feet in front of us.

He wanted to date me.

He swung his legs out of the car then leaned down to look at me. "Come on. Let me show you the cabin. I want you to be at ease staying here."

The quick change in topic allowed my brain to shift gears. I yanked the handle on my door as he closed his.

By the time I got out, he was standing by the hood, hand extended, palm up, waiting for mine.

My eyes flickered up to his.

He gave me a little nod.

I closed the door and took a single step away from the car. It was so much colder up here than it was in Sage Ridge but I barely felt it.

If I placed my palm over his, that would be it for me. I'd be gone. Claimed. Sunk.

Whether what we ended up being to each other was what he wanted or not, it would be all that was left for me.

Another step toward him.

March's bitter winds whipped around the treetops sending a fine dusting of snow spiraling down around us. A benediction or a curse?

If he left me again, my heart would never recover.

My fingers twitched, yearning for his.

Would Audrey accept his presence in our lives?

Would Aaron?

I swallowed.

What if Audrey's outbursts were too much for him?

What if he resented the demands on my time?

I closed my eyes. So damn afraid. Always so scared to make a mistake, then falling headlong into them anyway.

What if the reality of Max failed to live up to the dream? What if I'd wasted my life pining for a man who was never meant to be mine?

But what if he is?

"I swear to God, Wren, I'll catch you," he promised, his voice deep and sure.

My eyes flew to his.

Dark. Warm. Steady.

So serious. Thoughtful.

Purposeful.

Max never did anything without thinking it through.

The tension in my shoulders eased.

He rolled his lips between his teeth, that damned dimple calling to me like a siren's song.

I raised my arm, took the final step, and slid my palm over his.

"That's my girl," he said on an exhale, his shoulders dropping. Drawing me against his chest, he trapped my hands between us and wrapped his arms around my back. With his lips in my hair, he murmured harshly, "That's my good fucking girl."

With his cheek resting on top of my head, his hands traveled up and down my back, branding me as his even through the thick layers of my winter coat.

I trembled, desire and disbelief vying for supremacy.

"I know you're scared," he murmured. "I'm going to make this so fucking worth the risk."

Wiggling my hands down between us, I grasped his waist and pressed my body closer.

I couldn't remember the last time a man held me. I knew it was my ex-husband, but we'd slept in separate rooms for so long I couldn't remember the last time we touched.

But Max, there would never come a time I wouldn't want Max.

Closing my eyes, I breathed him in, hardly daring to believe I was in his arms.

I pressed closer, my fingers grasping.

He curled his body around me.

"I've got you, Tweet." He huffed out a laugh.

"What?" I asked softly, tipping my chin back to look up at him, mesmerized by the look in his eyes.

He grinned down at me. "Fucking finally."

I laughed and ducked my head, caught up in the wonder of the moment.

"Look at me, Wren."

I tipped my head back immediately.

His eyes glinted with satisfaction as he touched the tip of his nose to mine. "We're going to get it right this time."

I nodded, but I didn't believe. Not yet.

He smiled as if he knew. "What do you say I show you the cabin now?"

I blew out the breath I didn't know I was holding as he released his hold on my body but reclaimed my hand.

I walked beside him as if in a dream. The idyllic fairytale cabin ahead of me fully supported that notion.

Snow cloaked the roof and icicles sparkled along the eaves of the porch. An A-frame with an addition on the side, it boasted a wide porch that stretched the entire length of the front and down one side of the house.

"It's beautiful," I said. "I didn't expect it to be so big."

"The fourteen-year-old in me is dying to respond," he replied drily.

I guffawed. "Don't worry. Fourteen-year-old me heard you just fine."

Oh my.

We'd never had sex.

I'd never even seen him naked.

He'd certainly never seen me naked.

Which in retrospect was a good thing because, well, stretch marks and thirty-nine-year-old boobs could not hope to compete against the memory of my twenty-year-old body.

If he had one.

"Stop thinking so hard." He squeezed my hand and let me go to knock the icicles down before stepping onto the porch to unlock the door.

I stepped inside and stopped short. "Wow. This was not what I was expecting."

Warm, wood floors, reclaimed brick fireplace, and wide, pine trim claimed the perimeter of every cream-toned room and framed every doorway.

I walked down the hall ahead of him. Recessed lighting, bookshelves, and an entertainment center proved there would be no roughing it for anybody who stayed there. Peeking inside the kitchen doorway, I noted the modern appliances, cork flooring, and warm wood tones.

"For some reason, I expected it to be a lot more rustic."

"It was," Max admitted.

He looked around, a hint of sadness pulling the corners of his mouth down.

I moved closer. "What is it?"

"Hawkley and I fixed it up last year." His dark eyes found mine. "Hunter wrote a bucket list every year, things he wanted to accomplish for himself as well as things he wanted to do for us. Hawkley had Hunter's list for the year he died and renovating this place as a surprise for everyone was at the top of it. Hawk and I did it for him."

I returned to his side and slipped my hand into his. "I'm sorry, Max. Hunter's passing left a massive void."

His eyes flicked down to meet mine as his mouth quirked up on one side. "It messed us up. He was special."

I leaned in, suddenly brave in my desire to comfort him. "I wish I could have been there with you."

He squeezed my hand. "You were in the only way you could."

Did he know? Did he know about the food I prepared for all of them?

"Thank you for everything you made for us, especially the shepherd's pie and the muffins."

My breath caught in my throat.

"You'll have to make it again for my pops. He said it was the best he ever tasted." His soft smile did me in.

"I will," I replied quietly.

I'll do everything.

And I'll do everything right this time.

Max shook off the painful memories and showed me the rest of the cabin.

I could barely pay attention for wondering what came next. And when. Would he kiss me?

When it came time to leave, I was still wondering.

With one foot out the door, he tugged me back inside, closed the door firmly, and slowly backed me up against it.

His voice like gravel, eyes devouring my lips, he muttered, "Just a taste, Tweet. I've been fucking starving for you for twenty years."

Belying his rough words, he cupped my jaw in his big hands and gently touched his mouth to mine.

My eyelids fluttered shut.

The cabin disappeared. The wind outside stilled. There were no kids, no jobs, no passage of time.

Only him.

Us.

His kiss.

His breath.

His big hands holding me captive. His lips brushing over mine. Softly. Sweetly.

A thousand springtimes.

The first snowfall.

Autumn leaves and apple picking.

Summer sun reflecting like diamonds in the spray from the waves.

Everything good. Everything right. Everything I ever yearned for, and exactly as I remembered.

"Max," I breathed into his mouth.

"I'm here, Wrennie. I'm right here. Not going anywhere this time."

The tip of his tongue flicked out to gently caress the inside of my lip.

I moaned into his mouth, arched my back to press my chest against his. God, why did we have to have these thick winter coats between us?

My hips rocked. My body ached to strip down and give myself over to him right there in the front hall. Good girl upbringing be damned.

His fingers pushed through my hair to grip the back of my head while his other hand dropped to my waist and yanked me closer.

"Wren," he gritted out before slanting his mouth across mine roughly, forcing my lips open on a surprised cry as he delved inside.

Now, this.

This was no sweet, first-date, kiss.

This was hunger and yearning.

Apprehension and gratitude.

The end of a long, painful drought and the beginning of ever after.

It was the most desperate of hopes.

The scariest kind of all.

I tunneled my hands into his hair, giving as good as I got, my fingertips rejoicing in his thick waves as I held his mouth to mine, breathing his name between frantic kisses as if to reassure myself of this new reality.

I moaned as his tongue filled my mouth, stroking mine, tasting me, promising me more.

Promising me everything?

A tear streaked my cheek.

My body began to quake.

Max broke our kiss with a harsh grunt and pressed his forehead to mine as he drew in a shuddering breath. "We have to go. Now, before I do something stupid. I want to take this slow, Wren. I can't screw up this time."

His thumb brushed the tear away as his dark eyes held mine captive.

"Max," I breathed against his sweet mouth, my eyes closing. "Not too slow, okay?"

He grunted as his hands dropped to my ass and squeezed. "Definitely not too slow."

11

Mermaid Tears

The buzz in my pocket had me snatching the coffee pot away from my customer's mug and pulling my cell phone out in a panic. No one called me during the day except for Audrey's school. And Aaron would only call in an emergency.

My mom's name flashed on the display. *Oh, God*. What if something happened to my father?

Coffee pot in one hand, cell phone in the other, I hurried to the back hall between the kitchen and the bathrooms.

"Mom?"

"Let's have a girls' night in."

"What?" I answered stupidly. My brain, primed and ready to process the latest crisis, could not compute the benign request.

"Let's have a girls' night in tonight. You, me, and Audrey. I'll come to your place and bring everything we'll need."

"Tonight?"

Tonight, I wanted to moon over Max. Maybe even talk to him, or at the very least, text. When he dropped me off yesterday afternoon, he said he'd see me soon.

When was 'soon'? Today? Tomorrow? This weekend? Next?

I was bumbling around in alien territory and needed a few days to acclimatize myself.

"Yes. Tonight. Can you do it? I miss you."

My heart rate slowed, finally getting the memo there was no emergency. "Yes," I answered hesitantly. If she was negative, she'd burst my happy bubble. But Audrey would enjoy a girls' night in. We hadn't done it in forever. "I can do that. Audrey will love it."

She audibly exhaled. "Good. I'll see you later, honey. I'll bring dinner. I'll bring crafts. I'll bring everything."

"Mom?" I had to ask while I had the opportunity. "Susie wants me to take a course to help her with the business side of the restaurant."

"That's wonderful! When is it?"

"Um, well, the problem is that I'd have to go up north to take it. It's, um, three days of classes for three weeks in a row. I know it's a lot to ask, but—"

"It's not," she interrupted. "It's nothing. I'll take Audrey."

"Yeah?"

"Yes," she answered firmly. "I'd be delighted to have her."

I closed the call with a smile on my face, not my usual reaction to a conversation with my mom. Perhaps things between us were finally on the upswing.

Max's text came a few hours later while I waited for Audrey and Brooklyn outside the school.

Max: Did you have a good day?

Me: I did. How was yours?

Was this awkward? Was this what real couples did? Were we a real couple yet?

A flash of red caught my eye. I huffed out a laugh. Audrey had taken a shine to Daire Newman. Since yesterday, she'd talked of little else other than how he beat Harley in a swimming race. I felt my smile stretch my cheeks. Daire handled her, the dog, and his ragtag crew of four-year-olds with aplomb.

My phone buzzed in my mittened hand.

Max: Long and about to get longer. I was hoping to see you tonight, but I've got a situation with a patient that requires my attention. Rain check?

Disappointment wiped the smile from my face. Because even though I couldn't see him, I wanted to.

And I definitely wanted him to make the effort to see me.

I waved to Audrey from my usual spot, watching carefully as she navigated the parking lot. We'd been working on traffic safety for the past year and were finally at a point where she could leave school and cross the parking lot on her own.

The bright red coat and equally obnoxious yellow hat made her more visible, though there was no one in the pick-up line of cars who didn't know to be aware of Audrey.

When she made her way across safely, I dropped my eyes back to my cell and slipped my thumb out of my mitten.

Me: Of course. Anytime.

Max: Anytime?

Was he flirting with me? *Be brave, Renata*. I held my breath as I tapped out my next message.

Me: For you? Yes. Anytime.

Max: I'm going to hold you to that.

He could hold me to pretty much anything. The wall. My mattress. His mattress. A parked car. The desk in his office.

Audrey stopped in front of me, humming away, and reached for my hand. When she had a good day, she hummed. When the day was rough, she withdrew behind the shelter of her headphones and her music.

But today, she hummed, and I smiled.

On the way home, we walked past Artitude.

Artitude was Audrey's favorite place to go in all of Sage Ridge. Rachel, the owner, excelled in all kinds of glass art. Her front window, which she updated constantly with her new creations as well as those of her students, was a perpetual, riotous mass of color and reflected light.

It was also my favorite place.

And it was Rachel who gave Audrey the crystal on a string that she carried around in her pocket.

We stood at the window for ten minutes. I huddled beside her and waited, the bitter cold blowing up the backs of my thighs under my coat.

Finally, she stepped back from the window. "Can we go in?"

The bell over the door tinkled, and Rachel looked up from her seat near the back of the room. "Audrey! How's my favorite girl?"

Audrey glanced at me. "Isn't it funny how I'm everyone's favorite girl?"

I quelled my smile as I sucked in the achingly familiar scent of creativity. "And why wouldn't you be?"

"I don't know," she replied. "Why wouldn't I be?"

My smile won out. "No reason, Bean. No reason at all."

I quickly helped her off with her coat. This was not the place for Audrey to start swinging her arms around if she began to overheat.

Placing Brooklyn in a sit-stay at the front of the store allowed Audrey and me to wander back to talk to Rachel.

"Have I got something for you!" Rachel exclaimed to Audrey.

"I don't know. Only you would know that," Audrey replied with her head cocked to the side.

Rachel chuckled and swung out of her chair. "You're right, Audrey. I know I have something for you." She reached for a small box on the shelf behind her before sitting back down.

While Rachel chatted with Audrey, my greedy eyes took in every corner. So much of the shop had changed over the years, yet it still felt like home.

"Someone very special collected these. We made a beautiful sun-catcher out of them, but these were left over. I told her about how much you love pretty things, and she said you could have them."

There were treasures to be found in every nook and cranny of Rachel's studio.

Audrey peered into the box, her mouth rounding at the discovery of the frosted sea glass nestled inside. "Oh," she breathed. "So pretty. Can I touch?"

The wonder on Audrey's face matched my own. What a miracle it was to make something beautiful from little scraps of nothing.

"Yes," Rachel nodded vigorously. "Of course, you can touch. And if Mommy says yes, you can take them home."

As if I would ever deny her this. An even more familiar melancholy settled over me. I trained my face to hide it.

Audrey stirred them with the tip of her finger before taking them out, one by one, and lining them up on Rachel's worktable according to size and color.

Soon enough, she began holding them up to the light. "They trap the light inside," she mused.

Rachel smiled, her eyes soft. "Harley calls them Mermaid tears."

I knew the legend, and I could relate to it on a visceral level. Watching from afar, separated from my true love by time and space and circumstance.

But nothing lovely came from my tears.

Audrey perked up. "These are Harley's?"

"They were Harley's. She said they're yours now."

With Audrey occupied, Rachel turned her attention to me. "I've got an adult beginners class coming up. I think you should take it."

Immediately, I began to shake my head no, nodding to Audrey.

"She can come too," Rachel replied stubbornly.

My cheeks heated. "I don't have the money for a class right now, Rachel. I promise, I'm planning to take one in the summer."

I told her that every time she asked, but this time I actually meant it. With my program finishing, I would be able to afford to take a class by the time summer rolled around.

I'd taken art lessons from Rachel throughout my childhood and well into my late teens. It was only when I reached the age of eighteen that my father put a stop to them and insisted I work more hours at my part-time job.

"Bah," Rachel waved off my excuses. "You could teach this class better than I can. I always thought it was a shame you didn't keep up with your art. Let me give this to you. You can pay me back by helping me with the rest of the students."

I paused to consider her offer. Every fiber of my being wanted to take that class but having paid the fees for the last course of my program, money was tighter than usual.

Art classes are a frivolous waste of time.

I closed my eyes to block out the voice in my head.

My brows scrunched together. Would I be taking advantage of her if I took her up on her offer?

"You'd be doing me a favor," Rachel added hopefully, then pressed her lips together. "But I don't want to pressure you into doing something you don't want to."

"Oh, I want to," I replied without thinking.

Her face broke out in a happy smile. "Brilliant! It doesn't start until the end of April. Saturday mornings, and Audrey can come with you. I'll set her up with her own things." Rachel bustled around to my side of the table and gave me a one-armed side hug. "Thank you."

I walked out in a daze. Because as much as I wanted a piece of my dreams, Audrey and Aaron had to come first. I could not drop the ball. I had to remain vigilant. There was no room for selfishness.

My life was spinning out of control in the very best of ways. I only hoped I could keep up.

When we rounded the corner for home, Audrey pointed out my mom's car idling by the curb.

I tapped on the window as we walked by, and she greeted us with a big smile. I wondered if this night would be fun, the way it used to be, or if it would be another round of fending off autism cures and soothing her worries over Audrey's future.

As if I didn't have enough of my own.

Audrey tucked herself under my mother's arm as they walked and relayed the legend of the Mermaid's Tears while I carried Mom's bags.

Once inside, Mom bustled around, a small smile on her face while she unpacked her bags and cracked open her multitude of plastic containers.

"I made lemon-cranberry muffins for you, Renata. Chocolate for Audrey, and I found this recipe for protein-packed muffins for Aaron. Is he home?"

"He should be home soon."

"Good," she nodded to herself happily. "I haven't seen him in weeks, and I have something for him."

The kitchen counter filled quickly. "Mom, you've outdone yourself," I exclaimed.

She straightened, pleased. "You deserve a break, Renata." Turning, she slid three containers into the freezer. "Muffins and lasagna for next week."

I stepped back and allowed the familiar scene to unfold in front of me as if I wasn't a part of it. As if I was seeing it for the first time.

I watched my mother set up the craft project she brought for Audrey. Noted her patience as she walked her through the steps. Smiled when she allowed Audrey to find her own way of doing things.

My heart sang at the joy in her eyes when Aaron walked through the door, how she perched on the edge of her seat, unwilling to leave Audrey, yet yearning to get to Aaron.

I watched her eyes close as her lips tipped up in a smile when he leaned down to kiss her cheek.

And I realized two things.

One, my mother loved my kids.

And two, she just might love me too.

12

Believe Me

By Friday night, I still hadn't seen Max, though he texted me every morning, and we spoke on the phone every night after Audrey went to bed. Between my job, Max's practice, Audrey's needs, and Aaron taking extra shifts, there'd been no opportunity.

So, when he walked through the door to Susie Q's? I lit up like a Christmas tree. My feet sent me flying in his direction without a second thought.

His face beamed with pleasure and surprise. It was the surprise that re-engaged my delinquent mind and slowed my pace.

Maybe he wasn't even here to see me.

What seemed so sure, so certain, just five days ago, suddenly struck me as an impossible dream.

I pasted a polite smile onto my face.

"Hello, Max," I greeted him politely.

He narrowed his dark eyes on my face. "Don't do that, Tweet," he murmured. "Don't shut down on me."

I exhaled harshly, dropping my gaze to the floor before meeting his eyes. "I'm sorry. I'm nervous and I don't know if you're here to see me or just coming in to eat or maybe meeting someone else and I just don't know how to act."

He smiled and stepped closer. Reaching for my face, he brushed the backs of his fingers over my cheek. Dipping his head, he said, "I'm here to see you. I'm here to eat. And I'm here to meet up with a couple of friends."

"Female friends?" I blurted out before pressing my lips tight in humiliation. My cheeks blazed.

The corners of his mouth quirked. "Not female friends. The only women I hang out with are Harley and Noelle. Neither of whom you have to worry about seeing as Noelle's my sister and Harley may as well be. She's also married to one of my best friends."

I huffed out a breath, exasperated with myself. "I'm sorry." I shook my head. "I'm being ridiculous."

He stepped even closer, leaving only a few measly inches between my breasts and his abdomen, forcing me to crane my neck back to meet his eyes.

God, how I wanted him to kiss me.

His eyes traced my face. "Don't look at me like that in public, Tweet," he ordered softly.

My stomach flipped. Need billowed relentlessly as I hummed low in my throat. If he turned me around at that moment, I'd have gladly braced myself against the counter and dropped my knickers.

He gave his head a small shake and flashed his dimple. "This is a family establishment, Tweet." Stepping back, he continued, his voice serious, "There's no need to rush. We're going to beat the odds this time."

Could he see the doubt in my eyes?

His eyes crinkled so warmly I could not help but return his smile.

"Think I can steal you away for a couple of hours after your shift?"

Was Aaron going out? I didn't want to disrupt his plans. Would it be okay to bring Max home if Audrey was sleeping? What if she woke up?

"Wren," he murmured. "We can go to your place for a coffee if Aaron's going out. Otherwise, we can go to The Beaver Dam for a drink."

The Beaver Dam?

I did not have a single piece of clothing appropriate for The Beaver Dam. The last thing I wanted was to stick out like a country bumpkin amidst Sage Ridge's young, vibrant, and beautiful.

"We can have coffee at my place."

His eyebrows flew up. "You're okay with me meeting Aaron and Audrey?"

No. But it was the lesser of two evils.

"Audrey will be asleep, and Aaron knows about you."

He grinned, his dimple drilling a hole in his cheek. "I find this very interesting. What exactly does Aaron know about me?"

I tutted and smacked his chest lightly with the back of my hand before spinning around to grab three menus.

Seating him in a large booth, I plopped the menus on the table. "Want me to make you a shandy?" I teased.

"No!" he laughed and shook his head. "It served its purpose which was to give you a message and I never want to drink it again."

"And was the shepherd's pie a message?"

He cocked a brow. "Wasn't it?"

"Hm," I hummed. "Let's see what message I can send you tonight."

He grinned. "I look forward to it. Can you sit with me for a bit?"

I looked around the restaurant and chewed the inside of my lip. It was beyond full. "I wish I could," I said with real regret.

My eyes stung with disappointment as if I'd received the very best of presents, but wasn't sure how long I'd be allowed to keep it.

"Hey, hey, hey," Max called softly, his fingers wrapping around my wrist. "Everything is going to be fine. Better than fine, it's going to be great."

"There are so many things in our way."

It was true. We hadn't seen one another since Sunday. And it hadn't even been a busy week.

He shook his head and slid his hand down to intertwine his fingers with mine. "Not so many as you think. Trust me, Wren. We're going to have our shot."

I nodded and gathered myself together. I wanted nothing more than to believe him.

He squeezed my fingers, gave me his drink order, and let me go.

When I came back from the kitchen, two other men sat across from Max. I recognized Gabe. Older than Max by at least a couple of years, he was a good three or four years ahead of me in school. We never ran in the same circles, not even before I went to university. But I knew him in the same way everybody knew everybody else in Sage Ridge.

With his looks, he couldn't help but draw attention.

Black, messy hair. Startlingly bright blue eyes. Two full sleeves of tattoos, and only the most blessed among women knew where those stopped.

But I'd have been lying if I said I hadn't wondered.

When I reached Max's table, three sets of eyes perused me. I swallowed my trepidation and locked eyes with Max before setting down his beer.

"Hi," I said, finally turning toward the other two men. "What can I get you?"

Max smoothly intervened. "Gabe, Julian, this is Wren. I told you about her."

Gabe nodded and grinned wickedly. "You did," he agreed, his soft, raspy voice a heady contrast to that wicked smile. He peered up at me. "Are you sure you want to hang out with the boy-next-door? Is it too late to lure you to the dark side?"

Max scoffed. "The dark side. What's going on at your place tonight? Disney or Pixar?"

Gabe scowled. "The same fucking movie she's been watching for the past three weeks. I know every song by heart. I'm singing them in the damn shower."

I chuckled. When Audrey latched onto a movie, she watched it on a loop. "I know that feeling."

Julian extended his hand. "Hello, Wren. Max speaks very highly of you."

Julian had the deepest voice I'd ever heard. Just by looking at him, I could tell he was a different breed. Warm brown eyes, dark brown hair a little longer on top, and a sweet smile made him handsome in a perfectly ordinary way. But there was something about him that hinted at an invisible edge.

I shook his hand. "It's nice to meet you, Julian. Are you new to Sage Ridge?"

He shook his head but retained his grip on my hand. "I've been here about three years now."

I blushed to the roots of my hair. Three years? Had I been living under a rock? Well, I guessed I kind of was.

"You can let go of her hand now, Jules," Max interjected smoothly.

Julian gave me a smile that transformed his face from ordinary handsome to drop-dead gorgeous.

The small tug I felt in my womb prompted me to tug my hand from his grasp.

He chuckled and released me.

"Well, I hope you're enjoying Sage Ridge."

"I am." He eyed Gabe beside him. "Though it's hard to find civilized company."

Gabe grinned at me unrepentantly.

That man would be a handful, no, an armful, for any woman. Feeling intimidated by his attention, I edged closer to Max and immediately felt the warm, reassuring press of his palm against my back.

Where Gabe and Julian represented excitement and challenge, Max offered warmth, safety, and love.

Settling against his hand, I took their orders.

Max's eyes twinkled as his hand dipped lower, briefly skimming the cleft of my ass before asking me once again to surprise him with his.

I jumped and gulped audibly.

Safe?

I looked at him, wide-eyed.

He stared back at me, utterly calm. I wondered for a moment if I'd imagined it, or if the touch was accidental. His cocked eyebrow told me I had not.

I huffed out a short laugh, backed two steps away, then whirled around and headed for the kitchen.

As I walked away, I heard Julian's unmistakable voice followed by Gabe's throaty chuckle. "That's how you treat a woman, you uncivilized motherfucker."

When I came out with their meals, I made sure to place Max's down last in order to avail myself of a speedy escape.

I set Julian's steak and eggs down first, followed by Gabe's chili cheese fries.

Max eyed me curiously, watching his plate lower down in front of him. He froze for a second at the sight of his sausage on a bun, then barked out a laugh. I grinned madly as I hopped away before he could say anything. I'd have to go back and check on them, but hopefully by the time I served my other customers, I'd have gained a modicum of maturity.

Or at least, calm.

For the next half hour, I ran from one table to the next, and from the kitchen to the dining room.

When Shae and Bridge walked in, my hands were full of dishes. I called out that I'd be right with them. By the time I returned from the kitchen, Bridge was sitting beside Max, pushing him to the inside of the booth, and Shae had pulled up a chair seemingly as far from Julian as she could possibly get. I didn't blame her. The man was intimidating.

And just like that, I was back on the outside looking in.

I approached their table.

Bridge glanced up. "Wren! How are you?"

"I'm good, Bridge," I nodded like a pecking chicken, trying to lend credence to my words. "How are you?"

Instead of answering, she wagged her eyebrows at me. "We're going to crash book club. Are you in?"

Shae slung her arm around my waist.

I stiffened.

How were they so at ease?

Shae, her color higher than usual, squeezed gently and looked up at me. "Are you in?"

"In?"

"You're coming," Bridge asserted. "Noelle even convinced Harley to go, and Harley absolutely does not want to." She laughed. "Her mom goes."

"I'm not sure I can," I sputtered, reaching for my excuses.

"We've got a plan," Bridge continued. "Leave it with us. We're going to break you out for the night."

"I'm not sure…" I shrank inside myself, a wilting violet next to a couple of hothouse roses.

"Just think about it," Shae urged.

"I've been meaning to ask if you guys are hiring," Bridge asked.

I blinked in surprise. "For who?"

"Me, babe," she said. "If I'm going to hang out in Sage Ridge for a while, I need a job until I figure out what I'm doing."

"We are hiring," I answered slowly. Bridge had no qualms or reservations about asking to work at Susie Q's.

Oh my God. Had my father's attitude rubbed off on me?

"I'll talk to Susie. Maybe you could come in and meet her tomorrow afternoon after the lunch rush?"

No shame? No embarrassment?

No voice in her head screaming about her lost potential?

The money wasted on tuition? Or in her case, cooking school. Was there such a thing as chocolate school?

She smiled widely. "Awesome. My aunt wants me out of her hair. I'm driving her crazy and she's accusing me of trying to take over her kitchen."

"Are you?" Gabe asked with a cocked brow.

"Absolutely."

The whole table broke out into laughter.

I eased back, first one step then another and another until I made my escape.

Dipping down the hallway to the back hall, I leaned against the wall, dipped my chin, and closed my eyes.

Because I couldn't compete with women like that.

I breathed deeply.

It wasn't just about looks. Or confidence. Or personality.

I was barely available. A phone call was a stretch for me some nights.

This would end in disaster.

For me especially, but also for Max. I knew him well enough to know that it would break his heart to break mine.

And he would most assuredly break mine.

"Wren," his low voice called out to me softly.

I sprang away from the wall, pasted a smile on my face, and smoothed my hands down my apron. "Hey. Max. I was just—"

Before I finished speaking, Max had eliminated the distance between us. Cupping my cheek, he turned my face up to his and brushed his perfect mouth across mine.

My eyelids fluttered shut.

I exhaled against the promised heat of his mouth.

He whispered my name against my lips.

The frown smoothed from my brow as I relaxed into his hold.

"Max," I whispered back, his name pregnant with every hope, every dream, every ounce of yearning in my heart.

And every doubt.

His other hand framed my face. "I only see you." He dropped kisses to the corners of my mouth. "Believe me. I've waited almost half my life for you. I've had plenty of opportunities to move on. I don't want to."

"You're sure?"

He nodded and pressed his forehead to mine. "I'll see you after work."

13

Company

Holding the keys meant I was the last to leave. Locking the front door of Susie Q's, I ducked my head to ensure I tucked the restaurant keyring safely into my purse.

"Wren."

An embarrassingly high-pitched yelp burst from my lips. I stumbled backward until my back hit the glass of the door. The palm of my hand slapped down over my chest as I gaped at the tall, broad figure hovering over me.

"Max!" I gasped. "You scared me half to death."

Reaching for me, he yanked me into his chest. One hand circled to press against my lower back, the other cupped the back of my head. "I'm so sorry, Sweetheart. I figured you knew I'd be waiting for you."

Sweetheart.

Every sweet word from his mouth tumbled to the bottom of my hollow bucket, their tender echoes shoring up the walls of my heart.

With my chin tipped back, and my heart thudding in my chest, I stared up into his dark eyes.

Eyes serious, brow furrowed, he stared down at me. "We have a date."

"To give me a heart attack?" I wheezed.

He wagged his brows and grinned. "I'll do my level best."

I huffed out a laugh, my cheeks burning at the thought of what he might do to me.

It made me breathless. "Careful, I might hold you to it."

His grasp on me tightened as his eyes dropped to my mouth. "How do you feel about public displays of affection?"

Butterflies tripped in my belly.

Public displays of affection? From him? Yes, please.

This was a rhetorical question, right?

He stared at me expectantly.

"Um…I'm in favor?"

He grinned, his normally serious face boyishly handsome. "That's what I want to hear."

Dipping me slightly over his arm, his smiling mouth met mine.

My free hand swung up to grasp him behind his neck over the heavy layer of his winter coat.

His lips were cold, his breath warm, as he pressed his mouth to mine in a chaste kiss that stole the rest of my resistance.

God help me.

Pressing his forehead to mine, he teased, "Want to take me home with you?"

I snorted out a laugh. "You make it sound a whole lot sexier than it is. Are you sure you're ready for Audrey and Aaron?"

His eyebrows arched. "Are you?"

I pressed my lips together and nodded. "I'm scared, but I'm ready."

Turning me toward home, he slung his arm around me. "What are you scared of?"

So. Many. Things.

I sifted through the mess in my head, dismayed at what was left. "It pains me to say this, but my father finding out about us and ruining it is at the top of the list."

His eyebrows arched. "Your father?"

"He's critical of me. He'll see this as me shirking responsibility, or selfishly putting my needs before those of the kids."

"Really?" He maintained his conversational tone.

I nodded tightly, embarrassed my father was like that, ashamed that I allowed it to bother me. And ever so slightly relieved to admit it out loud.

"Hm," he hummed, his voice mild. "If that's truly how he feels, he's a dick."

I barked out a surprised laugh. "Is that so?"

He grinned down at me and squeezed me against his side. "It's an official diagnosis."

At my outside door, I faced him. "I didn't have a chance to prepare Audrey for you coming. I wasn't even expecting you to be waiting or I would have called home from work to warn Aaron. I'm not sure what kind of mood she'll be in."

"You want to call from here? Give them a heads up?"

I shook my head. "My battery is dead."

He shrugged. "This is her home. She doesn't have to be anything other than who she is. Aaron will be okay with me being here?"

I frowned. Shit. My eyes skittered back and forth. "I think so?" I huffed out a laugh. I'd never brought a man home before. "I have no idea."

Max brushed the backs of his fingers over my cheek. "Haven't done much dating?"

I swallowed my embarrassment. "None."

His hand stilled. "None?"

I nodded and snuck a glance at his face. A muscle ticked in his jaw. "Does that bother you?"

"Not for me it doesn't," he answered quickly. His eyes shone with something akin to pity that did not thrill me in the least, but his thumb running over my cheek provided a welcome distraction. "You're cold. Let's get you inside."

I opened the outside door and locked it again before heading up the stairs to our front door. Easing it open, I called softly, "Aaron, we have company."

"Company?"

I swung the door wide. "My friend Max is here," I answered, my voice unnaturally high.

Aaron grinned at me as he tossed his cell phone down on the coffee table. Springing to his feet, he crossed the room with his hand extended. "Hey, Max. Good to see you again."

My eyebrows rose. "You know Max?"

Aaron wagged his eyebrows and grinned. "I get around, Mom. I know everybody."

Max laughed and shook Aaron's hand. "It's good to see you, too."

Brooklyn stretched, her back end still on the couch while her front paws hit the floor. Stepping down, her entire back end wagged as she pranced over to Max.

He bent immediately, cooing, and running his big hands over her thick coat. She shamelessly rolled to her back.

What I wouldn't have given to trade positions with her. I'd fall belly-up and spread-eagled, too.

Giving my head a small shake, I glanced into the kitchen to check for Audrey and asked, "How's Audrey?"

"She was great. Passed out about 45 minutes ago."

Max asked Aaron a question about something that happened at the resort.

Aaron chuckled at the reminder.

I barely heard their words, struggling as I was with the juxtaposition of my real life intersecting with my fantasy life.

I held my hand out for Max's coat and hung it up beside mine on the coat hooks. The sight of our coats hanging side-by-side arrested me. His was made of fine quality wool, mine was discount polyester, but it didn't matter.

I quickly ran the palms of my hands down both, took a mental picture of them hanging side-by-side, and tucked it away.

"Mom?"

I spun around, realizing that was the second time he'd called my name. "What?"

His eyes crinkled at the corners. "Is it okay if I head out for a bit?"

My head began to nod before he finished talking.

He laughed, bussed me on the cheek and stepped into his shoes. Grabbing his coat, he said his goodbyes and left.

Max and I hadn't even made it past the front hall.

My shoulders hovered somewhere around my ears as I turned to face Max. "Would you like a cup of tea?" My face flushed at my lack of options. "Maybe orange juice? Or a soda?"

If this became a habit, I'd have to pick up some beer. Max's beer in my fridge. Max's coat hanging beside mine. Max taking the fourth chair at the table.

His hands cupped my shoulders and massaged gently, his face intent. "Tea would be great. Do you want to change first?"

My tension eased. "Yes. I'd love to get this off."

His dimple flashed. "That makes two of us, but I'll dream vicariously for now."

I laughed and shook my head.

"That's better," he murmured, then prodded me gently toward my bedroom.

What would he think about my bedroom? Heat rose in my face at the thought of sharing it with him. My room perfectly reflected my romantic heart. Plush furnishings, muted jewel tones, candles, scattered books, and soft lighting. He would see an inviting oasis with everything in its place. I snorted out a laugh. So long as he didn't try to open the closet.

I changed quickly, my options limited, and dashed back to the family room. I found him standing in front of the window. His forefinger gently spinning one of my glass hearts sent a pang to the living, breathing, heart in my chest.

Shaking it off, I bustled past him into the kitchen. Once my hands had something to do, I settled. Within a few minutes, we sat on the couch, homemade cookies on the table, mugs warming our hands.

And I was back to being awkward. "It's weird, right?" I blurted.

Sitting back, his big body sprawled out, he took a bite out of his cookie. "What's weird?"

I shrugged and forced myself to be brave. "My feelings for you are so strong, but I barely know you anymore."

"I don't know," he answered. "It's been my experience that people's personalities don't change all that much. You know me, you just don't know too much about how I've spent the years between then and now."

"I know you're a workaholic," I teased. Max's work habits were common knowledge. I couldn't count the number of times I'd heard Susie reprimanding him.

"Reformed," he rebutted, humming as he shoved the rest of the cookie in his mouth. "Who made these?"

My stomach warmed with pleasure. "Me. I love to bake."

He shook his head. "They're delicious. Better than Anita's. Don't tell her I said that, or she'll never serve me a waffle cookie again."

"It'll be our secret," I assured him, doubt already slithering in to steal my joy.

Did he really think my baking was good or was he just trying to make me feel good?

"What else do you like to do?" he asked.

"I like reading. Listening to music."

"The same things you liked back then," he said. "What about art? Do you still create?"

Brooklyn picked that most opportune moment to push her way in beside me on the couch, edging me closer to Max.

"Love that dog," he teased with a grin. "If I'm lucky, she'll stretch out and force you closer."

I rolled my eyes but couldn't hide the flush of pleasure on my face as I tucked my leg underneath me and shifted toward him. "What do you like to do?"

"I've always liked reading. Working out. I'm embarrassingly adept at home decorating." He grinned. "I'm a big fan of eating. Especially Mexican food" He paused. "To be honest, it's only in the past year or so that I've prioritized my personal life. Things were difficult for a long time, and I used work to escape." Taking a sip of his tea, he continued, "Then when I no longer needed the crutch, it had already become a habit."

"When you lost your mom?" I asked softly, wondering if I was overstepping.

"Losing Hunter was the first blow. Hawkley closed himself off from everyone, and Noelle ran. Harley was so angry but wouldn't talk about it. Then my mom got sick. When she passed, my pops fell apart. Eventually, he moved in with Dan and Lou for about six months. That helped him. As for the rest of us, it wasn't until Noelle came back last year that our healing truly took root." He paused then added, "We're not meant to fight alone."

We're not meant to fight alone.

Was that true? Sometimes, I felt like I was doing it all on my own, other times I felt like I was taking advantage of the goodness in the people around me.

I gave my head a small shake. This was a question for another day, and not one that would be easily answered.

"You're close to Noelle," I murmured.

"I love her to death," he agreed. "You told me a bit about your dad, how are things with your mom?"

I grimaced. "They're both good to the kids. My mom flip-flops between the mom who raised me and the mom who's more concerned with appeasing my dad. My father is the same as always."

"He must be proud of you for how well you've done with the kids?"

I scoffed. "No. No, he's not. He's still stuck in the past with all my lost potential."

"That's too bad," he answered, his dark eyes steady on mine. "If you were mine, I'd be proud."

If you were mine.

"Yeah?"

"Yeah." He set his mug on the table before leaning over to take mine from my hands to place beside his. "Come over here."

I edged closer, my head spinning with thoughts of Audrey shuffling out of her room at any moment.

He chuckled. "We'll keep it PG."

My face burned even as I laughed at myself. "I'm sorry."

"Nothing to be sorry for." He grasped my hip and shifted me to his side. "Anticipation is everything."

"Yeah, well, I've been anticipating for almost two decades," I grumbled.

Nuzzling his nose into my hair, his lips brushed the shell of my ear. "I'll make it worth the wait, Tweet. I promise."

Desire burned a path from his mouth at my ear to my womb. I pressed closer.

Heaven. Bliss. Joy.

Thunder and Lightning.

Perfect peace and a maelstrom of emotions.

And I'd waited so long.

14

Welcome to the Neighborhood

"We've waited this long." His lips continued to tease the curve of my ear. "We can wait a little longer."

My breath released with a shudder. "It's hard," I whispered.

"That's what she said," he whispered back.

It took half a second for his words to break through my sensual haze. I barked out a laugh and swatted his chest.

"Juvenile!" Twisting away to stare up into his grinning face, I could almost imagine I'd never lost this view. The fact that it had been twenty years since the last time choked my laughter off at the source.

"See?" he challenged with a wide smile. "I haven't changed all that much." His grin faded as his eyes turned serious. He brushed his thumb over my cheekbone. "And I'm willing to bet my future happiness on the fact that you haven't either. Not in any way that matters."

Doubt tightened its hold around my heart. "You can't be sure of that."

"Oh, but I can. You think I haven't watched you all these years? That I haven't seen the way you are with your kids? Your customers? Susie?" He dipped his chin and raised his brows. "And don't forget, Dan and Lou. They love you so very much."

I searched his gaze. "They talk about me?"

Dark eyes softened in understanding. "They speak very highly of you."

Touched, and exposed, I murmured softly, "They're the best kind of people."

"They are."

His gaze dropped as his thumb continued its journey along the line of my jaw, down the slope of my throat, to rest in the divot centered over my collarbone. He inhaled deeply and tilted his head to the side before widening his grasp and lightly collaring my throat.

The tiny hairs across my decolletage stood on end as my skin begged for more.

I tipped my chin back, shamelessly offering him greater access.

His touch, slow and certain, brought every nerve ending back to life.

My eyelids fluttered shut. I couldn't remember the last time I'd been touched. But it had only ever been like this with Max.

I loved my husband, but our union wasn't passionate. I assumed what I felt for Max was a product of youth despite the romance novels I devoured that suggested it could be otherwise.

But now, with Max's hand gently circling my throat, his finger stroking my pulse, I knew I'd been fooling myself.

And as much as I wanted to open myself up to him and sink into the oblivion his body would surely offer, I was grateful for the failsafe of Audrey in the next room.

Because my father's reaction was not the only thing that scared me.

How could I know what he felt for me was real? "Can I ask you something?"

"Anything."

I blurted out the question and possibility that had tortured me for years. "Why didn't you ever marry?"

He laughed softly and blew out a breath as he dropped his hand from my throat and took my hand in his. "Wow, right for the jugular."

I hurried to assure him, "You don't have to answer."

"It's not painful, it just surprised me that you got to the crux of my issues with your first question." He squeezed my fingers. "It's an easy, two-part, answer. First, I never met anyone who inspired that level of commitment. And two, I was afraid. Watching my family fall apart, especially my pops, made me question for a long time if love was worth the pain."

"Have you changed your mind?"

He brought my hand to his mouth and brushed my knuckles back and forth over his lips. "Yes."

"How?" My breath caught in my throat; my gaze trained to his mouth.

"Having a front-row seat to Hawkley overcoming his grief inspired me. Harley never had it easy, but she never gave up. Noelle came home and turned her life around. Even Daire, who I was convinced was a confirmed bachelor, didn't waste a single second once he set his sights on Harley. We could have what they have. And I don't want us to miss our chance."

I sighed, my eyes closed as he leaned forward, his warm mouth drifting back to my ear, his sweet words opening my heart.

"Now, how about you give my mouth exactly five minutes with yours, and then we'll cuddle up and watch a movie." He pulled back to look at me. "You're not working in the morning, are you? Do you need to get to bed?"

I shook my head, my eyes dropping to his mouth. "I'm good to watch a movie."

He grinned and dropped his mouth to mine. "First things first."

Four minutes later, I twisted around, slung one leg over his thighs, and dropped my ass on his lap.

"Fuck, Tweet," he groaned out a laugh. "You're not making this easy."

"Easy?" I panted. "I've never been so easy in my life."

His hands clamped down on my hips. Holding me still, he ground up into my heat. "It's not that I don't want to," he grunted. "I just don't want this to be Audrey's first impression of me."

I nodded and cupped my hands around his face. My head fell back as I rolled my hips. I don't know what came over me, but I'd never wanted anything as badly as I wanted him inside me. My body, mind, and soul, were on fire.

"One more minute," I gasped.

Pushing me up off his lap, he ordered, "Kitchen."

I wavered on my feet, my senses dulled by lust. "What?"

Standing up, he towered over me. "Kitchen." Without another word, he took my hand and dragged me after him.

The ten steps between the couch and the kitchen brought my brain back online and I saw Max through clear eyes.

And he was a man pushed to the edge.

Inside the doorway, he pushed my back against the wall. "I'm going to tell you what we're going to do. All you have to do is say yes or no, got it?"

I nodded, my eyes going heavy-lidded at the dark look in his.

With one hand, he undid the drawstring of my lounge pants. "I'm going to get you off with my hand, just once, and then we're going to watch a movie."

"What about you?"

"This is more than I expected for tonight and everything I want. When we take it further, I want to take my time with you. Yes or no?"

"Don't you want me to—"

"Yes or no?"

"I'm just making sure—"

Splaying his big hand across my naked belly, he closed his eyes and pressed his forehead to mine. "Yes or no, Tweet? Simple question."

I took the plunge. "Yes."

"Thank fuck."

Diving into my panties, he cupped my sex in his palm while his other hand fisted in my hair and pulled my head back. With his lips barely coasting over mine, he stared into my eyes. "Going to watch you come for me, Wren."

I gasped and melted into his hands.

With his foot, he nudged my feet further apart and drew slow, easy circles at my entrance. "That's it, baby. Let me in."

My eyelids drifted shut and my lips parted at the exquisite pleasure.

"Does that feel good, my baby?" he whispered against my mouth.

"Yes," my voice broke.

Pressing two fingers at my entrance, he promised, "Going to make you feel so much better in just a minute."

"Yes," I said again, my hips rocking in an effort to get him inside me. "Yes, Max. Just like that."

He chuckled darkly. "You going to coach me through it or are you going to let me have my way with you?"

Coach him? He had everything well under control and he'd barely started.

"Your way," I panted.

"That's what I want to hear," he praised. Dropping his mouth to mine, he licked across the seam of my lips and delved inside just as his fingers breached my entrance.

A long, low moan broke from my lips as I latched onto his wrist.

The tendons and muscles in his wrist moved under my hand, each movement corresponding to a delicious lick of pleasure derived from his fingers.

"That's my girl," he breathed, dancing his thumb back and forth over my clit.

The first flutter hit. He withdrew his fingers and slid his hand out of my pants.

My eyes sprang open in distress as my hands flew to his wide shoulders. "Max!"

He towered over me, dark, hungry eyes taking me in, wide chest shadowing me, his long legs braced between mine.

My heart fluttered in my chest at the sight. "Max," I whispered.

His other hand tightened in my hair.

"Close your mouth, Wren," he ordered, dark eyes holding mine.

I snapped my mouth shut.

A moment later, his fingers, slick with my arousal, coated my lips.

When my mouth fell open in shock, he took the opportunity to dip his finger inside and slide it along my tongue.

I stared up at him, unblinking and unsure. I'd never read this in any of my romance books.

He dropped his head, licked across my mouth, and groaned at my taste. "Open, my baby," he breathed.

I gave him my mouth as his fingers traced a line down my stomach and back into my panties.

His tongue, oh, God, his tongue filled my mouth, mimicking the dance we were slowly and surely headed toward.

With two fingers curled up inside me, his strokes slow and sure, his thumb went to work.

Waves of heat rippled outward while the pressure built. My hips rocked uncontrollably. Within thirty seconds, I combusted.

His mouth smothered my cries as his fingers gently coaxed me through to the end.

Releasing my hair, he cupped the back of my neck, and my head fell back against the wall.

His hand stilled, two long fingers still curled inside me.

Eyes heavy, I stared up at him. So dark, so serious, and so much more than I ever imagined.

He rubbed the tip of his nose against mine. "You okay?" he asked gruffly.

"Mhm," I hummed. "Just a little shocked."

"Shocked?" His eyebrows shot up. "Why?"

"You're, well, you're the boy next door."

My face heated. Now I blushed?

He slowly withdrew his fingers and circled my poor little clit once more before bringing his hand to his mouth and licking his fingers clean.

"Oh, my," I breathed.

He grinned down at me. "Welcome to the neighborhood, baby."

15

Debauchery

Max came over again on Saturday night after Audrey went to sleep and Aaron went out with his friends. We were like a couple of teenagers trying to cop a feel before my parents showed up. Only instead of my parents, it was my kids.

Sunday, he called wanting to take Audrey and me out for dinner.

I balked at the idea of going out in public. As soon as he realized my concern was dealing with my parents, he reversed course and took us to the movies where we would be less on display.

The excitement of the movies in combination with the extra socializing tuckered Audrey out. When we got home, Audrey scampered off to her closet.

Following me into the kitchen, Max pulled out his cell phone. "You want pizza for dinner? I'll order it for two hours from now?"

I spun to look at him in surprise. "You still want to be here?"

He frowned. "What do you mean?"

My cheeks heated. "I mean, you've spent all afternoon with us, and the past two nights with me. You're not, uh, bored?"

He dipped his chin. "Are you here?"

"Yes." I frowned back at him.

Stepping forward, he dipped his knees to meet my eyes head-on. "Then I'm happy to be here."

I smiled tentatively. "You're sure?"

"Positive." He flashed his dimple and dropped a soft kiss on my lips.

How crazy was it that we were in a position where he could do that? I tipped my chin back for one more and felt myself smiling against his mouth.

Max. He was standing right in front of me yet I still couldn't believe it.

"I'm going to go freshen up, okay?"

He grinned. "If Audrey wasn't here, I'd think I was getting lucky."

I laughed. "I wish you were."

What was the female equivalent of blue balls? Twitchy clit? Bitchy beaver? Cranky kitty? Crabby Clam? Blue bean?

Whatever it was, I had it.

Bad.

And yet, even if we had the opportunity, I wasn't sure how ready I was to follow through.

Max made the order, his deep voice a sensual caress as I made my way to my bedroom.

My relationship with sex was complicated. My first experience was not the best. Especially since it came with a healthy dose of public shame for getting caught with my hand in the proverbial cookie jar.

His hand in my cookie jar? His cookie in my jar? I snorted out a soft laugh.

With David, sex was fairly perfunctory. Only one of us regularly reached the finish line. And it wasn't me. In the beginning of our marriage, I broached the subject with him.

After a couple of hours of the silent treatment, he mansplained the female body, informing me that women don't always orgasm. And berated me for focusing on the physical. After all, 'there's more to sex than just orgasm.'

I slipped into the bathroom, closed the door, and forced myself to take a slow, deep breath. As much as I wanted Max, as much as I wanted him here, I wasn't used to having people in my space.

And I worried I bored him.

I ran the cold water over my hands and pressed my palms to my face. If he didn't want to stay, he wouldn't. I didn't have to be anything but myself.

I just wished myself was a tad more interesting.

Leaving the bathroom, I heard the murmur of male voices and the clang of dishes and cutlery in the kitchen.

Frig. Aaron was home? I glanced at the time. He was early.

As I approached the kitchen, I heard Aaron speak in the tone he reserved for the most serious of issues. Which wasn't used very often. "Don't hurt her. She's been through enough. If you're not serious, leave her alone."

A moment of silence beat between them before Max answered. "Your mom doesn't know this yet but I'm in this for the long haul. I'm taking things slow for her sake. I'm not going anywhere."

"Good to hear."

"I appreciate you protecting your mom."

Aaron made a sound I'd never heard from him before. "So far, the men in her life have been shit. My grandfather, my father, and

Audrey's father. None of them stuck by her. She needs someone who can stick."

"I'm going to stick, Aaron. Now that I know you're on board, I can pick up my pace."

Pick up his pace?

Oh, shit...oh, yay? I backtracked a few steps then made my presence known.

Max claimed the fourth chair at our tiny dining room table. Audrey was quiet but happy throughout dinner. Aaron and Max discussed sports, teasing me gently when I tried to participate.

"Stick to your books, Mom. You're embarrassing your sisterhood with these questions."

Laughter. Conversation. Gentle teasing. Was this what it would be like for us? Could it really be that simple?

Four days passed. Though we spoke on the phone every night, I'd barely seen Max since our impromptu family dinner on Sunday. With the weekend just around the corner, I looked forward to finally stealing some time together.

At the sound of the knock on my front door, I peered through the peephole and blinked in surprise before swinging it open. "Anita? What are you doing here? Is everything okay?"

I wracked my mind. Was there some reason Anita was showing up at my door on a Thursday evening?

Female giggles ensued. Harley poked her head around my door frame. "We're here to kidnap you. Anita's here to babysit."

My face paled as I drew back. "Babysit?"

Audrey did not do well with surprise changes in plans.

I never went out on a Thursday night.

Or at all.

My gaze dropped to the floor. Where were we going? What on earth would I wear? Susie Q's uniform would not cut it.

"It'll be fine, honey," Anita soothed. "I brought waffle cones and ice cream. Hauled the waffle machine out for just this reason."

"And if it can't happen, we'll just order a pizza," Noelle offered.

My head shot up at the effort they'd gone to.

"No pressure," Shae added.

"Well," Bridge interrupted with a grin. "A little bit of pressure."

At that, I laughed and stepped back. "Audrey, we have visitors."

Audrey opened her bedroom door and peered out into the family room. Her brows lowered then rose as she spotted Harley and Anita.

Harley grinned at her and waved.

Anita jumped right in. "How's my favorite girl?"

"Tired," Audrey replied, stepping further into the room. "What are you doing here?"

Anita gestured toward Bridge. "These ladies want your mom to come out with them tonight. I thought I could hang out with you."

Audrey's eyes skittered from me to the group gathered like a small beehive just inside our door.

Her eyes returned to me. "Are you going in your pajamas?" She narrowed her eyes on Anita. "Did you bring waffle cones?"

Anita brightened. "I did! Tell Mommy to go out with her friends and we'll have our own fun."

"Go out, Mom."

Shrugging at Anita, overwhelmed by my good luck, I scurried to my bedroom and pulled on my jeans and a sweater. Looking down the length of my body, I acknowledged it was no great improvement. Thankfully, I didn't have time to agonize over it because they were out there waiting for me.

That and the fear Audrey would change her mind propelled me to move faster.

Unfortunately, I had plenty of time to think on the drive to Michelle's house where the book club met.

I stopped behind Harley at Michelle's front door. She looked almost as dubious as I was.

"Are we sure this is a good idea?" I ventured.

"It's a great idea," Noelle enthused.

Shae held her fist up to Noelle for a bump and wagged her eyebrows. "And wait until you get a load of Michelle's man. He puts the hubba-hubba in hubby!"

"Shae! He's a married man!" Noelle scolded before turning to me with a smirk. "He's a firefighter."

"I don't know. I'm with Wren on this one," Harley admitted. Her voice dropped to a harsh whisper. "My *mom* is in there!"

"I know," Noelle's eyes gleamed with happiness. "I hope I'm in her group."

"Yeah," Harley snorted. "Because you have a thing for my dad."

Bridge chortled as Noelle gasped, "I do not. I mentioned one time that he's an attractive man."

Harley held her palm up in front of Noelle. "Please. Once was more than enough."

Shae entwined her fingers with mine and offered a reassuring squeeze.

I latched onto her like a buoy.

She squeezed again. Her voice low, she leaned closer to my ear. "It's hard, so hard, to get out there again. I understand. This is a good first step."

I made one last-ditch attempt to protest. "I thought they met at The Beanery or was it Novel-Tea?"

Harley snorted. "They used to. They got kicked out of both for being too loud."

"Really?"

Noelle laughed. "That and their vocabulary."

Harley scowled. "You're enjoying this far too much."

"You'll enjoy it, too, once the strippers show up," Shae assured her.

"What?" Harley hissed. "I cannot. Not with my mom in there."

Shae grinned. "Happy April Fool's Day!"

"That's supposed to end at noon," Harley grumbled.

"No more delays, ladies." Bridge leaned over and pressed the doorbell.

A few seconds later, Michelle swung the door open. Her eyebrows shot up as her mouth slackened with surprise. Then she burst out laughing. "Here comes trouble," she murmured, standing back with a happy grin. "Come on in."

Shae gathered all of our coats and dumped them in Michelle's den with the rest of them as Michelle ushered us downstairs to her beautifully finished basement.

I trailed a few steps behind Harley. The sound of women laughing and talking reached me before my foot hit the first step.

A moment later, Shae ran down behind me and placed a hand on my shoulder. She squeaked. "This is going to be fun!"

Halfway down the stairs, the wall dropped away, and I could see Michelle's set-up. There were two tables surrounded by chairs. In the middle of each table sat a wide selection of beverages and two trays of goodies.

We were coming in a bit late, and the room was already pretty full, so I assumed most of the women had already arrived. And all of them looked happy to be there.

For the first time, a frisson of excitement worked through me.

I was out. It was girls' night out. And I was part of it.

Me.

I spied Susie, Rachel, Lou, and *my mom*?

My mouth fell open in shock.

Her face lit up when she saw me. "Renata!"

My mouth slammed shut only for my eyebrows to fly up.

My mother is at Spill the Tea book club?

I gathered my wits and smiled back at her, then laughed, as her face fell.

She slapped a hand over her eyes and began to laugh behind her hand.

I grinned.

This was the mother I remembered from my childhood.

"Don't worry," Michelle assured everyone with a snort of laughter. "We're separating into groups. No one wants to know their mother's kinks."

A collective groan worked its way through three generations of women.

Three generations who presented a universal truth. The yearning for love and romance did not flicker out once we reached a certain age. If at all.

We were made to love. And I was well within my rights to long for my share.

I crossed the room quickly and offered my mom a hug.

She gazed up at me. "I'm so glad you're here." Her eyes flitted over to Harley, Noelle, Shae, and Bridge. "Those are good girls, Wren. I like them for you."

"I like them for me, too," I agreed softly.

"Is Aaron home with Audrey?" Her brow furrowed. "I thought he worked Thursday nights?"

"Anita's with her."

Her lips rounded in an 'O'. A hint of regret flashed in her eyes as they flickered up to mine. "I love it that you guys have Anita." She squeezed my hand. "Now go to the other side of the room before Michelle sticks us together."

I widened my eyes in agreement and nodded before making my way back to my group.

My group.

I had just sat down between Shae and Harley when a deep voice called down from upstairs. "Michelle? I'm bringing the food down."

Rachel snorted. "He's giving us a heads-up this time."

"Why?" I asked.

Michelle guffawed. "Because last week we had just finished an alien romance. We didn't hear him coming down and he caught us with the measuring tape."

"He asked if he could help us with something," someone wheezed with laughter.

"Susie filled him in," Lou snickered.

Michelle shook her head. "Yeah, yeah. Yuck it up. You guys weren't here for the fallout."

"Kind of wish I was," someone teased.

Michelle's smile did little to dissuade the notion that the fallout was anything less than satisfactory.

Heavy footsteps landed on the stairs.

I watched as long, jean-clad legs appeared first, followed by deliciously veined forearms, a flannel shirt, and a cheeky grin.

"Hi Nathan," Lou chirped. "Did you bring us some grub?"

Nathan looked around the room warily. "Everybody behave until I get back upstairs."

He stopped beside Michelle and dropped a brief kiss on her smiling mouth.

Rachel whistled.

He grinned and shook his head before heading back upstairs. The room was silent as he left.

Then his deep voice rang out once again, "The door is closing. Resume your debauchery."

16

Cock-Blocked

Saturday morning, the phone rang bright and early while I was still cozied up on the couch with Brooklyn and my morning coffee.

This time when I saw my mom's name on the display, I didn't panic. "Hi, Mom. Is everything okay?"

"Everything is fine, just fine. Um..."

It wasn't like her to peter off like that. I tensed. "What is it?"

"I have a small favor to ask you."

"Sure," I answered slowly. "Go ahead."

"It's just that, your father doesn't know about book club." She paused then went on in a rush. "He thinks it's a bible study."

For a pregnant moment, I was stunned silent. Then I laughed. "Mom!" I jokingly scolded. "Shame on you!"

She giggled like a schoolgirl. "I'll have you know, Renata Lynn, that almost every single one of those ladies goes to church."

The idea of my mom circumventing my dad's boorish ways to go out and have fun with her girlfriends tickled me pink.

"Good for you, Mom. I mean it. Your secret is safe with me."

What was happening? It seemed in the past couple of weeks my whole world had flipped onto its head. Everything I thought was set in stone, everything I believed to be irrefutable truth, had crumbled and fallen.

First, Susie's offer of more hours in addition to support with Audrey. Then, Max walked back into my life. Dan and Lou making it possible for me to finish my course. I suddenly had a group of girlfriends, and my mom belonged to a smutty book club. One I was pretty sure we were all going to join if we could convince Harley.

To top it off, today Audrey was coming to work with me. We would keep it short this first time, but she was excited about it. Especially when Susie offered to let her help roll the cutlery into napkins.

After my shift, Max picked up chili and cheese buns from Beach Buns and met us at home. We spent the evening teaching Audrey to play poker. She was enthralled. And she had the best poker face by far.

She took herself to bed shortly after eight, and Aaron went out with his friends right after work. After watching a movie, I tip-toed into Audrey's room to check on her before easing her door closed and returning to Max.

We'd hear her if she woke up.

"Come here, Tweet," Max murmured.

I padded across the floor until I stopped right in front of him.

Leaning forward, he grasped my hips and pulled me forward, placing my bum on the couch beside him, my chest against his.

"Hi," I whispered.

His serious eyes traced my face. "Hi, yourself. I missed you this week."

"Me too." I scrunched my brow. "These next three weeks are going to be busy."

He nodded and brushed my hair back from my face. "I know. Don't be worried. I understand. What can I do to make it easier?"

"You've already done so much, Max. You, and Susie, and Dan, and Lou... I can't thank you enough."

"It's the least of what I want to do for you. You know that, right?"

I nodded slowly. "I think so."

He smiled. "Are you going to miss me while you're living the student life?"

I smiled. "I will."

"Are you a little bit excited?"

"I've mostly been worried, but now that it's time, I am excited." I squeezed my shoulders up to my ears as I grinned, then swallowed, feeling suddenly so very guilty. "I don't get much time to myself. I'm looking forward to reading and, I don't know, maybe going shopping for some new clothes?"

It was long overdue. My jeans had faded away to nothing, and my tops were at least a decade out of style.

"Good for you. You deserve it. You going to let me give you a little something to think about while you're gone?"

You deserve it.

I pressed my breasts against the hard wall of his chest.

My brain wanted to mull over his words, my body readied to get down to business.

His eyes darkened as his free hand dragged down the length of my side to rest on my hip before continuing its journey over my ass to the top of my thigh. His voice was gruff. "That feels like a yes."

I tipped my chin back, watching his face from beneath my lids as his eyes followed the path of his hand up to my back. Pulling me tight against his chest, his other hand tugged my head back, and his mouth lowered within a whisper of mine.

"I'm going to need verbal confirmation, Tweet. You going to let me send you away with a sweet memory?"

His wide chest pressed warmly against mine.

The steady beat of his heart.

Solid.

Strong.

Immoveable.

Unshakeable.

Max.

"Yes."

His firm lips seduced mine open as he delved inside, his tongue pushing mine back inside my mouth to play with his.

I closed my eyes, melted into his hold, and gave myself over to him.

He grunted his approval and shifted my body closer. His hips rolled underneath me, telling me in ways words could never adequately express just how much he wanted me.

His hold left me no room to move. Fire coursed through my veins. This was what it felt like to be taken and it was just a kiss. My, God. What would it be like when he finally took me to bed?

My entire body hummed with pleasure.

He broke the kiss and tugged my head back further before dragging his teeth down the side of my neck, his scruff sending shockwaves of pleasure straight to my nipples.

So focused was I on his mouth, I yelped in surprise when his hand cupped my breast over my sweater.

His hand froze in place as he lifted his head. "Okay, Wren? You want to stop?"

"God, no," I protested, my voice guttural.

"That's my girl," he praised. Holding my gaze, he released my breast and skimmed his fingers under the hem of my sweater and up over my abdomen. With no hesitation, he tugged the cup of my bra down and captured my nipple between his fingers.

"Yes, Max," I hissed.

His hips thrust up beneath me.

"What about you?"

"What about me?" he murmured, his hooded eyes on my face as he kneaded my breast and rolled my nipple between his fingers.

"You're going to be frustrated," I worried.

His lips curved into the faintest of smiles. "I'm a big boy, I'll handle it. This, you, is all I want right now." He brushed a kiss across my lips and spoke against my mouth. "Believe me when I tell you, my time is going to come."

I drew in a sharp breath. "I look forward to that."

The promise in his dark eyes made it a certainty. "You and me both. For now, let me play with my girl. I want to learn your body. See what it takes to make you come. Let me make you feel good."

"Shouldn't I learn your body?"

He laughed and dipped his face down to mine. His eyes alight, he assured me, "By the time you get me naked, you'll only have to look at me to get me off."

I snorted out a laugh.

He tugged the drawstring of my lounge pants.

Relentless need burned away my laughter as his talented fingers dipped under my waistband and brushed across my mons.

My breath caught in my throat. How long would it take before his touch stopped feeling like a miracle?

How long before the craving for him would fade?

How long until I could accept this as part of my normal everyday life?

My next thought burned through the fog of my desire. How long before his craving for me would fade?

"Tweet," he murmured, his fingers stroking the curve of my inner thigh. "Stay with me. Take what I'm giving you. It's yours. It's all for you."

Sincerity shone from his dark eyes.

I nodded and relaxed in his arms, only realizing at that moment that I'd tensed up.

"Better," he whispered.

I softened further under his praise.

"Let your legs fall open for me," he murmured, aligning my chest with his.

I wrapped my arms around his neck and let one knee fall to the side.

He rewarded my compliance with a soft nip at the corner of my mouth before dragging three fingers over my clit in a slow circle.

I moaned into his mouth, my legs spreading further, hips flexing.

Where my mind flittered around worried about the past and the future, my body held no such compunction.

"Max," I breathed.

Just saying his name, knowing it was his hand working between my thighs, his heart beating against mine, his tongue tracing the seam of my lips, sent me higher.

"So wet, so sweet," he murmured.

My arms tightened around his neck as my pelvis rolled, chasing his fingers, wanting more than the teasing touch he gave me.

I cupped the back of his dark head and pulled his mouth down to mine. My tongue darted inside his mouth, begging him to play, to take, to enter me.

Instead, he licked across the bow of my top lip before gently drawing the bottom one into his mouth and releasing it with a soft scrape
of his teeth.

Frustration rolled through me.

I wanted more.

Needed more.

Digging my heels into the couch cushions, I pushed myself further
up so that my ass was almost in his lap, giving me a better hold on his
head. I held his face and pressed my mouth to his.

His body shuddered underneath me, and a flare of feminine satisfaction fueled me.

Flipping to my knees, I hovered over him. Grasping his wrist, I
pressed his hand against my sex and dropped my forehead to his. Half
of me was appalled at my brazen behavior. But the other half, the half
that mindlessly drove me onward, gave no fucks.

Rocking back and forth, I dragged my heat over his fingers that so
sweetly teased my entrance in shallow circles.

That was better. I had him where I wanted him. "Mm," I hummed
low in my throat in satisfaction, cupped my hands around his gorgeous
face, and took his mouth while my hips rolled over him like a woman
possessed.

He firmly circled my entrance. "You want to ride that, baby?"

"Yes, Max," I panted. "In me." I demanded, adding a belated,
"Please."

The tendons of his wrist flexed in my hand as he slid one finger then
another inside me while his thumb found and strummed my clit.

Both of my hands found his strong shoulders as my head fell back.
"Yes, Max, yes."

"That's perfect, baby," he praised. "Look at you taking what's
yours, taking what you deserve."

Pleasure unraveled deep in my womb and spread outward.

Max gripped my waist and steadied me as the smooth roll of my hips began to stutter.

He yanked me forward over his hand again and again. "Give it to me, Wren."

Oh, God!

"I want it, Wren," he demanded, his voice tight.

So sweet.

"It's mine."

So hot.

"Let go," he ordered with a growl. "Flood those fucking panties."

Yes. I cried out as my body bowed over him.

He gentled his touch to drag out my orgasm. His other hand left my waist and pulled me forward by the back of my neck. Taking my mouth, he swallowed my cries until the tremors stopped, leaving my body limp and sated.

Easing me forward into his arms, he cradled me.

"Bossy little thing, aren't you?" he teased softly.

"Max!" I gasped and hid my face, half laughing, half mortified.

Tangling his hands in my hair, he tugged my head back to meet my eyes.

My face flamed.

His dimple winked for a brief second then his serious dark eyes met mine.

"That's what I want for you, Wren. I want you to have everything you've ever desired, know without a shadow of a doubt that it's yours to have, and have no qualms asking for it."

"I—"

Oh, God. I nearly told him I loved him.

It was too soon.

I mean, it had been nearly two decades, but we hit the reset button. That meant the timer started again, right?

Eyes wide, I stared up at him.

He raised his brows in challenge, then his attention shot to the front door.

The lock turned and I scrambled to right myself, smoothing back my hair, pulling down my shirt, and swinging around to sit beside Max, who leaned back, cool as a cucumber, on the couch.

Aaron took one look at us, covered his eyes, and pretended to stagger backward. "My eyes!"

"Oh my gosh," I wheezed, my face turning crimson, while Max chuckled.

Aaron scrunched his nose and scrubbed the top of his head. Sighing, he dropped his hands to his hips, dipped his chin, and shook his head back and forth. With an exaggerated sigh, he lamented, "Cock-blocked by your own kid."

"Aaron!" I sputtered. "You're a menace!"

Aaron, eyes full of life and laughter, peered up at me and grinned.

Max barked out a laugh and pulled me into a side hug.

The contagious rumble of his laughter vibrated against my back.

I lost the fight and began to laugh.

Aaron grinned wider. "Next time, Mom, leave a sock on the door."

17

History

Harsh words slapped me across the face as soon as I walked through the front door.

"What could she possibly be doing for work that's more important than looking after her child? She's a waitress for Pete's sake."

"Hello," I called out to alert them of my presence. Not that it would deter him.

Mom bustled down the hall to meet me, her face already ruddy with stress. "Renata! We're happy you're here, honey."

"Hi, Mom."

Her eyes searched my face. It was an effort to maintain the façade of blank neutrality that served me best when he was around, but the relief on her face told me I'd managed.

"Where are the kids?"

"Aaron took Audrey swimming at the resort."

"They're coming though?"

"Yes, they should be here any minute."

"Dad's waiting for us in the kitchen. I'm very excited to have Audrey stay here." She grabbed my hand and pulled me to a stop. In a much softer, quieter voice, she added, "I'll take good care of her, Wrennie." She grimaced. "And despite his bluster, Dad will too."

Without giving me a chance to respond, she tugged me into the kitchen where I slid into my usual spot at the table.

My father leaned forward and braced his elbows on the table in front of him. "So, you're leaving your kids for three weeks in a row for what exactly?"

I traced the scratch marring the otherwise pristine surface with the tip of my finger. This scratch was like me, the solitary blemish on an otherwise perfect surface. The one deviation that couldn't be covered up or erased.

More and more I recognized how toxic the dynamic was between my father and me. Asking a parent for help shouldn't be that hard.

My face carefully blank, I met his eyes. "Susie asked me to do some training to help her with other aspects of her business."

He scoffed. "And will this training result in a higher pay?"

"Yes."

His eyebrows rose, my answer rendering him momentarily silent.

Perversely satisfied to catch him by surprise, I smiled back at him benignly.

My mom sat on the edge of her seat, her attention winging back and forth between us as if she was watching a tennis match.

He grunted. "Well, there's that at least. If you're going to be pawning your parental responsibilities off on someone else, it better be worth it for the kids in the end. I trust the extra money will go toward their care?"

The anger I'd all but forgotten about over the past couple of weeks due to the sweetness of being with Max flared to life. Like a forest fire moving uphill, it devoured all my good intentions.

"Doesn't it always?" I bit out.

He leaned back in his chair and crossed his arms, his eyes hard. "Shouldn't it?"

My entire wardrobe flipped through my imagination like hangers zipping past on an imaginary clothing rack. The highest quality item I owned was my Susie Q uniform.

As much as I believed the kids had to come first, surely I deserved some benefit of a personal nature from all my hard work.

I took in my father's attire with a single glance. Not one scuff on his shoes, pants creased within an inch of their life, pristine shirt.

No. He did not go without.

The front door opened.

Mom leaned forward and forced a false laugh. "The kids are here. Is everybody hungry?" She stood. "I made a pot roast with potatoes, carrots, and Brussels sprouts. Do you like Brussels sprouts?"

I swung my gaze over to my mother. She, too, was dressed impeccably. My lips trembled with the effort to hold in everything twenty-year-old me longed to scream at them.

At that moment, Audrey and Aaron entered the room, Brooklyn padding along beside them in her service vest. With her headphones on, Audrey was oblivious, but Aaron scanned the room with wary eyes. When he greeted me, it was with a grim smile and a raised brow.

I deflated. Because I needed their help.

I'd made my bed when I chose Aaron, and I wouldn't have it any other way.

My father softened immediately and held up his hand to get Audrey's attention. "Audrey, honey. Come show Grandpa what you're drawing on your iPad."

Turning his attention to Aaron while Audrey set herself up, he smiled. "How are you, Aaron? How are your studies going?"

"No complaints, Grandpa. Mom is the best cheerleader you can imagine. And she makes me the best lunches. I'm almost embarrassed to bring them. Everyone else fends for themselves and they're all salivating over mine."

"Well," he responded drily, his eyes dropping to Audrey's drawing. "At least she learned something working at that diner."

Aaron's eyes narrowed.

Catching his attention, I gave an infinitesimal shake of my head.

He pressed his lips together tightly. "She's the best," he clipped. "Audrey and I couldn't have asked for a better mother."

The rest of the evening, due to Aaron's presence, ran smoothly until it was time to leave.

Aaron went outside to warm up the car while I got Audrey and Brooklyn ready.

"I have to go pee," Audrey danced back and forth from one foot to the other.

"No problem," I assured her, spinning to whip off her coat and help her out of her boots.

"I'll make sure she has everything she needs," my mom offered holding out a hand to her. "Come on, Audrey, honey."

Audrey shoved her hand between her thighs and ran after her.

Left alone with my father, I dropped to my knees and worked on getting Brooklyn's booties on.

"I heard you've been seeing that Brevard boy," my father stated, his tone hard.

I froze for a moment, then, my hands shaking, I continued to look after Brooklyn who began to lean heavily against me.

"Yeah? Where'd you hear that?"

"Word gets around."

"Well," I stood up and smiled brightly, forcing it up into my eyes in an act of bravado that took more energy than I had left in reserve. "It's very new, but I'm hopeful."

"Isn't he the one you were hanging around with on the beach the summer before you got pregnant? Is he Aaron's father?"

After almost two decades, he was still furious that I refused to reveal Aaron's father's name. I didn't want someone who considered me, or Aaron, a burden. And my father would have done everything he could to tie him to me in order to save the family from my disgrace.

My mouth fell open in shock. "No! If Max was Aaron's father he would have *been* his father."

He shook his head angrily. "I don't care for that family. They interfered in our business."

"It was the Bennett family who helped me. Max is a Brevard."

His thick index finger stabbed the air. "You need to keep your priorities in order."

My knees went weak as my entire body began to quake. "What makes you think they're not?"

"You have a history of getting distracted."

The front door swung open. "Mom? Are you coming?"

"Take the dog out, Aaron," my father ordered. "Your mother will be out in a minute."

Aaron stepped inside the front hall, lifted my coat off the hook, and held it out for me to put on. "Here, Momma. Put your coat on."

My sinuses burned with shame. "Thank you, son."

"Go on and take the dog—"

Aaron cut him off. "I'd just as soon stay here, Grandpa."

My head whipped up to look at him.

His face was a wreath of smiles. "I'm terrible at getting Brooklyn into her seatbelt. Mom's the best at it." Turning his smile to me, his eyes softened as he added, "You want me to wait for the Bean and you can get Brooklyn into the car?"

Taking up Brooklyn's leash, I turned toward the door.

"Aren't you forgetting something?" My father snapped. "Have you lost your manners hanging out with that boy?"

I turned slowly, my blood boiling, knowing exactly what my father wanted. "What did I forget?"

His eyebrows rose in challenge. "Dinner?"

Audrey bounced back into the hall followed by my mother whose gaze bounced nervously between my father and me.

I met his eyes briefly before dismissing him and turning purposefully toward my mother and offering her a smile. "Thank you for dinner, Mom. You outdid yourself as usual."

I would pay for that insult, but it felt good not to cow down to him for once.

Aaron barked out a laugh then covered it up by joking with Audrey.

And I, like the needy, clingy, weak-willed woman I'd turned into, took the dog out to the car.

18

Spoiled

B y the end of the first day of classes, I knew two things.

One, I needed new clothes. Desperately.

And two, I could use a haircut.

In a classroom full of twenty-year-olds, I stuck out like a red, swollen, festering, thumb.

I hadn't realized how much *life* I'd missed out on until I came face-to-face with it.

These people had plans and passion and time, so much time!

They laughed, they smiled, they made jokes.

Bought ridiculously over-priced coffees and talked about music and books and movies.

They got together for lunch and dinner, sometimes on the same day. Their weekends were filled with dates and drama and furious sprints of homework and study wherever they could fit it in.

I missed out on all of that.

I didn't regret my children. Not for a minute.

I didn't want their fancy coffee, and I didn't care to spend my weekends running from one bit of excitement to the next. I definitely didn't envy them their fucked-up internet dating debacles, although their sense of ease about their own sexuality urged me to embrace my own.

But I envied their easy comradery, the friendships they seemed to treasure above all else, and the assurance with which they chased their dreams for the future.

And I wondered if I'd ever get a chance to chase mine.

Because getting a business diploma to manage Susie Q's or any other restaurant was most definitely not my dream.

I shook away the selfish thoughts. My life left no room for dreams, especially those that would lead me away from my primary purpose. I had a family, a beautiful family, to look after.

Thank God this was the last course. If I had to brave the classroom again, I wasn't sure I could have hacked it.

As soon as I stepped over the threshold into the cabin, my cell phone rang.

I snatched it up. "Audrey? Bean?"

"When are you coming home?"

Tears stung my eyes. "Two more sleeps. I'll be home after dinner, in two more sleeps."

"I don't like the bed here."

"Maybe Grandma could sleep with you at our place?"

"Grandpa said no. He said, 'it's time she learned she can't have everything her own way.'"

"Well," I cleared my throat and forced my jaw to unclench. "That's crazy, isn't it?"

"Yes. Grandma doesn't get anything her way. Grandpa is bossy. Really bossy."

I smiled. Audrey thought he was referring to my mom instead of her. Or maybe it was me? Frig. I didn't even know who he was talking about for sure. I suspected it was Audrey. You know, all my lax parenting that caused those pesky autism symptoms.

"What did you do today?"

Audrey gave up a few more sentences before losing interest in the conversation and handing the phone off to my mom.

"Hi, Renata, honey. She's doing fine."

"Thanks, mom. I guess she wanted to sleep at home?"

"Yes, but your dad...you know how he is. Stuck in his ways."

"Hm. Well he's well used to having his own way, isn't he?"

Her false laugh grated against my eardrums. "He's just concerned."

"About what?"

"Well," she began, and I braced myself. "A child is not a part-time job. Audrey needs more care than most."

"So, you wouldn't have me do this course?" My voice was pitchy with disbelief. I began to run through my options.

Was there anyone else who could take Audrey? Maybe.

Was there anyone else Audrey would feel comfortable staying with? No.

"No, no, not that. It's about Max Brevard. Are you sure you should be focusing on a relationship when Audrey needs you? Won't a boyfriend be a distraction?"

"Mom," I clipped. "Are you kidding me right now? Was dad a distraction when you were raising me? Should we all be single moms?"

"No, but dad is your father. He was just as committed to you as I was. Max is interested in you, not your kids."

I sucked in a deep breath. "Max has been nothing but kind to Audrey and Aaron. Not once has he inferred that they were in the way.

And if he did, you should trust me to put my children first. I always have. I always will."

Silence rested between us on the line.

"I'm sorry, Renata," she said. "You're right. I don't know what I was thinking."

She wasn't thinking. Not for herself. Whenever he went on one of his rants, she became his parrot, so bent on calming him that she sacrificed me.

And herself.

"Thank you for looking after Audrey, Mom. I'll talk to you both tomorrow."

"Don't leave like this, Renata," she chided.

"I'm not leaving like anything. I need to check in with Aaron and Susie, and I also have homework to do."

"I suppose you'll be calling Max Brevard as well?"

"I suppose that's my business, Mom. If I thought you could be happy for me, I'd share. For now, I'll keep things to myself."

"It's not that I don't want you to be happy—"

"I really do have to go, Mom. Thank you for looking after Audrey. We'll talk tomorrow."

She sighed. "Goodnight, Renata."

"Goodnight, Mom."

The next two days flew by. Before I knew it, I was home again with Audrey and Aaron. I worked all day Friday and Saturday, falling into bed exhausted at the same time as Audrey with only enough energy to check my email and send off a few quick texts to Max before dropping off to sleep.

Sunday, Aaron had to work, and Audrey refused to leave the house. She hadn't been sleeping well due to the changes in her routine. Between sleeping at my parents' house three nights a week and going home with Susie on the days I worked her shifts, she wasn't coping well.

I was exhausted. And I still had homework to complete.

Then Max showed up with dinner for all of us and a Lego set for Audrey.

After we ate, Audrey went to take her bath.

"I'll clear," Max said. "You head into the kitchen, and I'll bring everything to you."

This was the dream. Just this. Sometimes I could almost touch it, other times I swear I felt it slipping through my fingers.

I filled the sink and added dish soap. There was no room in our tiny apartment for a dishwasher. With only three of us, we didn't need it.

Max dumped the dishes into the sink and caged me in from behind.

I leaned back against his wide chest and closed my eyes.

"You're tired."

"Sorry," I winced.

He swept my long hair away from my neck and dropped a scruffy kiss to my nape. "Nothing to be sorry about."

Oh, God. This. Just this.

I closed my eyes.

If I hung on tight, if I did everything right, I might be able to keep it.

"I'd like to stay. Would you like to sit at the table and do your homework while Audrey and I build the Lego set?"

"I feel bad," I confessed.

He huffed out a laugh, his breath tickling my ear and sending a delicious shiver through me. "Why do you feel bad?"

"She's not your responsibility."

His arms wrapped around me from behind. "No. She's not. Not yet. But you? You are."

By the time Audrey was ready for bed, I still wasn't finished so Max left. I yearned to share a home with him. How sweet it would be to climb into bed with him every night? To feel his arms around me? Would we make it to that point?

Monday, I worked all day then dropped a miserable Audrey off at my parents' house and drove up to the cabin. Max had packed three bags of groceries into the trunk which saved me a boatload of time. And took no time at all to unload. As tired as I was, the cabin offered an oasis. I curled up on the couch and read for two glorious, uninterrupted hours with the heat from the wood stove warming me clear through to the marrow of my bones.

Mom texted me updates throughout the day and called me every afternoon. Unlike the first phone call when she questioned if I could handle a relationship, she was supportive.

"Are you enjoying your course?"

A shard of guilt stabbed me. I shouldn't be up there enjoying myself when other people were picking up my slack. I stuttered out a reply. "I don't know if it's enjoyable exactly, but I'm really glad I'm able to do it. Thank you so much--"

"I'm not looking for thank you, Renata." She sounded tired. "You deserve to enjoy yourself. I never got a chance to go to school. I think that's why I was so devastated when you got pregnant—"

I couldn't have this conversation again.

"Mom—"

"No, wait, I'm glad we have Aaron. Our life would be so much emptier without him. And I'm glad I can look after Audrey so you can take this course. I should have done this for you years and years ago. I'm sorry."

"It's okay—" I rasped.

"It's not, honey, and I know that. Just know that I'm proud of you. Really proud of you for taking this course."

"It's just something Susie wanted me to do—"

"I saw the registration on your kitchen table. I know you've been working on this for years. I'm so proud of your determination. I'm ashamed you couldn't tell me about it, but I know that's my fault. I wish I'd helped you sooner."

I didn't know what to say so I said nothing.

What if she told my father? I'd never hear the end of it.

"How's Max?"

Just when I let my guard down, she struck. I rolled my eyes. "Mom—"

"Is he good to you?" she blurted.

"What?"

"Is he good to you? You don't have to answer me. Just...make sure he's good to you. Don't settle for anything less."

I softened. "He's good to me, Mom. It's still new, but he's good to me."

"That's good, honey." She sniffed. "Here, say goodnight to Audrey and I'll talk to you tomorrow."

Before I could process my mother's words, Audrey came on the line. And true to form, she said 'goodnight' and immediately hung up the phone.

I laughed and settled back against the couch. For the first time in forever, I could hear my own thoughts.

And they were hopeful.

Before I went to sleep, just like every night, I called Max.

He was the first thing I thought of when I woke up in the morning, and the last person I spoke to every night before I went to sleep.

The next day, a few of the girls who I had worked on an assignment with the week before cajoled me into going out for lunch with them. They took me to a restaurant inside the local mall.

Not much older than Aaron, they were sweet. And funny. And liberated as hell.

I don't know where they got their confidence, but I wanted some for myself.

Throughout the rest of the afternoon, my thoughts spun. After school, I drove back to the mall, treated myself to an iced coffee, and spoke to Audrey for a few minutes. When she hung up, I tucked my phone back into my purse and went to work.

It was long past time.

When I got back to the cabin, I sat by the wood stove and ate my take-out dinner. Another extravagance I should not have indulged. My bags, plural, sat on the couch across from me like a living, breathing, accusation.

Faced with the results of my spree, I wasn't sure what came over me.

That night in bed, I told Max about my day. "I got my hair cut."

"Yeah?" His pleasure warmed his tone. "Do you like it?"

"I love it," I admitted softly. I swung my head gently, delighted at the feel of my soft curls bouncing around my neck. I'd forgotten my hair took on a bit of a curl when it was shorter and lighter. "It wasn't expensive. I just went to one of those drop-in places, but they did a good job."

"Even if it was expensive, you deserve to get your hair cut, Tweet."

I waited a beat or two then admitted, "I also got a mini makeover. That was free with the purchase of the cosmetics."

"Good for you," he replied adamantly.

I bit my lip.

He chuckled. "Is there more?"

"I bought clothes, too."

"Tweet, you're entitled to get your hair cut, buy makeup, and get new clothes when you need them. Or even when you don't. You're a person just like everyone else. All these small luxuries are not just for other people." He sighed heavily. "I'm going to spoil you to death."

"Oh my gosh," I snorted. "I don't want you to spoil me."

He laughed. "You'll love it. I promise. You're way overdue some spoiling and I'm ready to make up for lost time."

"Lost time?"

"I've missed a lot of birthdays, Christmases, and anniversaries, Tweet. I don't intend to miss any more."

19

Rattled

Pulling the truck into my parents' driveway Thursday night, I was too exhausted to worry about my father. With any luck at all, he would be out like the week before and I wouldn't have to hear it about borrowing Dan and Lou's truck.

Swinging my legs out, I jumped down to the driveway and plodded my way up to the door.

Audrey swung it open before I had a chance to knock. "Hi, Momma. I'm ready to go home." She stopped suddenly and looked at my face. "You look weird."

I barked out a laugh. "Thanks, Bean. Is Grandma here with you?"

"Hi, honey." My mom rushed down the hall to the door then stopped in her tracks. Her face lit up like a beacon. "Your hair!" She rushed toward me, her hands outstretched to touch my new do. "It's gorgeous!" Her eyes scanned my face and her smile gentled as she met my eyes. "You're gorgeous."

I scoffed and rolled my eyes to hide my pleasure. "Okay, Mom."

"No, I'm serious." She grabbed my hand. "You look great. This time has been good for you. Do you have half an hour to come in for a cup of tea?"

At that moment, there was nothing I wanted less, but I'd barely seen her since I started the course. It was the least I could do.

"Is Dad home?" I asked nervously.

She shook her head. "I don't expect him for another hour. He's usually not home before I leave for book club." She rolled her eyes and winked at our shared secret.

I laughed. I loved this new version of my mother. I bent over to pull off my boots. "Sure, Mom. I can come in for a bit." Turning to Audrey, I winced at the dark frown on her face. "Can you watch one episode of your show and then we'll go home?"

"I already had my TV time."

"This one will be a bonus. Unless you don't want to…"

I watched as she weighed her options. "I'd rather watch it at home."

I shook my head. "We won't be watching any more TV at home. I'm giving you a bonus episode so I can have tea with Grandma. If I'm not staying for tea with Grandma, you don't need a bonus episode."

"Fine." She stalked away, and I followed my mom into the kitchen.

This room gave me mixed feelings. Countless craft days, tea times, and baking lessons took place on or around that table. But it was also the scene of one of the worst confrontations of my life and countless uncomfortable family dinners.

Mom bustled around the kitchen happily.

Every few minutes, she looked at me and exclaimed, "I can't get over the change! I love it!"

By the time the kettle boiled, she had my favorite vintage teapot and the matching cups set up and ready to go. She poured and offered me mine.

I wrapped my cold hands around the base to warm them. "How's book club going?"

She laughed and blushed, then admitted, "You know, it's fun. So much fun. The books are fine, some of them are great, but it's the ladies I love. They're so..." Her eyes darted back and forth as she sought the right word. Her gaze returned to mine. "Genuine. They are genuine."

I thought about Bridge and Shae, Harley and Noelle, how they didn't pretend to be anything they were not. "It was fun," I agreed.

"Will you go again?"

I thought about Audrey. It was unlikely. "I'm not sure." I cocked my head to the side. "Would it bother you if I did?"

She shook her head vehemently. "No. Not at all. In fact, I'll drop out and sit with Audrey if you want to go."

Her offer surprised me. And warmed me. "No, Mom. I've never seen you laugh so much as you did that night. If I decide to go, I'll find a way."

"The offer is there for you if you want it."

I smiled, and I didn't have to force it to reach my eyes. "Thank you."

The front door swung open. My father. "Renata," he barked.

My mother jumped.

He continued, "You blocked the driveway!"

Lurching to my feet, my hip hit the edge of the table and sent my teacup rattling in its saucer. "I'll move it right now."

He stomped into the kitchen, his eyes scanning a scene that should have brought a smile to his face.

"Don't worry, Robert. I'll take your car to bible study instead of mine. That way you won't have to go back out to move it when Renata leaves."

His gaze zeroed in on my hair.

"Doesn't she look great, Robert? She got her hair cut!" My mother, forever in denial, exclaimed.

His angry gaze met mine. "Is this part of the course work?"

I shook my head, my stomach full of lead. "No. Of course not. But I needed one."

"Your mother's not looking after Audrey so you can get your hair done," he grumbled as he tossed his wallet and keys into the bowl on the counter.

To my eternal surprise, my mother answered. "Actually, I would happily look after Audrey so Wren can get her hair done. Or her nails. Or go out with that nice young man she's been seeing."

He scowled darkly. "If you've got time and money to be gallivanting all over the place it's time you stand on your own two feet."

"Don't I stand on my own two feet?" I challenged quietly.

He could say what he wanted about past me but present me was doing everything she could to look after everybody. My children were happy. I couldn't be doing that bad of a job.

"Of course you do," my mother interjected with false cheer.

"Perhaps it's time you took over the car insurance payments."

A prickle of fear chased the blood draining from my face. My teeth chattered once before I managed to grit them together.

Aaron was a young driver. For that reason, his insurance payments were high. The fact my father refused to buy him a used car and registered the new car in Aaron's name made them higher still. Aaron and I would both have to take on extra shifts to cover the cost.

A lot of extra shifts.

"If that's what you want, I'll tell Aaron tonight that we are taking them over."

"Robert, your dinner is in the microwave. I'm sure you're hungry. You can discuss car insurance with Aaron at a later time. It is his car

after all, not Renata's. Right now, I'm going out to meet my friends."
She turned to me and waved me toward the door with a flourish.
"Renata, it's time for you and Audrey to go."

I rose from my seat. My teacup rattled in its saucer as I cleared it
over to the sink. "I'm going to get Audrey ready to go."

Walking into the family room, I cringed in dismay.

She was locked onto her episode. There would be no leaving until
it finished. Not without a fight.

"Audrey, honey, how much time is left in your episode?"

"Six minutes."

I swallowed.

Six minutes.

If my mom left me here with him, it would feel like a lifetime.

Their voices, his harsh, hers cajoling, reached me from the kitchen.
"Audrey, honey, we have to go."

"Six minutes."

My hands shook.

He would never forgive me for disgracing him.

And I would never apologize.

Looking around the room, I noted Audrey's things scattered
around and took a deep, steadying breath. By the time I finished
packing her up, the show would be over.

In the truck, it became apparent that Audrey's dark mood had not
lifted. At home, it got worse. Brooklyn stayed on her, but her agitation
would not be soothed.

After an hour, I coaxed her into the bath which usually had a
calming effect. For whatever reason, that night it didn't work.

I missed both of Max's attempts at calling but managed to shoot
him a text explaining Audrey needed me.

She finally drifted off to sleep shortly after eleven with me lying down beside her. This did not bode well for an easy morning.

I knew these changes in routine would throw her.

I knew it would be hard.

I wished I didn't have to depend on my father.

One more week.

We could do it for one more week.

We had to.

20

Chill

While Friday morning had been rough for both Audrey and me, Susie was surprisingly correct. Audrey did just fine kicking about the restaurant after school for an hour before wanting to go home. And she was more than willing for Susie to take her.

By Saturday morning, she had settled.

Bridge finished her one week of training and was set to take over the Saturday shift. Which was wonderful because as much as I needed the money, I was beginning to crack under the pressure.

I spent the morning cuddled up with Audrey watching movies and coloring. She was back to her usual self. Unfortunately, Max and I had plans to go to his sister's place that night and I worried it would set her back.

I put the finishing touches on our lunch and carried the plates to the table while Aaron finished getting ready for his shift.

Reaching up, he grabbed a straw from the cupboard. "Is it okay with you if Nadine comes by tonight?"

"Of course, but I might not be going out."

"Why not?"

"Audrey just settled down and I don't want to wind her up again."

"Mom." He put his protein shake down on the counter and gave me his full attention. "You deserve a life."

"I have a life," I retorted.

He snorted. "You do now."

"Aaron," I began, but he cut me off.

"No, Mom. Hear me out. You gave up everything to be a mom. And you're killing it. You're the best mom, but you need your own life. And Max is good for you. You can't expect him to sit inside every night to make life easier for Audrey. She has to adjust."

"She's had to adjust to a lot already."

He nodded. "And she's doing just fine."

I shook my head. "She wasn't doing fine last night."

He shrugged. "So? Even when you keep to her routine she still has those nights."

"True." I narrowed my eyes on him. "When did you get so smart?"

He grinned. "I inherited it. Can I ask the Bean who she'd prefer to be with tonight? If she picks you, I'll back off."

I smiled. "Go for it."

"Bean!" he hollered.

"What!"

"Who do you want to hang with tonight? Max and Mom? Or me and Nadine?"

"Nadine is coming over?"

Aaron smirked. "There's your answer."

I pretended to scowl at him, eliciting the laugh I loved to hear before calling Audrey, "Lunch is ready!"

The three of us sat around the table that had seen its share of action. Lego builds and craft days, tabletop hockey and science projects. Even the occasional tea party. The conversations and confrontations that took place here, sometimes accompanied by tears, ended with hugs. But that was life. Sometimes it hurt. The key, as a parent, was to limit the damage.

Several hours later, sitting on Noelle's couch between Shae and Max, the guilt had yet to abate.

"Are you okay?" Shae murmured softly.

"I'm good."

She smirked. "Let's try that again. I'll explain how it works. I ask if you're okay, and you tell me the truth."

I huffed out a laugh.

She took my hand in hers. "I'm a safe person, Wren."

I nodded and tucked my chin in. "I feel guilty for forcing so much change on Audrey all at once. I feel like everything is going to backfire."

She squeezed my hand. "Well, in all honesty, you've dealt with a lot of backfires. It only makes sense to expect more. But what if it all works out?"

"There's the hope," I admitted. "But sometimes it all seems a bit far-fetched."

"Five years ago, did you dare to dream you'd have 3 days left and you'd be finished your program?"

I shook my head. "Absolutely not. I wasn't even sure I'd make it through the first course."

"And here you are," she replied softly. "A seasoned fire fighter."

I smiled. "I like that."

"I wouldn't mind a fire fighter," she joked.

"I know of a couple," I joked. "Maybe Michelle's hubby, Nathan, can take you on a tour of the station and hook you up."

She laughed. "I've heard worse plans."

I turned to find Max watching me, a small smile on his face. "You okay?"

I smiled back. "I'm good."

And I was.

Looking around the room, I enjoyed a slice of the pie I never dreamed I'd have a chance to eat.

One entire wall of Hawk and Noelle's house was completely made up of glass. The moon hung low and bright over the forest outside, and fire blazed in the wood fireplace. Pretty glasses filled with wine coolers sat on coasters on the coffee table, and beer bottles dangled from strong, masculine hands.

Across from me, Daire sat with his arm around his tiny bride, his broad palm cupping her round hip.

Baby Hunter nestled snug and warm in Harley's arms.

"That baby looks good on you," Max teased, his thigh pressed tightly to mine.

Harley's eyes twinkled back at him as Daire smiled lazily, tugging her closer. "That's good to hear because we're going to be having one of our own pretty soon."

"What!" Noelle and Hawkley both exclaimed at once, looking shell-shocked.

Noelle laughed and clasped her hands together under her chin while Shae and Bridge jumped up to give her a congratulatory hug and fired off their questions.

"How far along are you?"

Harley smiled happily. "Almost 15 weeks."

"When are you due?"

"September 25th."

"Do you know if it's a boy or a girl?"

"We're keeping it as a surprise," Daire interjected.

"Only because you bullied me into it," Harley groused.

He only laughed and hugged her to his side. If she got any closer, they'd meld into one body. By the look on that man's face, I didn't think he'd mind.

It was early, but there was already a soft glow about her that could not be denied.

I refused to allow my smile to slip from my face despite the sadness that beckoned me. Because neither of my pregnancies were met with this level of joy and anticipation. My children deserved better.

I deserved better.

On the big, comfy chair to my left, Noelle sat perched on Hawkley's knee. Even as I watched, his thick arm looped around her waist and pulled her back to cuddle against him. Their eyes met and crinkled. Noelle huffed out a soft laugh and shook her head as Hawkley eased her back to lean against him, his eyes turning back to his sister.

Bridge, sitting forward on the edge of the couch beside Harley, kept us in a fit of laughter with her stories.

And Shae sat beside me with my hand in hers, her easy-going smile a façade for the gentle, intuitive spirit residing inside her.

And Max.

Max lifted my knuckles to his mouth and brushed his lips across them.

"Oh, my freaking Lord," Bridge exclaimed.

My head snapped up, but Bridge was looking at Shae.

Shae laughed. "I know, I know. It's painful."

"What's painful?" I asked, lost.

"All the mushy love hormones you guys are giving off," Bridge complained then fell back on the couch. "I need some sort of vaccine to keep me immune."

Shae laughed. "I hear you, sister."

For once, I was the object of envy. It was unfathomable. And I wanted the same for both of them.

Not surprisingly, Max and I were first to leave. When we opened my front door, we found Aaron asleep on the couch with Audrey sprawled out beside him. Due to the time, Nadine was long gone.

Max tugged me into the kitchen and tipped up my chin. "I had fun tonight and I think you did, too."

"I did," I admitted. "I just felt bad because I've forced a lot of change on Audrey all at once."

"I know." He drew me into a hug. "You've only got one week to go. Three days."

"We can do it."

He tightened his hold. "Of course you will. Your family, what you've made, Wren, it's beautiful."

"Is that your professional opinion?" I teased to cover up the pleasure that unfolded inside me at his words.

He drew back with his eyebrows raised. "You want my professional opinion?"

My eyebrows scrunched. "Why wouldn't I?"

"Boundaries, remember?" He wagged his eyebrows. "My mother drilled them into my head."

"So, you've been holding back?" I asked suspiciously. What did he have professional opinions about? Was it Audrey? Her progress?

"When you want my opinion, you'll ask for it. But as for what you've made here, the family you made, the home you created, it's a thing of beauty. Be proud."

"Is it about Audrey? What you're thinking about, is it about Audrey's progress?"

"No, Tweet. It's not. You're doing a wonderful job with her. She's thriving."

I drew in a deep breath, feeling like I dodged a bullet. Instead of pushing to know what he was thinking about, I let it go.

There was only so much a person could take, and I was at my maximum.

After he left, his words stayed with me.

They warmed me as I roused Audrey just enough to get her to bed.

They touched my heart when I quietly urged Aaron to stretch out on the couch, tucked his pillow under his head, and covered him with a blanket.

They fueled my steps as I went through my nightly routine of washing my face and getting ready for bed.

They covered me as I slipped into my bed and retrieved my phone.

It was only when I opened my email that the chill set in.

21

His

I braced the shovel against the wall just outside the front door and hustled back into the welcoming heat of the cabin. Rubbing my cold hands together, I looked through the sidelight. The driveway and front path were clear for now, but I didn't expect it to last. It wasn't abnormal for us to get a load of snow this late in April, especially this far north. Living in an apartment, shoveling snow wasn't something I had to deal with. Certainly, I rarely drove in it.

And it was calling for more before the night was out.

Leaving my coat on the hook and my boots by the door, I detoured to the kitchen and flipped the kettle on.

Time was a luxury I had not afforded for years, but up here by myself, it was abundant. I could hear myself think, and my brain spun on overdrive.

Being away gave me perspective and allowed me to see that Audrey was getting older and gaining more independence. And I could maybe take a little time to breathe.

Maybe have something for me.

Like Max.

As for Aaron, I was so damn proud of that kid. I didn't take credit for everything he was, but surely I had something to do with how wonderful he turned out. He was on his way, nothing but open road and dreams ahead of him. And I'd do everything I could to ensure it.

So it wasn't that I didn't appreciate the time away, or even that I wouldn't appreciate a few more days.

Just not with a storm of this magnitude threatening to roll in.

I poured boiling water over the hot chocolate and added the marshmallows Max bought before taking the heavy, ceramic mug to curl up in the chair by the window.

Pulling the blanket up over my legs, I snuggled in. The picture window framed a winter wonderland straight out of a Hallmark movie. There was no denying its beauty, and as it washed over me, the tension in my shoulders eased.

I was safe. Lonely, but safe.

My cell phone dinged, and I snatched it up off the side table, certain it was Max. My stomach tightened with anticipation, then fluttered at the sight of his name.

Max: Are you keeping warm?

Tweet: So far so good.

Max: It's going to get pretty cold tonight. And they're calling for more snow.

Tweet: You're not helping my nerves.

Max: I'm not worried about your nerves. I'm worried about you staying warm.

Tweet: You're a psychologist. Feelings are literally your job.

Max: Keeping you warm and happy is my job.

Tweet: Then somebody's shirking their responsibilities.

Max: Open the front door.

My feet hit the floor before my brain fully registered his message. "Max," I breathed.

I dropped the blanket and ran to the door. Swinging it open, seeing Dan's and Max's smiling faces, I burst into tears.

Dan let out a big boom of a laugh before pulling me into his arms. "Aw, Wrennie! Don't worry! I'm leaving!"

I snorted out a laugh and hugged him back.

"That's my girl," he murmured then set me away from him where Max stood ready to claim me, pulling my back against his chest. Jerking his chin up at Max, he continued, "This guy came over all in a tizzy about getting up here before the storm hit. If you're okay with this bossy lug staying with you and bringing you home tomorrow, I'll take the company car back now."

My entire body went rigid. I felt Max flinch as I stared at Dan, my jaw hanging open.

I gaped at him. "You...you...you would do that for me?"

"Wrennie," he answered, his voice gruff. "It's the least of what I'd like to do for you. But Max here says you're his to look after. I'm just along for the ride."

Tears sprang to my eyes.

I didn't know what to do with this level of care and kindness from a man.

Max's arms tightened around me as he pressed his lips to the top of my head. "Just say thank you, Tweet. That's all you have to do."

"Thank you, Dan." I moved to wriggle away from Max, but he pulled me closer.

"She'd like to hug you, Dan, but I'm not inclined to let her go at the moment so you'll just have to let her thank you be enough."

Dan laughed. "It was always enough." He pulled his gloves back on. "Welp! I'm off. Need to get home to Lou before she starts panicking." He turned to me and winked. "Besides. She wants all the good Max and Wrennie gossip."

Dan laughed softly as I blushed to the roots of my hair.

Max's chest vibrated against my back. His deep chuckle in my ear sent a frisson of heat straight to my poor, neglected, nipples.

"Enough, Dan." Max rumbled good-naturedly, his arm around me tightening. "I'm going to feed our girl. Text me when you get home if you wouldn't mind."

"Will do."

And with that, he was gone, leaving Max and me alone in a secluded cabin, insulated from the rest of the world by rapidly falling snow.

We stood quietly.

Unmoving.

His lips moved in my hair. "Are you nervous?"

"A little," I admitted.

His palms went to my shoulders and smoothed down my biceps to cup my elbows as he stepped back. "Hungry?"

In more ways than one.

I rubbed my own palms over my goose-pimpled arms. "I could eat."

You, I tacked on silently.

My Lord, I was needy.

"Come on," he linked his fingers through mine. "I brought take-out from the new place. We need to warm it up."

My eyebrows shot up. "New place? Sage Ridge has a new place?"

He chuckled and shook his head. "When you say you don't get out much, you really don't get out much."

I guffawed. A few weeks ago, a comment like that would have made me cry bitter, bitter tears. Now? With Max in my life? He was all the excitement I needed or wanted.

"I'm working on changing that," I surprised myself by saying. Even more surprising, it was true.

These past few weeks had allowed me to grow in ways I hadn't considered. Hair, make-up, journaling, broadening my expectations for Audrey, I'd even bought myself new clothes for the first time in I didn't know how many years.

I nibbled on the inside of my bottom lip. I still felt guilty about the clothes. But it's not like I could walk around naked.

"I'm glad to hear that. I'm all in to help you with that endeavor."

I smiled up at him. "I'm counting on it."

Hooking an arm around my neck, he tugged me into the small kitchen and set the take-out bags on the table.

"Are you kidding me?" I exclaimed. "We have a Greek place, and I didn't know?"

"You like Greek food?"

I slapped my palm over my chest. "I love Greek food. I haven't had it in years, Max. *Years.*"

He pinched my chin between his thumb and forefinger. Leaning down, he brought his mouth within a hairsbreadth of mine. "Well then," he murmured, "you're long overdue."

His eyes dropped to my mouth, and my lips parted in invitation.

Snapping his gaze up to mine, eyes hooded, he smirked and pulled away.

I gasped, "Tease!"

He chuckled and nudged the take-out bags toward me. "Eat."

I dove in and started pulling out containers. "My God, Max, you brought the entire menu!"

"I kind of did. It's a couples' sampler platter. A little bit of every-thing. I'll take you when we get home. We'll take the kids with us. Nadine, too. Do you think Audrey would like it?"

Two hours and half a bottle of wine later, tummy full and happily curled up on the couch, Max's cell phone lit up.

"Good," he murmured. "Dan is home."

Placing his cell phone face down on the table, he sat back and looked at me. "Now we can go to bed."

I jumped up from my seat and spun away, gathering our glasses as I went. "Sure. Yeah. Early morning. Lots of snow."

"The snow has stopped. I'll get up in plenty of time to clear the driveway and get you to class," Max answered easily.

What I'd give for an ounce of his calm.

I hustled into the kitchen. Plopping the glasses on the counter, I braced my hands against the sink.

Oh my gosh.

Now what?

He's 41. I'm 39.

We're allowed to have sex.

I seriously might combust if we don't.

But his driving up here was not for that. He was just being kind. He was just being Max. I couldn't just assume.

I took a deep breath. I'd simply offer him the other room that was made up. Offer him? I'd offer him a room in his own cabin?

I smacked my hand against my forehead. *Pull it together, Renata.*

Squaring my shoulders, I washed our glasses and set them on the drainer to dry. Max moved around in the other room. The door of the woodstove clanged shut. The drapes slid across the windows. The light extinguished.

Nabbing my cell phone and my book off the end table, I shrugged on a false cloak of confidence and sailed into the hallway leading to the bedrooms.

As I passed the open door to the second bedroom, I asked, "Did you want to sleep in here?"

I turned to look at him as the words left my lips. The look on his face halted me in my tracks.

He stood in the middle of the family room, his fingers tucked into the front pockets of his jeans.

I swallowed hard as my heart thudded in my chest.

He dipped his chin, his heated gaze steady on mine as he rolled his lips between his teeth, that damned dimple just begging for my tongue to dip into it. He untucked his fingers and prowled toward me, his long legs eating up the distance between us.

"No, Wren. I do not want to sleep in that room."

22

It's Go Time

I sucked in a breath and met his eyes. "It's go time?"

His footsteps faltered as he barked out a laugh. "Go time?"

I slapped my hands over my cheeks to hide my face. "Oh my God." I laughed through my mortification. "I'm nervous, okay?"

He stopped right in front of me. Reaching behind my head, he angled his chin toward me and began to gather my hair into a ponytail. "Drop your hands and look at me, Tweet."

Doing as he asked, I scrunched my nose and smiled up at him awkwardly.

His face serious, he dipped his knees to bring his gaze level with mine. "I'm nervous, too."

That got my attention and steadied my nerves. "You are?"

His lips curved into a small smile. "Of course." Straightening to his full height, he continued to run his fingers through my hair as he stared down at me. "You beautiful, beautiful girl. I've waited my whole life to gather the courage to be with you. Of course, I'm nervous."

I grasped his waist and breathed his name, disbelief and wonder coloring my tone, "Max."

"I'll go slow." He began backing me down the hall to the bedroom I'd been using, and the wide, comfortable bed still rumpled from my sleep the night before. "I'll be gentle," he murmured. "I'll be the boy-next-door you need me to be, this time, and I'll make sure you're more than ready." Cupping the back of my head in his palm, he dipped his knees to meet my eyes. "There won't be a single thought in your head other than the craving to have me inside you."

My heart thrummed at the warmth and tenderness in his eyes. "Okay," I whispered, my nerves abating.

He stopped us beside the bed, our only light from the muted antique lighting in the hallway on one side, and the moonlight reflecting off the snow through the window on the other.

With only inches between us, he released my hair and reached back in that delicious way all the heroes did in romance novels and grasped the back of his sweater before pulling it off over his head.

My greedy eyes took in his mussed-up hair, dark eyes, wide shoulders, and sculpted chest before following the trail of crinkly hair that tempted me to flick open the button of his jeans and help myself.

This was not the first time I'd seen him shirtless. As I ran my palms over his strong shoulders and muscled chest I acknowledged it wasn't even the first time I'd touched his chest. But that's all I'd touched. And the chest I remembered was that of a young man.

Now he was thicker. More heavily muscled. And less defined.

I pitched forward, pressed my face to his chest, and breathed him in. Turned my head to the side to press my ear to his heart, I closed my eyes.

His strong hands ran up and down my back and pulled me closer.

It was ecstasy.

It was agony.

I clung to his back. "Max."

"I know, Tweet," he whispered back. "I know."

Gently he raised my chin and brushed his lips over mine. "I love you, Tweet. I've always loved you."

A soft, hiccupping, sob broke from my throat. "I feel the same, Max. I always have."

His lips fluttered across my face, gathering my tears. "Don't waste your tears. We're here now."

I nodded, swallowed the memories of painful yearning, and yanked myself into the present.

Gathering the hem of my sweater, he lifted it up and off, then immediately snapped open the front closure of my bra and pushed it off over my shoulders.

He brushed the backs of his fingers over one aching breast. "My beautiful girl."

With trembling hands, I reached for his waistband, opened his jeans, and pushed them down past his thighs.

With his hand under my elbow, he stopped me from lowering myself to the floor, and stepped out of his jeans. Tucking his fingers into the waistband of my leggings, he dropped to his knees and peeled them down. Tapping first one foot, then the other, he freed my legs. Without waiting, he hooked two fingers into the sides of my panties and pulled those off as well.

I stood in front of his kneeling form, bare, vulnerable, open, and ready.

There was nothing I had I wouldn't give him.

Beginning inside my ankle, he trailed his fingers up the inside of my leg and along the crease at my thigh. Bending, he planted a row of wet, open-mouthed kisses across my soft tummy.

Utterly mesmerized, lips parted in wonder, I watched.

I watched his hands slide up and down the outside of my legs, from my ankles to my waist where his fingers tightened their hold, and his mouth opened over my flesh, the tip of his tongue circling my belly button.

I watched, a huffed breath escaping me as he drew back to take me in, then dipped his head to lick along the crease of my thigh.

I watched as he grasped the back of my knee and urged my thigh up over his shoulder as his other hand came to rest firmly on my lower back, steadying me, holding me immobile.

My hands flew down to his head. "Max, I've never…"

His eyes flashed as they met mine, and I could see the same hunger that paced and growled and roared inside me reflected in their dark depths.

To be wanted like that, how would that feel?

Now I knew.

And it was everything I dreamed it would be.

In his eyes, I was beautiful.

In his eyes, I was worthy.

In his eyes, I was everything.

"If you don't like it, I'll stop," he promised, then lowered his dark head.

At the very first flick of his tongue, my hand fisted in his hair, my hips jerked forward, and my head flew back as I cried out in shock and pleasure.

If I thought I was ready for the second touch of his tongue, I was wrong. My knees buckled.

He stopped and wrapped both arms around my hips before twisting me to sit on the bed. "Lie back. We'll do it this way."

Standing, he dropped his boxers and rolled a condom over his length.

I couldn't speak, could barely breathe. I lay back on the bed and my pelvis rocked, wanting more. "Sorry!"

He dropped back to his knees between my legs. "No, Wren. I want you to tell me what you want. What you like."

Encircling my ankle, he lifted it to his mouth and pressed a sweet kiss to the arch of my foot before guiding it over his shoulder. Then, he draped my other leg over his other shoulder. Starting at my knee, he trailed his tongue up the inside of my thigh.

I gasped, my body trembling in anticipation.

Both of his arms wrapped around my thighs, and his big hands splayed over my womb. Shifting closer, he forced my legs wider.

Just as I lifted my head, he dropped his, and the sight of his beautiful mouth closing over me intensified the exquisite pleasure he elicited.

Lips nipping, tongue circling, the scruff of his beard an intoxicating abrasion against the inside of my thighs, I moaned, "Oh, God. Max, Max, Max..."

I was no stranger to orgasms, but I'd rarely been gifted one. And it was building fast.

My hips rocked faster.

He groaned against me, his tongue spearing my center before returning to lave my clit.

I rocked against him mindlessly, lost in a waking dream.

One hand soothed over my hip and under my thigh, then two fingers found my entrance and curled inside. Slowly pumping in and out, his fingertips dragged across the world's worst-kept secret. A sensual heatwave rippled outwards before drawing back tightly into a single, pinpoint of intense pleasure.

My breath froze.

My body bowed.

One second balanced on the precipice, the next flying free, his soft, thick, hair captured between my fingers, his name a prayer on my lips.

Lost in a sensual haze, I was barely aware of his arm snaking under my waist and yanking me up the bed. With one hand locked around the back of my neck, the other wrapped around my hip, he pushed inside me.

My neck arched back, and I cried out at the fullness of his intrusion.

He stilled, his mouth dropping frantic kisses along my jaw, my neck, my throat. "Wren," he rasped. "Tell me when I can move."

I slowly released my breath, and my body yielded to his. I wrapped my legs around his lean hips, tilted my pelvis to take him deeper, and dug my fingers into his back to hold him still.

"Wren..." He pushed up on his hands and turned his face away. His gorgeous chest and wide shoulders shadowed me. The muscles in his jaw rippled as he closed his eyes.

I watched, fascinated, as he fought for control.

He squeezed his eyes shut and blew out a harsh breath before getting hold of himself.

I looked down the length of his body to where it joined with mine before moving back to his beautiful face. Experimentally, I rocked my hips.

His lips parted and his chin dropped.

"Oh, wow," I whispered, drunk on my power.

He turned back to face me. "I'm trying to hold on, my baby, but it's hard."

I twinkled up at him. "That's what she said."

He barked out a laugh and dropped down to his elbows, pressing more of his weight onto me. "You're killing me."

"Move, baby."

"Yeah?" His eyes studied mine. "You're good?"

My smile split my face. "I've never been so good."

He smiled down at me, kissed me sweetly, and began to rock inside me.

I broke the kiss and urged him with my hands. "You can move, Max."

He chuckled. "I am moving. Hold on. I'm going to blow your mind."

Shifting up until his chest lined up with my eyes, he rolled his hips.

Immediately, my knees flew up to hug his sides. I clung to him as the base of his cock dragged across my clit. "Max!"

A shudder worked its way down his long body. "Oh, God. Don't talk to me. I'm dying, here. I'm going to embarrass myself," he huffed.

I began to laugh, then, as if my brain finally caught up to what was happening to my body, tears stung my eyes. Because I was wrapped around Max, and he was finally inside me.

Not one of my dreams prepared me for the reality of him.

Not one.

I trailed my fingers down his broad back. "You're so beautiful, Max."

"For fuck's sake, Tweet! I'm trying to make this good for you." He laughed then groaned, all traces of humor falling away. He closed his eyes. "Fuck but you feel good."

"Take what's yours, Max. I've been dying to give it to you."

His eyes locked with mine as he rolled his hips slow and deep. "Are you mine?"

"Oh…" I breathed, my eyelids fluttering shut as he did it again and my pussy fluttered around him.

"Are you mine, Wren?"

"Yes, Max. I'm yours."

"Hang on, baby."

I wrapped my arms around his back reveling in the power of his hips and the muscles in his back undulating as he drove inside me.

"Fuck, fuck, fuck…" he grunted.

I tilted my hips, absorbed the shock of contact and the first astonishing flutter of my release. "Max, oh, God, Max," I cried out in surprise.

"That's it, baby. Give it to me."

"Holy moli," I gasped in awe.

"You better fucking believe it," he grunted back. "Fuck. Wren." His hips stuttered. He yanked one of my knees up and buried himself inside me as he came with his face tucked into my neck, my name on his lips.

23

Appendage

Waking up with my naked body half sprawled over an equally naked Max Brevard topped my recently reconstructed list of favorite things.

Well, it definitely made the top five.

Nestling closer, I encountered my favorite appendage. And it appeared ready and raring to go.

His voice, gritty with sleep, tightened my nipples. "You awake?"

"Yes. You?" A beat of silence passed, then I slapped my hand over my face. "Oh my God. You've reduced me to this. You and that appendage of yours."

He laughed, his chest vibrating. "Appendage?"

"Yeah, you know..." I petered off and drew an air circle over the sheet failing to mask his erection.

"Cock," he emphasized.

My hips rolled, and I squeaked.

Chuckling softly, he hugged me closer. "Say it, Wren. Say 'cock'."

"I cannot," I answered primly.

Laughing full-out, he claimed, "I'm going to teach you a whole new vocabulary. One day soon, you're going to tell me exactly what you want me to do to you and you're going to use words like cock, clit, pussy, and maybe even cu—"

I reared up and slapped my hand over his mouth. "Don't say it!"

His eyes danced as I glared out a warning.

When he nodded, I slowly withdrew my hand.

Smiling, he tucked my hair behind my ear. "Are you sore?"

I assessed for a moment then replied, "No. Not at all."

He flexed his hips. "Want to hop on?"

"Hop on? On top?"

"Yeah. Hop on top. Grab a condom off the nightstand and roll it on me."

"Roll it on you."

His eyebrows arched. "You want to ride my cock?"

I flushed. "Yes."

"Then cover it." He grinned. "It's go time."

I rolled my eyes even as I flushed further and reached for the condom. "I'm never going to live that down."

"Nope," he replied unrepentantly. "I love it. It's my new favorite saying."

Ripping open the package, I carefully withdrew the condom.

"Pinch it at the center."

It's not like I'd never seen a condom, I'd just never put one on. I pointed at the middle of the circle of latex. "This little nipply part?"

His dimple dug into his cheek. "Yeah. Pinch the little nipply part, press it to the head of my cock, and roll it down my shaft with your other hand."

With only the slightest hint of trembling, I did what he asked. As soon as I reached the base, I froze. "Max, I haven't even gotten a chance to touch you, yet. Do we have more condoms? Can we start over?"

"I don't have any more with me," he replied. "You can play with me as much as you want next time." He tapped the side of my thigh. "Up you get, baby. Swing your leg over."

Reaching down, he grasped his cock to hold it steady for me as I began to ease myself over him.

When I thought I'd taken him all the way, he pushed my shoulders up so that I sat upright.

"Oh," I exclaimed, shimmying my hips. "That's...deep." I wiggled, my eyes going wide. "There's a spot in there..." I ground down against him, "that feels really, really, good." I met his eyes, my own rolling slightly back in my head. I'd never been on top.

A flash of anger ripped through me at the thought I'd been so woefully neglected, but I extinguished it to focus on the joy of discovery with Max.

Max lay back, hands clasped behind his head, sleepy, hooded eyes watching me. My God. The muscles in his arms stood out in stark relief against the pillow behind his head. Black hair messy, mouth soft and sensual, he looked like he dropped off the cover of a romance novel. The kind I'd never dared to read.

And he was waiting for me, who was so woefully inept, to do something.

"What do I do? How do I make you feel good?"

"You don't," he replied, his voice gruff. "You use me to make yourself feel good while I watch. When you get yourself off, believe me, I won't be far behind you."

I pushed myself up on my knees and slowly sank back down, my body, starved for affection, eagerly sucking him back inside.

"Experiment, Wren. Figure out what feels good and do that."

I did. I rocked my hips one way, then another. Ground down and rolled, then rose on my knees and slowly eased back down. Everything felt good, but some things felt infinitely better, and when I found that motion, I kept at it. Within a minute, my hands were flexing on his chest, my chin tucked down as I dragged myself back and forth over his *cock*.

I shuddered. Even the thought of that word made me hotter.

"You need a little help?" he asked, his voice deep and rough.

"Maybe," I flustered, unused to speaking so openly.

"Want me to give it to you? Or you want to do it for me?"

"Do what?"

"Rub your clit, Wren. Let me see you make yourself come on my cock."

I sat up straight, my head lolling back as he hit that spot. My brain finally processed his words, and I slapped a hand over my cheek. "You want me to *touch myself* in front of you?"

He flashed that damned dimple. "Well, I sure as hell don't want you touching it without me."

I rolled my hips, wondering if I could make it to the finish line without my hands. "This is baptism by fire!"

He drove his hips up once, and again. "You love it."

I was close. "I do."

Taking hold of my wrist, he brought my fingers to his lips and pulled them into his mouth. After rolling his tongue around them, he drew my hand to the apex of my thighs and rolled my fingers over my clit.

I moaned.

"That's it," he praised, releasing my wrist. "Show me how you like it, Wren."

After only a few circles, I began to clamp down.

He reared up and captured my nipple in his mouth and sucked. Hard.

My body combusted and then I simply hung on as he wrapped his hands around my hips and took over, driving inside me again and again, his lips pressed tightly together, face flushed, until he came with a deep groan, the lines in his face smoothing as he emptied himself inside me.

Pulling me down to his chest, he wrapped his arms around my back and held me tight. His heart thudded against my own.

I closed my eyes. If there was a heaven, and I believed there was, it must come in as a close second to this moment.

Just as I began to drift off, my body languid, he slapped me on my ass. "Let's go, Tweet. Can't be late on your last day of class."

I snorted and rolled off him.

He laughed at me as I attempted to back my way into the bathroom to hide my butt.

His eyes lit with challenge. "That's like waving a red flag in front of a bull, baby."

I spun and ran into the bathroom with my hands covering my bum, squealing, "I have class!"

The last day of classes was a half day.

Max dropped me off and then went back to close up the cabin. By the time he was done, so was I.

"Can I take you out for lunch before we go back?"

What I really wanted was to go back to the cabin and roll around between the sheets for an hour.

He chuckled. "I can read you, you know."

I laughed and turned to him. "Oh, yeah? And what am I thinking?"

He cocked one eyebrow. "That you'd prefer to go back to the cabin and take advantage of me one more time before I bring you home."

"What?" I squawked in mock dismay. "Me take advantage of you? I think not, sir. I fell for the boy-next-door routine. You pulled a bait and switch."

Nothing in my very limited experience prepared me for a man who handled me the way Max did last night. I mean, throwing my legs over his shoulders? Yanking me up the bed? I closed my eyes and flushed as a thousand butterflies rampaged through my belly at the memory. Entering me like that? And when he pulled my knee around his hip? I almost had a heart attack.

Never mind what he had me doing that morning.

Swinging the car through the parking lot to the road, he tossed me a grin. "That *was* my impression of the boy next door."

Reaching for my hand, he confessed, "I'm so damn proud of you, Tweet. You're a strong woman."

I looked away from him, training my eyes on the snowy landscape beyond the windscreen.

"Why do I feel like that was the wrong thing to say?"

I sighed. "So many people have said that to me, or some rendition of it. And I hate it, really despise it, when someone says, 'you're stronger than I am. I'd never be able to do what you do', or, 'you're so patient. I could never be that patient' because it infers I had a choice. Like because I was super strong and patient, I decided to take this on. Or that there's something inherently special in me that makes the struggle easier for me than it would be for someone else. And that's just not true. The truth is we all do what we have to do. I'm not special. Or strong. Certainly not stronger than anyone else."

"What would you want people to say?"

I huffed in exasperation. "I don't want sympathy or pity, but what I wouldn't give for someone who understands what I'm dealing with and tells me I'm doing a good job. That's all."

"And who can do that for you?"

I thought about it. "No one, really. No one can understand the stress of maintaining a state of constant vigilance. There's no rest. No real break. Chaos can disrupt at any time and often does."

He squeezed my hand and murmured, "For what it's worth, I've treated many families with similar stressors. I've witnessed their struggles. I'm not unfamiliar with yours. And I can tell you, truly, you're doing a great job."

His words washed over me, taking away my anger and cleansing the taste of my bitter words from my mouth.

I inhaled. Deeply. And something inside me released with that breath. "Thank you."

24

Compelled

By the time we rolled into Sage Ridge, it was nearing five o'clock. Almost three hours earlier than I had returned home the past two Thursdays. I hoped Audrey would be happy to see me this time rather than be bent on punishing me for my absence.

It wasn't her fault. Regulating emotions doesn't come easy to a lot of people, and it was excruciatingly difficult for her.

"There's hardly any snow here at all," I exclaimed.

"Two hours north makes a big difference. Should we swing by and pick up Audrey?"

I bit my lip. "If my father is home, he might be rude to you."

Max smiled grimly. "I can handle your father." He glanced at me quickly. "I know your relationship is strained. I don't want to say anything that will make things more difficult for you, but I wouldn't mind him knowing you have me in your corner."

"He, uh, he doesn't like you, Max."

His eyebrows rose. "He doesn't know me."

"He connects you to Dan and Lou. He's never forgiven them for putting me up in the cabin."

His jaw dropped. "Would he rather you'd been homeless?"

I shrugged. "I don't know. I've thought about it so many times over the years. Maybe he wanted me to beg for forgiveness? Maybe he would have let me back inside eventually? I don't know. He believes I owe him an apology. But will never apologize for Aaron's existence."

Max shrugged. "You shouldn't. His problem, and it is his problem Wren, is his to solve. It has little to nothing to do with you."

"How can you say that? It was me getting pregnant that caused all this."

"Are you sure?"

"Uh, yeah," I snapped. "I was there."

"Okay, let me ask you something. If you had dropped out of university, would he have been embarrassed? What if you failed a course? How about if you got drunk as a teenager? How many things set him off?"

"A lot. There were a lot of things that set him off, but only one thing made him kick me out of the house."

He chuckled. "Just how much bad did you get up to, Tweet? What are all these bad things you did that set him off?"

"I..." I opened my mouth to answer and snapped it shut just as fast.

"Yes?" he prodded, his eye soft and expectant. Knowing.

I looked out the window feeling inexplicably sad all of a sudden. "I really didn't do anything. Wore the wrong outfit to church. Got a 'C' on an English paper. Forgot to do my chores. I missed curfew once."

"By how long?"

I barked out a bitter laugh. "Ten minutes." Before he could ask his next question, I answered it. "He grounded me for a week."

"See? His problem. Not yours."

"He's not all bad. He bought Aaron a car and pays for his insurance. He also covers Aaron's tuition. He's very good with both kids. He bought Aaron's crib, and they are very generous with the kids at Christmas and on birthdays."

"What about with you?"

I flushed. "Not so much."

I was grateful he didn't say anything else. Who wants to admit their parents don't value them?

Does Aaron feel valued? Does he feel like he has to help with the bills? Like he has to earn his keep?

Max pulling into my parents' driveway arrested my thoughts. My stomach sank at the sight of my father's car in the driveway.

"He's home."

Max threw the truck into park and turned to look at me. "Let's go get your daughter and take her home."

Staring straight ahead, I raised my hand to knock the door. Swallowing my anxiety, I prayed my mother would answer the door.

No such luck.

My father's expression slid from irritated to furious to blank in the space of a single breath. Swinging the door open, he waved us inside.

"Max."

"Robert. It's been a while."

"Oh? I can't seem to recall a time when our paths might have crossed."

Max smiled easily but his eyes remained hard. I shivered at the coldness reflected there. Would that icy fury ever be directed at me?

"Men's breakfast a couple of years ago at your church. Your pastor invited me to speak on the subject of bridging the gap between parents and their young adults. I've never forgotten the speech you made about the importance of supporting your children even after they reached adulthood." He paused and the temperature in the front hall dropped ten degrees. "It was...inspired."

Astounded by my father's audacity considering his brand of support, I narrowed my eyes on my father's face as I thought about what Max revealed.

"Yes, well," my father answered just as coldly, "not all children are capable of achieving financial independence."

It took a moment for his words to sink in. I gasped and made to step back but Max's hand at my back held me steady.

Max tilted his head to the side and smiled. "But that's not what you said, was it, Robert? You spoke about being friends with your adult children, treating them as equals, extending respect to them just as readily as you would to anyone else."

My jaw fell open.

"Renata?"

At the sound of my mother's voice, I snapped my mouth shut and stuttered out an answer. "H--hi, Mom."

She bustled into the hall with Audrey's bags. Her smile and her steps faltered when she saw Max, but she recovered both quickly.

"Max! Hello!" She extended her hand. "I'm Lorraine, Renata's mom. Come in. Please."

Max's smile warmed. "Pleasure to meet you, Lorraine."

Audrey wandered into the hall, her crystal swinging from her fingers. When she caught sight of Max, her whole face lit up. "Hello, Max. Do you want to build Lego today?"

Max smiled warmly. "Hello, Bean. I'd love to build Lego with you today. How about we go pick up pizza so Momma doesn't have to cook tonight and go home to eat dinner first?"

"I like pizza."

I shuffled from one foot to the other.

My father had yet to speak to me.

My mother was flustered by Max's presence.

And we hadn't made it past the front hall.

"Whose home are you going to exactly?" My father asked harshly.

"Mine," I clipped, and that something I tried so hard to keep under lock and key broke out. "The one I pay for with my paycheck. The one filled with food and toys and music and games that I purchase. The one where laughter bounces off the walls. That home."

My mother gasped. "Renata!"

"I'm sorry, Mom." I softened my tone because she did deserve my thanks. "Thank you for looking after Audrey. I never worry about her when she's in your hands. Knowing she was with you made this course possible. I hope you know how much I appreciate it."

Max collected Audrey's bags and handed me Brooklyn's leash.

Mom's eyes darted back and forth between me, Max, and my father. "Your father helped, too."

"Yes. He's always *supportive*. Thank you, Dad." I turned to go, then felt compelled to add as I met his furious gaze with my sincere one, "I do appreciate everything you do for my children."

I waited a beat for him to respond. When he turned around and walked away, so did I.

"Robert."

The sound of Max's voice stopped me in my tracks. I lifted wary eyes to Max's face, hard and unyielding, as he looked at my father.

"Be sure to tell your pastor I'd be happy to come back anytime. I'm sure you're not the only one who missed the message."

My father took a threatening step toward Max, and Max smiled, an icy challenge in his hard eyes.

I gasped and laid my hand on Max's chest.

For the first time in my life, I witnessed my father back down from opposition.

As usual, my mother chased after him as he stomped away.

My body was a riot of emotions. I didn't know if I was going to shit my pants or climb Max like a tree and order him to fuck me against the door. The same door my father closed in my face when I was pregnant and vulnerable.

A completely inappropriate giggle burst from my lips. I slapped my hand over my mouth.

Max shifted his attention back to me, his gaze warm, and something inside me thrilled.

His hand a gentle guide at the small of my back, we walked outside.

"Is it like this for you all the time?" Max murmured calmly as we settled into the car.

Shrugging one shoulder, I sighed. "It's not always that bad." I offered him a genuine smile. "Usually only when he gets riled up about your family or Dan and Lou."

He grinned at me. "Glad I could be of service."

At that, I laughed out loud, relieved not to be on the receiving end of his pity.

It deeply shamed me that my father did not even try to curb his hostility in front of Max. Even still, Max's presence blunted its sharp edges and gave me a smidgeon of courage to defend myself. Watching Max's eyes darken with anger was strangely validating.

Witnessing him stand up to my father, without once raising his voice, blustering, or causing Audrey even an ounce of alarm, showed me like nothing else what a bully my father was.

I didn't feel so alone.

25

My Max

It took a couple of days to settle Audrey down, but after assuring her, repeatedly, that I was finished school and wasn't going away again, she settled.

By the time Saturday rolled around, she was excited for her first day at art class. With Bridge working Saturdays with Susie, I had my much-needed Saturday mornings free again.

And with Spring crawling her way in, we could finally dump the heavy layers of clothing Audrey so despised.

"Hello, Rachel. I'm here for art class. My Max is picking us up after and taking Mom and me to his house."

I flushed.

Rachel laughed. "Nothing like a kid to air all your secrets!"

I shook my head but could not help my smile. "It's not that he's a secret, it's just that..."

"What?" she teased. "New?"

"Yes," I admitted.

"I wouldn't worry about it. A man like Max? When he makes up his mind, he makes it up but good."

Audrey cocked her head to the side. "Do you know my Max?"

She started calling him 'my Max' Thursday night. There was a kid named Max in her class, who was now called 'school Max'.

"I do know your Max," Rachel replied. "He came in last year asking for help with a garden project for his sister."

My eyebrows flew up as I repeated her statement. "Max did a project."

Rachel laughed. "His first and I suspect his last. Creative flexibility is not his strong suit."

"No, I suppose it wouldn't be," I mused.

Rachel's students filed in quickly leaving little room for talking.

Rachel had planned a simple, beginner's stained-glass project for this first class. The students handled the glass with such care it sent me into the past to my first time handling glass.

It was a medium I'd never even considered, but once tried, I was hooked.

I taught them how to cut and shape their pieces to fit, then witnessed their delight when they got it right.

There was something magical in creating something beautiful from scraps of nothing. Being back in this room after so many years of denial unlocked a part of me I thought I'd lost. A sense of wonder, passion, excitement.

When I lost my art, a lot of the magic seeped out of my life and left me hollow. I didn't know if I could have made it back to the art room any sooner, but I vowed not to leave it again.

The class passed quickly with nary a peep from Audrey. When it was time to go, she still wasn't ready.

"Good," Rachel exclaimed. "This gives me a chance to show you something."

Taking me into the back room, Rachel uncovered a utility table against the wall.

"Is that my..." I stopped. It wasn't my anything, but back in high school, Rachel decided my talent needed more of an outlet and taught me lampworking.

"Yes. It's still yours." Peeling back a protective sheet, she uncovered all my old tools. "It was all in storage. When you agreed to come back, I pulled it back out for you."

"I can't believe it," I murmured. "I don't even know if I can still do it."

"Only one way to find out. Anytime I'm here, feel free to come in. I'll get you a key so you can help yourself."

"Mom! My Max is here!"

"Rachel," I stressed her name. "Thank you."

"Aw, you're welcome. And welcome back."

Max's home, as he warned me, was impeccably decorated. Situated on a quiet side street in Crystal beach, its white clapboard siding with blue trim depicted a quintessential beach house.

"Max," I breathed. "It's beautiful."

He smiled and squeezed my hand. "I can't tell you how much it pleases me to hear that."

Sprawled out over one story, the kitchen, dining room, and large family room blended together and spilled down a hallway to the bathrooms and bedrooms.

From the moment I stepped through the door, I felt welcomed. There was not an ounce of unnecessary clutter. The paint on the walls was soft, muted, a perfect backdrop to the vibrant rugs and throw pillows.

With the blinds pulled back, the windows offered an unimpeded view of the street in front, and the beach in the back.

The kitchen, with its white cabinetry, glass-tiled backsplash, and spacious butcher block counters had my fingers itching to bake. The large kitchen table fairly begged for a family to sit down to eat.

Instead of a dining room, Max had a library. "I could spend hours, days, weeks in here!" I wandered through his space to the family room. "Oh my gosh, you've got a turntable, too."

"I told you," he laughed and tugged me onward. "I want to show you the rest."

Audrey had claimed a corner of the couch and Brooklyn had helped herself to the other side.

I gasped. "I'm so sorry. She never does that at someone else's house. Brooklyn, floor."

His warm hand came down against the back of my neck and he squeezed lightly. "Don't worry about it. I want Audrey to be comfortable here. That means she has to treat it like her own house."

I didn't know how to answer him. "I can't believe you did all the decorating," I murmured instead. "It's truly stunning!"

"I'm glad you like it."

"I love it."

He hummed and looped his arms around my waist loosely. "Could you see yourself living here?"

I blinked. "With Aaron and Audrey?"

He chuckled and pressed a scruffy kiss to the nape of my neck. His deep voice in my ear provoked a riot of goose pimples to storm across my flesh. "Well, I think they're a bit young to live by themselves."

His question unlocked all kinds of yearnings, so I deflected to something I was sure about, even more sure after what he'd just said. "I'd like us to be by ourselves soon," I murmured.

"On that note," he teased. "Let me show you the bedrooms."

The house boasted four large bedrooms. The master and ensuite were the only ones that looked lived in.

Two of the other bedrooms were set up as guest rooms with only the basics, and the third was a mess.

I laughed out loud when I saw it and stared at him incredulously.

He scrubbed a hand over his head and smiled widely, his dimple a defined crater in his handsome face.

"What happened to this room? It's almost as bad as my closet."

He tilted his head to the side as he perused it as if through my eyes.

A folding craft table covered in a mishmash of this and that took up half of one wall. A ladder leaned against the other wall beside a short, squat bookcase. A tower of boxes littered one corner, and a few loose items covered a small side table and the floor at the foot of the adjacent wall.

It was everything the rest of the house was not.

"This room became a kind of catch-all." Max began slowly, staring into space. "There were so many things my dad cleared out of the house after my mom passed that I just couldn't part with. I told him I'd take them to the reuse center, and I did eventually, but they came here first until I was ready." Back in the present, he looked around the room at everything that was left. "Some stuff I was never able to let go. Some stuff was Noelle's that I held onto for her though those are all gone now that she's settled with Hawk."

My voice softened in understanding. "And the gnome in the corner? Is he one of the things you couldn't let go of?"

He smiled, his eyes soft with memories. "Mom had a beautiful garden," he chuckled, "and a serious gnome fetish. She left them to Noelle. When Noelle moved away from Sage Ridge, I brought the gnomes here along with everything else Dad wanted out of the house.

He just couldn't stand seeing all her clothes and shoes knowing she'd never wear them again. Everything else in the house is exactly how Mom left it."

I walked closer and picked the little fellow up off a discarded side table. "This little guy has a missing arm. Did you kidnap him?"

"Rescued, more like. Noelle lost it after Mom died and took a baseball bat to the gnomes. I saved them. When she moved in with Hawkley, and had her own garden, I set them up for her."

I ran a finger over the rough edge. "Why not this one?"

With a few easy strides, he reached me and ran a hand over its little head. "I didn't want her to have the memory of the pain. And I couldn't bear to throw any of Mom's gnomes out."

"I like him," I declared, suddenly fiercely protective of the little guy. "He deserves a spot in your garden. Maybe we can find a place where he can thrive. Maybe we can get him a few gnome-buddies to keep him company." I cocked my head to the side in thought and mused, "Maybe a bird house?"

Laughing, he slung an arm around my shoulders and squeezed me into his side. "You might just be right."

God, it felt so good to be near him. This room, this room housed all his pain, and I wanted to take it all from him. I looked around. "What else do you have in here?"

He released me and retreated to lean against the doorframe. "You can look around if you want. There's nothing much left of great importance."

I picked an envelope up off the top of the bookshelf.

He huffed out a surprised laugh. "Except that."

A tan craft-style envelope, it had Max's name handwritten across the front with three doodled hearts.

"Is this a love letter?"

"Yes. From my mom. She wrote it shortly before she passed."

Turning it over in my hands, it didn't even look like the seal had been broken. "Have you read it?"

He shifted his weight. "Once about a year after we lost her, and again not that long ago when I cleared out all of Noelle's things."

Every fiber of my mother's heart yearned to read this last love letter from a mother to her son. But the tension in Max's body told me he wasn't ready for that.

I gently traced one of the hearts, placed it back down on the bookcase where I found it, and crossed to him. Snaking my arms around his waist, I laid my head on his broad chest. "I'm so sorry you lost her."

His body trembled in my arms.

Some losses, no matter the passage of time, never fade.

26

All I'd Failed

I anxiously paced around the family room as I waited for Aaron to get home from work. With each pass of the window, I looked out onto the street to search for him. Those delicate glass hearts, lit by the streetlights outside, mocked me with their fragility. My teeth worried the inside of my lip so much it was beginning to feel like ground beef.

Because, after opening a third email, I had to accept that Kian wasn't prepared to wait any longer to meet his son.

After Audrey went to bed, I tried everything to distract my mind from the upcoming conversation with my son. I baked two batches of muffins, cleaned the bathroom, and wiped down the kitchen cabinets.

Still, my heart thudded in my chest.

I opened my book and reread the same page so many times I finally gave up and tossed it aside. Moving to the one thing that never failed to lift my mood, I turned on the lamp and flicked the switch on the turntable before leafing through my albums. Finally finding one of my favorite feisty women, I slid the vinyl into place and allowed her raspy voice to wash over me.

Just as my nerves began to settle, Aaron's key turned the deadbolt on the front door.

His easy grin faltered as he took me in, then his brows lowered ominously as he closed the door behind him. "Mom? What happened?" Shucking off his coat and boots, his face darkened. "Is it Max? Did he do something?"

"No!" I waved him off and forced a smile. "It's not that, and it's not bad," I grimaced because who was I to say if it was bad or not, "but I do need to talk to you. Let's go into the kitchen."

Flicking on the harsh overhead light, I immediately wished I'd opted to have this conversation in the warm, gentle light of the family room. The bright kitchen that had been the scene of countless rounds of cards, board games, and conversations, suddenly felt like an interrogation room.

Barely taking his eyes off me, Aaron washed his hands at the kitchen sink, then grabbed a muffin and sat at the table.

"Milk?" I grabbed a glass out of the cupboard and swung the fridge door open.

"Sure."

My hand shook as I poured the milk into the glass. Returning the pitcher to the fridge, I took a silent, deep, breath to steady myself before spinning around to face him.

Instead of devouring the muffin as usual, he picked at the crinkled wrapper surrounding it. His wary eyes found mine.

Quickly, I set his glass on the table in front of him and slid into the chair next to him. "Okay. It's not necessarily a bad thing, and I don't know how this could have happened, but Kian emailed me."

"Kian?"

"Your father."

Aaron's face blanked of all expression as he drew back. A myriad of expressions filtered across his face too quickly for me to identify.

I rushed in to fill the silence between us. "I'm sorry. I know you're not ready for it, and I can't even begin to think how he found you."

He swallowed and his eyes darted away before coming back to mine. "I think I might know."

My eyes widened. Did Aaron somehow track him down? I didn't think it was possible. Even when I offered Aaron to help him find his father when the time was right, I wasn't sure I would be able to pull it off.

He cleared his throat. "Nadine and I, for fun, we, uh... we did one of those ancestry kits." He looked away but continued slowly. "I don't know if I secretly hoped he would find me, but I thought the chance was so small that it wasn't worth telling you."

"Like a dare to the universe," I murmured.

"Yeah."

The fog began to clear as understanding filtered in. "But how did he get my email?"

Aaron winced. "The half of me that wasn't ready put your email instead of mine." He paused. "I'm sorry."

I replied quickly and covered his hand with mine. "Don't be. I don't mind. Not at all. I was just afraid this would be an unwelcome surprise."

Meeting my eyes, his mouth twisted. "What did he say?"

My voice softened. "Would you like to read it?"

He nodded.

Opening my email, I passed him my phone.

His eyes scanned the message then dashed back to the beginning to take it in again, slowly this time. Finally, his fearful eyes met mine. "He wants to meet me."

I nodded. "That doesn't matter. The real question is, do you want to meet him?"

"How do you feel about it?"

I felt my way slowly through the maze of my conflicting feelings. Guilt. Shame. Regret. Remorse. Embarrassment. Hope. Fear.

Cornered.

I blinked slowly.

Cornered.

"It doesn't bother me," I cleared the lie from my throat, "as long as it's positive for you."

His gaze bounced around as if the answer could be found hanging just out of reach. "I'm not sure. I think so?" He faced me, his hands stilling. "What if he's horrible?"

"Then you inherited all your goodness from me."

He barked out a rough laugh and grasped the back of his neck. "Wow. Okay. Yeah." He stared into space, then nodded. "Yeah. Let's do it."

"Do you want to write him back?"

He winced and scrubbed a hand over his face. "Can you do it? Can I give you a list of questions and you ask him?" He shook his head. "I'm just not ready to dive in but there are things I'd like to know."

"Yes, son." I nodded, took back my phone, and opened my notes. "I'll tell him you're willing to meet with him but that you'd like to ask a few questions first."

He nodded and leaned his elbows on the table. "Okay. What should I ask first?"

"Maybe how he tracked you down?"

"Yes, ask that. Also, is he married? Does he have any other children?" Relaxing into his seat, he took half the muffin top off in one bite. "Where does he live? And work? What did he study in school?" Breaking off another piece, he stared off into space as my thumbs typed furiously.

I never imagined he had so many questions.

Of course he has questions, I berated myself.

"What does he like to do? What are his hobbies?"

Standing, he crumpled the wrapper and tossed it into the garbage. Next, he gulped down his milk, washed the glass, and set it down in the dish drainer.

"Does he have a favorite movie?"

"I think that's probably enough to start," I murmured, my thumbs flying.

He paused by my chair. "Can you forward his email to me so I can read it again?"

"Absolutely."

He grinned suddenly. "I wonder if he's like me?" He laughed and rolled his eyes. "Or if I'm like him?"

I smiled through the pain and answered with a lilt in my voice. "I guess we'll find out!"

Bending low, he bussed me on the cheek before heading to his bedroom. "Goodnight, Momma."

Sitting at the table, I struggled to make sense of the storm inside me.

Sticking his head back in the kitchen, voice strained, he added, "And Mom? Can you ask him if he ever thought about me?"

A lump in my throat the size of a small cantaloupe stole my voice. I nodded.

"Thanks, Momma. You're the best."

I waited for the snick of his door quietly closing before giving in to the tears that choked me. I laid my head down on the cushion of my crossed arms on the table and grieved for all I'd failed to give him.

27

Spill the Tea

Since telling Aaron about Kian, the hits kept coming.

First, Brooklyn got another eye infection. Knowing she was prone to them, I simply took her to the vet to pick up another prescription for eye drops. Instead, the vet recommended a minor surgery to stop her bottom lid from curling in causing her eyelashes to irritate the sensitive membrane of her eye.

Pet insurance would cover most of the cost, but Audrey would not handle being separated from Brooklyn for any length of time. And I didn't think Brooklyn or Audrey would react well to the stitches.

Next, Aaron called and confessed his car brakes had been squealing like baby pigs for a week. That bill we had to cover ourselves. And I didn't have the first clue where to pull the money from.

To top it off, I hadn't seen Max since Sunday.

And now I sat in Michelle's basement surrounded by women who were snorting and laughing over the latest steamy romance they'd chosen for their book club. So many times, I had dreamed of being a part of something like this, but lost in a maze of worry, I barely paid any attention.

Finally, Noelle leaned over and whispered in my ear, "Let's get out of here."

Startled, my head snapped up. "What?"

Harley, Shae, and Bridge surrounded Noelle. "Let's go," Noelle urged again.

"No," I protested as my cheeks began to burn.

You ruined everybody's fun.

"We're going to The Beanery," Bridge smiled.

Some of the other ladies looked over at us curiously, probably because we were leaving early.

I caught my mother's worried look from the corner of my eye, and though the guilt weighed heavily, I could spare no extra energy to soothe her anxiety.

I stumbled to my feet. "Are they open? I thought book club wasn't allowed at The Beanery?"

Harley laughed and pointed to the other side of the room that was fairly bumping with laughter. "They're not allowed at The Beanery. We've yet to be kicked out."

Bridge wagged her eyebrows. "The night is young."

"I don't know guys," I began, trying to let them off the hook. "I'm not really feeling up to it."

Shae handed me my coat and tucked her hand in the crook of my elbow. "All the more reason to go."

At The Beanery, Shae led me directly to a table while the others cleared out the last of the chocolate croissants in the display and ordered coffee.

There were two couples seated near the front window, so we settled in the back corner.

"Spill," Bridge demanded. "You look like you ran over your best friend who borrowed your favorite shoes to walk your dog."

"There's a visual," Harley commented, looking at me over the rim of her hot chocolate as she took a small sip.

I jerked in surprise when Shae's hand covered mine. "You don't have to tell us anything, but we just want you to know that you can."

"A steel vault." Noelle turned an imaginary key at her mouth.

"We're here for you," Shae added.

Under the table, Harley pressed her knee against my thigh, her steady presence in my life lending me strength.

"And we're safe," Bridge declared. "There's no point in keeping everything cooped up."

Needing a moment to think, I looked away and took a breath before facing them.

"When Aaron started school, my father bought him a car. He put it in Aaron's name, but he pays for the insurance and any repairs. It's a new car, so there hasn't been much up until now in terms of repairs, but Aaron is a young driver, so the insurance payments are high. My father is angry with me and is threatening to withdraw that support." I inhaled deeply. "And Aaron's brakes need to be replaced."

Harley winced. "Ouch."

Shae's lips pressed into a tight line. "Asshole."

I laughed. Maybe it was wrong because my father wasn't all bad, but I craved the warmth of their solidarity.

Noelle twirled her hand. "Continue."

"Brooklyn needs minor surgery on her eye. Most of that cost is covered by insurance, but Audrey doesn't handle change well and I'm not looking forward to managing her anxiety while Brooklyn is recuperating."

"Understandable," Harley declared.

I took a deep breath and released the next bit in a long stream of words. "And Aaron's birth father contacted me. He wants to meet Aaron."

Shae's mug hit the table. "Well, fuck a duck."

"Wow," Harley murmured.

"How does Aaron feel about that?" Noelle asked.

I shrugged. "He's curious."

"And how do you feel about it?" Shae murmured.

Tears sprang to my eyes. "I feel like I failed him. Like maybe I should have done something different to keep his father in his life." Now that the cat was out of the bag, I couldn't stop talking. "My father, he's already pissed about Max. He thinks he's distracting me from being a good mother. This development will just give him more material to beat me over the head with." I smiled ruefully at Harley. "He despises your family for what he calls your interference in our family affairs, and he lumps Max in with you guys."

Harley's eyebrows scrunched in confusion. She opened her mouth to speak then seemed to think better of it and snapped it shut.

"That's a lot," Shae said softly.

"It is," Noelle murmured.

"I've narrowed down the path to happiness," Bridge boldly declared, drawing all our attention. Holding up one finger at a time, she continued. "First, you cannot care about what other people think of you. Two, you must preserve the bits and pieces that make you who you are and feed your soul no matter the cost. And three, if you're looking for love, make sure to find yourself a man who frees you to be your dirtiest, filthiest self, walks on the outside of the sidewalk, and kisses you on the forehead."

Shae, her long, blond, ponytail swinging, threw her head back and laughed. "Amen!"

"A little manhandling doesn't hurt either," Harley smirked.

I tilted my head to the side. "Manhandling?"

Max's words echoed in my head. *That was my impression of the boy next door.*

"Oh my God," Noelle exclaimed. "She's thinking about my brother!" She held up a palm. "Nope! Nope! Nope!"

Harley laughed and wiggled back in her seat, her tiny feet failing to reach the floor. "Isn't that great, Noelle?"

"What?" I asked, dumbfounded by their reaction.

Harley jerked a thumb in Noelle's direction. "This one has threatened one too many times to tell me about my brother's... skills." She pretended to gag, then her eyebrows flew up. "She's even commented on my father!"

Noelle laughed and covered her face while Harley shot her an evil grin and continued. "How does it feel now?" Then looking at me, Harley teased, "Do tell...how is our Max between the sheets?"

Both Bridge and Shae leaned in, unabashedly interested in the answer.

Harley continued, "He's 100% into manhandling, I know it. If ever there was a control freak, it's Max. Fess up!"

My face flamed as I rolled my eyes.

Noelle cried, "Mercy!"

Harley sat back, a satisfied smirk on her face. "My work here is done." Pointing to me, she declared, "You're my secret weapon! Noelle can't threaten me anymore."

I laughed, how could I not?

The fact that they took all my news with such ease allowed me to admit to more.

"You know," I pulled my napkin into strips, "I'm so angry. I push it down, but it flares up with almost no notice. I've tried so hard to please my father with zero success. My mom is constantly brokering peace between us, which requires me to keep my mouth shut, but I'm just not sure I have it in me anymore to care what my father thinks."

"You've got no more fucks left to give," Shae stated with a knowing nod.

"Down to your last fuck," Noelle agreed, shoving the last bit of chocolate croissant into her mouth.

"You've got to budget your fucks. You can't just give them out willy-nilly all over the place." Harley grinned.

Bridge slammed her palms down on the table, drawing the attention of the other two tables. "You're fresh out of fucks!"

I barked out a bitter laugh. "I wish!"

Harley leaned in. "What do you mean?"

"I mean," I stressed irritably, "if anything, I give too many fucks."

"Explain," Harley demanded.

My face scrunched with the effort not to break down in front of these special women.

Shae rubbed a slow circle over my back.

"I feel like I'm missing the mark in every single aspect of my life. I cut my son's father out of his life because I didn't want him to treat us like a burden or an obligation. At the time, he was happy about it. But I left no room for him to change his mind." I couldn't look at them, but the urge to purge was too strong to ignore. "My father is still pissed I got pregnant and brought shame to our family. He loves Aaron but somehow doesn't connect that bright spot in his life to my pregnancy. It burns him that I never apologized." I held out my hands. "But how can you apologize for your child's existence? I won't do it."

"And you shouldn't," Shae agreed quietly.

Noelle hummed her agreement.

"I feel like", my cheeks burned with the upcoming admission, "Sage Ridge's token charity case. It's not that I don't appreciate the help," I rushed to add, "I just wish I didn't need so much of it."

I drew in a shuddering breath. "And Max...he could do so much better than me."

"I'm going to stop you right there," Noelle interrupted softly. "I've never seen my brother so happy. Honestly, the last time he was this happy, he was with you."

"Yeah?"

She studied me quietly. "He cried, you know."

My head snapped up. "What?"

She winced. "When he broke up with you, he came home and cried." Her eyes took on a faraway glaze. "Mom encouraged him to call you and patch things up, but he said he couldn't jerk you around until he was sure." She looked at me. "He was sure. He was just scared."

Harley sniffed and wiped a finger under her eye. "Everyone needs help sometimes, Wren. I get so much support from my family. You've had none. You deserved every bit of help you got. And it wasn't all that much. It definitely wasn't as much as my parents wanted to give you." She held her hands up then let them flop back down. "How could we just sit back? Especially knowing how important you were to Max. Never mind the fact you were abandoned."

My eyes darted to meet Shae's soft gaze. "Abandoned?" I whispered, not liking the sound of that word.

"What else would you call it?" Harley whispered back.

We did not get kicked out of The Beanery, but we did close it down.

The next morning when I opened my front door to leave for work, a small gift bag bumped against the doorframe. I slipped it off the outside doorknob and withdrew a tiny glass jar from inside the bag.

I held it up to my face and burst out laughing.

Inside, carved out in tiny wooden letters, dangled the word 'FUCK'.

A sparkly label wrapped around the outside of the glass: 'Down to My Last Fuck – Break in Case of Emergency'.

28

Pops

"I'm so freaking nervous," I admitted. Tucking my hands under my thighs to curtail my fidgeting, I took a deep breath.

Max reached across the center console of the car to rest his palm on my thigh. "He's nervous too."

My eyebrows flew up. "He is?"

Glancing my way, Max flashed his dimple and laughed. "You're the first girl I've brought home."

I grinned back at him. "You're a late bloomer."

Flicking on his indicator, he took the turn onto his father's street. "Lucky for us," he murmured.

"Are you close to your dad?"

"He's my best friend," he replied simply.

My God, what would that have been like? "He was a good father."

"The best."

Did Max want to be a father? The idea of carrying his child occurred to me, and the thrill of it hit me like a ton of bricks. But starting over, could I do it? Did I want to?

My gaze dropped to my lap. The sun filtered through the trees lining the street and dappled across my denim-clad knees.

And if I didn't want to start over, would that be fair to him? To deprive him of a child of his own while bringing my children, my dog, and my baggage into his life? My heart skipped a beat as my breath came faster.

"Relax, Wren. It's all good. I promise."

I nodded, attempted to wipe the worry off my face, and slowed my breathing. "Do you want to be a father?"

His eyebrows shot up as his eyes darted over to me before returning to the road. "Do you want another child?" His brow furrowed. "I assumed you would be done but I'll give you one, happily, if that's something you want."

He wasn't answering my question. "What do you want, Max?"

He shrugged. "I'm not opposed. Obviously, I'd love any child we made, but I'm just as satisfied with the crew we have now."

Was he telling me the truth? Did I want to start over with a new baby?

My eyes ran over Max's profile, his lean physique. God, how I'd dreamed of carrying his baby. A baby with his deep dimple and dark eyes. A sharp shard of regret stabbed through my chest. If only we'd come together again a few years ago.

I peered into the backseat where Audrey drew on her iPad, her chin dipped down. Brooklyn sat up straight, buckled into her doggy seatbelt, wet nose pressed against the window.

My brow furrowed. "I'm sorry, Max. Brooklyn's messing up your window."

His eyes flicked to the side view mirror. "That's fine, Wren. It's long past time I had a little mess in my life."

"I wouldn't describe our mess as little," I worried, chewing the inside of my cheek.

He shook his head. "I'm a big boy, Wren. Your mess is not even a stretch for me. Trust me to know what I want, what I need, and what I can handle."

Without thinking, I snorted.

He chuckled. "Try."

Pulling into the driveway, I startled. "This is the same house you grew up in."

In fact, it was only a few blocks away from Max's own house. I would never want to live that close to my father but Max never had a harsh word for anyone in his family. I used to wonder if Max's family was as beautiful as Lou and Dan's. Now I had my answer.

"You didn't know that? I thought I told you my pops didn't change anything after Mom passed."

"That must have been so hard for him," I mused, my heart throbbing. Losing Max hurt like the devil and we'd only had one sweet summer. I couldn't imagine what it must have been like for his dad.

"It was bad. He couldn't function without her and ended up moving in with Dan and Lou for about six months. Eventually, he healed as much as a person can from a loss like that, and came home. Now, you couldn't get him out with a crowbar."

Taking off my seatbelt, I asked, "Should I put Brooklyn's vest on? That way she'll be in work mode instead of pet mode. Does he like dogs?"

"You don't have to, he does, and this is a safe place for Audrey. And Brooklyn. And you. I promise."

Audrey climbed down from the backseat. "This is not your house, my Max."

"This is where I grew up, my Audrey. My pops lives here."

Love flowered in my chest at his sweetness, sweetness Audrey accepted as her just due.

Without waiting, she began walking up the path. Since she'd been hanging out with Susie, she'd become more adventurous.

The front door opened before she reached it and an older man, almost as tall as Max, flashed his own dimple as he smiled at Audrey. "You must be Audrey."

"You must be Pops."

He laughed. "I am. It's a pleasure to meet you. Would you like to come in?"

"Yes. I brought my iPad. Would you like to see my art?"

"I would indeed."

Max's father was everything I imagined Max would be in the future, a future I desperately wanted to be part of.

Max laid his hand on my shoulder and turned me into his large frame. "It'll all be good, Tweet. You've got nothing to worry about. Being with my Pops is like being rolled up in cotton wool. He won't do a single thing to cause you pain or anxiety. And he'll take care with Audrey and Aaron, too."

Once inside, I surreptitiously slipped my homemade meatloaf into the freezer.

"If that's meatloaf, I hope you're not putting it into the freezer," Pat teased gently.

I spun around, my face flushing. "I didn't want to assume," I began.

Taking the casserole dish from my hands, he smiled, his eyes kind. "Feel free to assume when it comes to meatloaf. Especially yours." He tilted his head to the side. "I wanted to thank you so many times, but

Max told me to leave you be. Said if you wanted me to know it came from you, you would have told me."

If possible, my face flushed further, this time from guilt. Because while I assured myself I was only helping a grieving widower, it was my love for Max that compelled me to do something, anything, to ease their pain.

And I had been a married woman. Married or not, I owed those two families too much to ignore their pain.

"We appreciated it, Wren. Thank you."

I swallowed. "You're welcome."

He winked and flashed the dimple his son inherited. "Feel free to assume with any of your baked goods as well. Those muffins are legendary."

I laughed. "Max told you?"

He shook his head. "Lou. She takes them to the women's shelters. When you bake too many, she pinches one or two for me and my sweet tooth."

"Oh," my hand fluttered to my chest, "I love that. Thank you. I'll make you your own batch."

"I'm counting on it."

"Pops?"

My mouth dropped and I huffed out a laugh.

Picking up my hand, Pat kissed the back of it. "She's quite comfortable already. I'm happy to finally have you home, Wren."

My eyes filled with tears. Gentleman that he was, he pretended not to see.

"I understand Audrey's favorite food is pizza?"

I cleared my throat but could not find my voice, so I nodded instead.

"Max gave me that bit of intel. Pizza is on its way."

"Thank you," I rasped.

"My pleasure." He gave his head a small shake as he headed back to Audrey and Max in the family room. "Pineapple on pizza. What's the world coming to?"

29

Adrift

Saturday night, Aaron and Nadine stayed home with Audrey so Max and I could go out.

Sitting across from him at the cozy Greek restaurant in town, his knees caging mine under the tiny table, brought me back to our beginning. With how strict my parents were, it was almost as difficult to see him back then as it was now.

Almost two decades had passed since our first date. I spent just as much time getting ready now as I had then. And with my haircut and new clothes, I was just as ready.

Being with Max swept my boatload of worries out to sea. For a while. But like worry is wont to do, they crept back in.

"You have something on your mind." He leaned back against his chair and studied my face.

I squirmed in my chair at the thought of unloading all my baggage on him.

Finally, he offered me a smile. "You never could hide your thoughts. I can help or I can listen. I can also do both. What do you need from me?"

He cared.

He cared then, and he cared now.

And in all the years between then and now, he'd never stopped caring.

Letting him into my life wasn't selfish. Sharing my worries wasn't weak. I wasn't whining or complaining. And I certainly wasn't asking him to take on my burdens.

Noelle's revelation from the other night sprang to my mind. "Noelle told me you cried when you went home that night," I blurted.

Bringing that up must have seemed out of the blue. But I needed confirmation it hurt him as much as it hurt me. Confirmation that he cared for me the way I cared for him.

His eyes widened in surprise, and he looked off into space for a moment before returning the full impact of his attention to me. "I did. Even then, my mother knew what you meant to me. She used to tell me that our story wasn't over yet." He opened his mouth to say more then seemed to think better of it.

"What? What were you going to say?"

He winced. "That was nothing compared to my reaction to your pregnancy, engagement, and marriage." He shook his head, his brow furrowing ferociously. "I wasted so much time. And I hurt you so desperately in the process. I'll never forgive myself for that." Leaning forward, he reached for my hand across the table. With his strong fingers encircling my wrist, he lifted my palm to his downturned mouth and kissed its center. Returning it to the table, his fingers wrapped tightly around mine. His dark eyes held his promise. "I'll spend the rest of my life making it up to you."

My heart melted for this man who took responsibility for my choices. "You have nothing to make up for."

Stroking the tender skin of my wrist, he waited patiently for me to speak.

I sighed in resignation. It couldn't hurt to share. "My father is threatening to stop paying for Aaron's car insurance."

His brows lowered.

"Aaron's brakes need replacing."

His lips thinned.

"And to round it out, Aaron's birth father emailed me. He wants to meet Aaron."

His eyebrows hit his hairline and he whistled softly. "Wow. Is that all?"

I laughed, feeling infinitesimally lighter about the whole mess for the first time. "Brooklyn needs minor surgery. And that's all."

"I didn't know you still had contact with Aaron's birth father?"

I offered him a rueful smile. "I didn't. Seems Aaron and Nadine did an ancestry test." I raised my eyebrows. "Then Aaron registered his results and used my email."

Max's sharp brain missed nothing. "You think it was his way of looking for his father."

Huffing out a small laugh, I agreed, "I think he was testing the universe, putting it out there to see what happened."

"Is he happy about the results?"

I pressed my lips together. "Yes. Nervous, but yes."

"I know I said I could just listen." He smirked at himself but held my gaze. "Wren, I don't want you to suffer needlessly. Please. Let me help."

"Max…" I turned my face away, needing a moment to think away from the influence of those dark eyes that could convince me to do anything. "If I can't figure it out on my own, I'll come to you."

"Deal," he replied quickly.

I laughed, my eyes returning to his. "That was fast."

He shook his head and chuckled ruefully. "I wasn't going to give you a chance to think twice."

After dinner, we practically flew to his place. We were still so very new that my nerves had not yet abated when we were alone.

Several record albums lay scattered across the coffee table. Sliding a familiar one out from the bottom of the pile, I held it up and exclaimed, "I have this album!"

Max grinned. "I've seen your collection. We have a lot of the same albums."

I ran my hand over the sleeve. "Listening to this one takes me back to a much, much, simpler time."

Taking it from my hands, he crossed to his turntable and slipped it on while I made myself comfortable on the floor.

"I don't know if it was simpler, or we just had fewer responsibilities and maybe we were too dumb to realize what we were risking." Turning toward me, surprised laughter burst from his lips. "What are you doing?"

I smiled but didn't move. "Some music you just have to lie down under and let it seep through to your soul."

Looking down at me, he rested his hands on his lean hips. "When I pictured you spread out before me like dessert, it was on my bed, not my floor."

I blushed. My mouth opened and closed. How the hell was I supposed to get from the floor to his bed without looking like a total eager beaver?

Eager beaver. Ha.

Chuckling, he folded his muscular frame down and stretched out beside me. When his fingers found mine, I closed my eyes in contentment.

A sweet memory surfaced. "We used to lie down like this and watch the stars."

He brought our interlaced hands to his mouth and brushed a kiss over the back of my hand. "Those were some of my happiest moments."

A bittersweet ache throbbed in my chest. "Mine too."

Behind my closed lids, the sting of tears threatened to ruin this most perfect of repeats. I swallowed hard, unwilling to ruin the sweetness of lying next to him. But, God, how many nights I'd cried when his hand had let go of mine!

His thumb stroked the pulse in my wrist. "Why didn't you ever date after your divorce?"

"Oh, boy." I opened my eyes and stared up at the ceiling as I blew out a breath. I guessed we were at that stage in our relationship where we opened the closets and allowed the past to tumble out. "There wasn't much time or opportunity. Audrey in those years...she wasn't easy." I shrugged. "Occasionally, a man would come into the diner and ask me out for coffee. Part of me wanted to go but you get called out often enough for being a disgrace to your family because of your pregnancy, it tends to screw with your perception of your sexuality." Shame burned my cheeks, still, but I continued, ready and willing to break through the cage of my upbringing. "In combination with the way I was raised, dating seemed like a bad idea. Sex seemed like a terrible risk."

With my husband, I'd never been able to break through the mental barrier to enjoy it. Not that he put in much effort. Looking back, I wasn't even sure what compelled him to pursue me. His interest in sex was perfunctory at best. He didn't want children. And in the end, he didn't want me.

Talking about it brought clarity to my reasons. "It felt selfish to focus on myself when my kids needed so much. Aaron was hurting and acting out." My throat grew thick at the memory. "God," I spat. "David leaving left a huge, gaping hole in Aaron's life."

"He was like a father to him."

"No," I corrected vehemently, "he *was* his father. He had been his father since Aaron was three years old. Aaron barely remembered life without David." I swallowed the tightness in my throat. "Aaron was just beginning to realize he didn't have a father like other kids when David came into our lives. He clung to David like a happy, little barnacle."

"How old was he when David left?"

"Ten. I had no idea David planned to leave. He didn't even give me time to prepare the kids." The ceiling faded away as I stared into the past. "One night I put the kids to bed and by the time I came back to the family room David was standing in the front hall surrounded by suitcases."

Closing my eyes, I winced. How could I have missed the signs? He must have been planning his escape for weeks.

Max rolled me onto my side and tucked me against the length of his body. Safe within his embrace, the memory I'd worked so hard to suppress rose to the surface.

The sight of those suitcases, so unexpected and out of place, stopped me in my tracks. "David?" I asked, confused. "Where are you going?"

Meeting my eyes, he held his palms away from his sides and then let them fall. "I can't do this. I thought I could, but I can't."

I gave my head a shake, doubting what I heard.

My eyes traced his face and the suitcases at his feet. When had he packed them? Why hadn't I noticed anything amiss?

The first tendrils of fear unfurled in my chest, their icy touch chilling the blood in my veins. The part of me bent on self-preservation refused to accept it. "This? What do you mean, 'this'?"

Everything around me looked exactly as it had when I'd left him to put the kids to bed. The TV droned on in the background, the canned sound of sitcom laughter grating my nerves.

"All of it. Kids. Family." *He paused.* "You."

It took me a moment to remember my question, then I stepped back as if pushed. I covered my heart with my palm as if to protect it. "Me?" *I rasped.*

His cheeks flushed bright red as he looked away.

My mind spun, unable to grasp what was happening, unwilling to face the hurt. My gaze dropped to the floor to trace the pattern on the rug we had so painstakingly picked out when we bought our house.

Oh my God. Audrey. Aaron.

My eyes snapped up to his. "What about our kids? How are you going to tell them?"

He shook his head, his jaw set. "I'm not."

I snorted then, incredulous, and threw out my arm. "What? You think they won't notice when Dad has his own house across town? When they have one bedroom here and another in your house?"

"I was hoping we could sell the house."

A sharp puff of air parted my lips.

The TV droned on.

The bulb in the kitchen, the one I'd asked him to change, flickered.

Of course. Of course we couldn't stay here.

I struggled to make sense of it all. My children, they were going to lose everything, their whole world, in one fell swoop. My eyes filled with tears, and he blurred in front of me.

I swiped my wrists across my eyes.

"Renata..." he trailed off, his eyes darting away before coming back to meet mine head on. "I'm not going to be here."

My breath stuttered from my lungs. "Not going to be where?"

A car turned onto our street, its headlights streaming through the front window, momentarily blinding me.

I forgot to close the curtains again.

I stepped closer to him, as if proximity could wring sense from the chaos. "You're not going to be in Sage Ridge?"

Did he get a job transfer too good to turn down? Why couldn't we do long distance? Was there someone else?

The blood drained from my face at the thought, but the reality was worse.

He shook his head. "I'm not staying in Sage Ridge...and I won't be seeing the kids."

My jaw flapped ineffectually. An icy wave of panic washed over me, dragging the rest of the blood in my body to my feet. I was being set adrift, like a raft on the open sea, for the third time.

Worse, he was doing it to our kids.

My kids.

In a flash, I sparked back to life. "You can't do that," I whispered savagely. "You can't just walk out on them."

He shook his head and looked down at the floor. "I can't stay."

A woman's strident voice elicited more canned laughter.

My book lay open on the coffee table.

The washing machine buzzed, signifying the end of the wash cycle.

The end of us.

I have to put David's dress shirts in the dryer before they wrinkle.

The thought barely registered before I realized he wouldn't be there to wear them. Rage, raw and unfiltered, bled over my vision.

Closing the distance between us, I twisted both of my fists in the front of his shirt. With sick satisfaction I noted the alarm on his face. My whole body shook with the force of my desire to hurt him the way he was hurting me.

The way he was hurting them.

Then Aaron, his sweet, sleepy voice, sliced clear through my fury.

My heart skittered in my chest as I released David's shirt and spun on my heel to face our son.

My son.

"Dad? Where are you going?" His eyes darted between David and me, his expression slowly morphing from confusion to suspicion to horror.

Another tear rolled down my cheek as I flitted back to the present.

"He didn't even answer him," I whispered. Max's lips moved in my hair as I hung suspended between the pain of the past and the safety of Max's arms. "He just put on his coat and pulled his bags out the front door." I began to shake, the memory of Aaron in his favorite Batman pajamas that still fit his waist but stopped three inches above his ankles. I huffed. "He was wearing his favorite pajamas. Sometimes it's the smallest things, those that mean nothing and everything at the same time, that stand out in those painful memories."

"Visceral memories," he murmured, his hands running over my back and side. "Give me the rest of it."

"Aaron's childhood ended that night." I clung to Max, the pain of watching Aaron grasping onto David's coat as fresh as if it happened yesterday. My face crumpled. "I tried to pull Aaron into my arms, but he pushed me aside. He wanted David. He *needed* David. And it was so cold, Max, it was so damn cold, and he was standing outside on the icy concrete in his bare feet, pajamas flapping around his skinny ankles, toes digging into the concrete as he tried to wrestle David's suitcases back inside."

That moment left me hollow with the knowledge that I could never take the place of the father he loved.

"Fuck, Wren." Max wrapped his body tighter around mine.

My brow smoothed as Max's scent surrounded me, and I nodded, compelled to tell the rest. "I had to physically restrain Aaron from running after David's car. I couldn't get the front door closed and hold onto him at the same time. We just sat there in the hallway in front of the open door while David drove away and Aaron screamed for him to come back. He didn't look back."

Realizing it was Max's shirt I now had twisted in my fist, I loosened my hold and sucked in a deep breath. The night had gone from bad to worse when Audrey woke up. "David left him like a fucking stray dog on the side of the road. I'll never forgive him for that." I closed my eyes but not my ears to the echoes of the past. "The sounds, oh God, Max, the sounds that came from his little body. I'll never forget."

"How could you?" he responded gruffly, his hands running over my back, pressing me tight to his wide chest. "How could anyone forget something like that?"

Something loosened inside me, a knot I never knew existed unraveled, and I breathed easier. "I've never told anyone about that night." Pressing my forehead against his chest, I murmured, "Thank you."

Retelling that memory stripped away the shame of it. Watching it unfold through Max's eyes, there was only raw, unfiltered, anger at David.

"Has he contacted the kids at all since then?"

"No. He contacted me about a year later and offered to terminate his parental rights. He admitted he never really wanted to be a father, wasn't cut out for it."

Max's entire body stiffened at my revelation.

I twisted my neck to look at him. "What?"

He stared down at me incredulously. "He didn't pay child support?"

"No. When you terminate your parental rights, you don't have to. He did owe back pay for the year and I took that. I didn't want anything else from him. My kids are nobody's burden."

"Wren," he muttered harshly, his fingers digging into my hip. "I had no idea. I can't even comprehend the home and family you've built. You're the strongest woman I know."

"I don't feel very strong most of the time," I admitted.

He barked out a harsh laugh. "You're strong, Wren. You're a fucking tank."

"Max!" I laughed, the sound rasping and rough. "Never, ever tell a woman she's a tank!"

Huffing out a harsh breath, he shook his head. "I'm not ready to laugh about this yet, Wren."

Oh no.

I scrunched my eyes closed. "I'm sorry for laying all of that on you."

"No. Never be sorry for telling me anything. I want it all, Wren. All of it. I'll carry the whole fucking lot of it for you. Gladly."

Safe in his arms, that bitter sliver from my past worked its way out, and I allowed the music to sweep it away.

Lighter, freer than I could ever remember being, I realized I wanted so much more than I'd been given.

"Max? Are you okay?"

"Of course. Are you?"

"Yes."

My unspoken thoughts stretched taut between us.

He waited.

"Max?"

"Wren."

"Do you think you could drop the 'boy-next-door' act?"

Propping himself up on his elbow, he stared down into my face. His brow deeply furrowed, he asked, "Now? After all of that?"

I nodded. "I want it. I want everything." I searched his eyes and struggled to find the right words to express my feelings. "I want you to be with me the way you want to be with me. I want you to use my body."

His eyebrows flew up. "Use?"

I huffed and stumbled over my words. "Maybe use is the wrong word. Enjoy. I want you to enjoy my body." I shook my head sharply. "Not enjoy it for the purpose of giving me pleasure--" I thought for a moment, adrenaline surging as my desires sharpened to crystalline clarity. "I want you to take *your* pleasure from *my* body."

He nuzzled his nose against the side of my face then dropped his lips to my ear. His deep voice tightened my nipples; my pelvis rocked forward seeking his. "You want me to play with you like you're my favorite toy?"

I inhaled roughly. Latching onto the strong forearm locked across my abdomen, I squeezed.

"I'm going to need verbal confirmation," he muttered low in my ear.

"Yes," I gulped.

His tongue traced the shell of my ear and he murmured, "And you don't care if I give you pleasure? You're just going to give yourself over to me for mine?"

My eyelids fluttered shut.

Yes. Take me out of my head.

A deep, sensual shudder worked its way down my body. My back arched; the points of my breasts desperate for the hard planes of his chest.

"God, yes."

30

No More Mr. Nice Guy

Left aching and stripped raw from my journey into the past, I only wanted to feel. Dark desires, the kind I'd never voiced aloud spilled from my lips.

Use me.

Take everything from me.

My body.

My will.

My thoughts.

My pain.

All of me.

Max rolled to his feet and pulled me up to mine. With his hand braced firmly against my lower back, he guided me to his bedroom where his wide, welcoming bed beckoned me forward.

My eyes darted around his room before returning to the bed. I longed to slip between his sheets and open myself up, lock him inside the circle of my arms and between my thighs. A quiver of longing and apprehension danced down the length of my spine.

His hand chased it back up to the base of my neck, his thumb stroking my nape before tunneling into my hair. Stepping back slightly, he denied me the heat of his chest as he gathered my hair back into a ponytail. The tingling pleasure parted my lips, and the slight sting as he tugged elicited a low hum from my throat.

He dropped his mouth to my ear, his deep voice sending a lightning bolt of shameful lust straight to my groin. "When you're begging me for release, remember you asked for this."

I swallowed back a moan.

This was not the Max I knew. This Max was unknown, unpredictable, and uninhibited.

Exactly the way I wanted to be.

His hand wrapped around my hair, he angled my head to the side, and his scruffy chin hit my neck. Goosebumps raced across my flesh, tightening my nipples. "Oh, God," I breathed.

I'd never been so aware of my body, so grateful for its joyful response under his hands. When his mouth opened and his teeth clamped down on that most sensitive of curves, my hands shot back to his thighs to steady myself.

"I'm going to take everything from you, Tweet, everything you didn't know you had in you to give."

Yes.

I nodded.

This was my body to do with as I willed. My body to share. My body to indulge. My body to pleasure.

For him. With him. By his hands and mouth and body. Only him.

"Teach me how to please you," I forced out in a whisper.

His hands rose to cup my breasts over my shirt. "Everything you are pleases me."

"Yes, but—." His fingers twisted my nipples and stole my breath, the pleasure-pain pushing my breasts further into his hands, seeking more, even as every muscle in my body tensed.

"See," he murmured darkly. "You're already pleasing me."

The tone of his voice brought all my senses online at once, sharpening my awareness of him as a bigger, stronger, being. Soft lips brushed down the side of my neck. I blew out a breath and relaxed into his hold. This was Max. There was no need to be tense or afraid.

His big hands soothed me as they followed the curves of my body and crept to the neckline of my blouse. Dipping under the soft fabric, he caressed my sensitive skin.

I lifted my chin to give him greater access, sighing and leaning back against his chest as his fingers danced across my flesh.

Suddenly, I was roughly yanked forward as he grasped the edges of my blouse and tore it open clear down the middle.

I yelped in shock, staring down at my body with my mouth agape.

Wasting no time, he dragged the two halves back over my shoulders, pulling my arms together behind me, and wrapped it around my wrists.

"Max," I gasped, my breath escaping in sharp pants.

Licking a path up my naked spine, he pulled my earlobe into his mouth, and murmured, "You still with me?"

"Yes." My breath rattled out.

Gripping my upper arms, he drew me back to lean against his chest. "Put your head back on my shoulder."

As soon as I complied, his hand encircled my throat.

"Oh, God," I breathed, my panties flooding.

His other hand flicked open the button of my jeans and drew down the zipper.

I whimpered in his hold, shuffling from one foot to the other.

"Anytime you want to stop—"

"Don't you dare stop," I ordered.

Before the last word left my mouth, his fingers curled inside me.

My head shot forward, my body bowing, until his hold tightened on my throat, and he yanked me back against his chest as he circled my clit.

My legs began to shake.

He was a fever, a drug.

I wanted more, wanted it to last, but I was already there. The first flutter hit, my pelvis tilting, offering him more. Offering everything.

And he withdrew his hand.

"Max," I gasped.

"Now, now, Tweet," he murmured. "You said this is for me. And I haven't even taken my clothes off."

I closed my eyes. He was right. This was not what I had in mind. I wanted to watch him take his pleasure, witness his release as he came undone.

"Take them off," I urged.

"Suck."

My eyes snapped open as his wet fingers pulled down my lower lip. Responding immediately to his tone, I opened my mouth. Before I even understood what he was asking, I tasted myself on his fingers as he firmly stroked them along the length of my tongue.

A groan vibrated in his chest. "Taste your sweetness, Wren. Wrap your lips around my fingers like it's my cock and suck. Do it for me."

A riot of butterflies took off in my stomach. My face flamed. Still, I closed my lips around his fingers, stroked them with my tongue, and sucked them deeper into my mouth.

"That's it," he praised. Releasing my throat, he tangled his fingers in the back of my hair and angled my face toward him.

Dark eyes hooded and lit with a near feral desire, a desire for me, fell to watch his fingers pumping in and out of my mouth.

His unmasked need had me rolling my hips as he ripped his fingers away and slammed his lips down onto mine. The angle he held me at prohibited the slightest movement. I could barely kiss him back. I could only take, take whatever he wanted to give me.

Yes.

My entire being settled.

This.

My eyes fluttered shut.

"That's it, Wren," he praised, his lips moving against mine. "That's my good fucking girl."

I smiled against his mouth.

With a soft chuckle, he dropped the sweetest of kisses onto my top lip, so sweet it brought tears to my eyes, then abruptly pushed me forward and bent me over the mattress.

Every move kept me off-balance. One moment, I thought I knew where he was headed, the next, he pivoted away. Tender and rough. Sweet and Wild. Uninhibited and free.

The sound of his zipper sent me up onto my toes, my back arching, body pleading.

Strong fingers caressed my hips and pulled my jeans down to my thighs.

I shuffled my feet and wiggled my ass, wanting them off.

With one hand on each cheek, he spread me open. Never had I been so exposed. My hands fisted as I turned my face to hide in his thick duvet.

His erection nestled between my cheeks, his weight falling on me as he twisted his fingers in my hair and turned my head. "No hiding from me," he demanded, then smoothed my hair back from my face as I complied. Standing back up, he spread me open and dragged his erection over my most secret of places. "You are just as alluring and intriguing here as everywhere else."

As if to prove it, he dropped to his knees and pressed his mouth to my cheek, licking a path down to my sweet spot.

"Max! God, Max," I panted, shocked, my body shaking as he dragged his mouth lower. His tongue speared my center, lapping up my arousal. When I could take no more, his lips gently encased my aching clit, taunting me as he failed to deliver the friction I required to come.

I bucked underneath him, my hips moving of their own accord. Eyes closed, mind free, nothing existed save the lash of his tongue and the thunderous need barreling through me.

He breathed deep, then groaned, "You smell so fucking good." With one last lave of his tongue, he stood up.

I cried out at the loss, my immobilized fingers stretching to reach for him.

The sound of the condom wrapper brought immediate relief. I closed my eyes and pushed my hips back.

He smoothed his hand down my back, over my hip, and across my rump, and I tilted further. "That's it, baby. Offer me that pussy."

"Oh, God," I moaned. "Max..."

Filling his hands with my ass, he notched himself at my entrance, teasing me with shallow thrusts. "What do you need, Tweet?"

I shook my head. "You. Just you. Want to please you."

Pressing his thumb against my back entrance, he rolled his hips, and I nearly shot off the bed. "You please me. Immensely."

Frustration mounted as he held his position. I wiggled my body toward him, rocking my hips but he pulled back, his cock a mere tease.

"You think I'm going to allow you to fuck yourself on my cock, baby?"

So unexpectedly dirty. I had no idea. I wanted my pants off. I wanted my arms free. I wanted to flip him onto his back and ride him. Abandon all my good girl common sense and fight him for my release.

The muscles in my thighs quivered. How did I think this was a good idea? I couldn't hold out. Every ounce of me pleaded for him to finish me.

"I'm going to melt," I panted, the head of his cock teasing my entrance.

"Not yet you're not," he promised darkly.

"Please, Max," I breathed as my vision blurred and my ears filled with the roar of my blood. Reduced to a wanton ball of need, my only goal in life was to take his cock inside me and milk it dry.

I cried out as he finally breached my entrance, bottoming out inside me in one unrelenting push. My hips circled wildly, seeking the friction he denied. "Now, Max," I ordered. "Take what you want now."

When he pulled out and dropped to his knees, I nearly cried, but his mouth covering my pussy appeased me.

Mindless, I pressed my hips back, rocking against his face.

His hands kneaded my cheeks as his mouth continued to lick and suck, leaving me poised on the precipice but unable to take the fall.

Every time I pushed back, he withdrew.

When I gave up, he swirled his wicked tongue inside me.

Melting into the mattress, I nodded my head. "Okay, Max," I breathed. "Okay."

"Perfect, sweetheart," he murmured against my swollen flesh, swollen and tight and oh so ready to take him. As if he read my mind, he circled my entrance with his fingers. "So pink and puffy, ready to swallow everything I have to give."

Unable to speak, I simply nodded.

His mouth left me empty, and I waited.

His hands released their hold, and I waited.

He stood and notched his head at my entrance, and I remained still, my breath sawing in and out of my lungs.

When he filled me, my eyelids fluttered shut, and I held.

And when he began to rock against me, I took what he gave.

Flames of pleasure licked at my walls with every stroke. Heat built in my core. My muscles trembled uncontrollably.

Max grunted behind me, his fingers digging into my hips.

My arousal coated my thighs, the obscenely wet sound of my body sucking him inside only making me wetter.

My eyes flew open as something foreign lashed at my insides. "Max," I gasped. "Something is happening."

"Let go, Wren. Fucking give it to me."

Eyes wide, mouth falling open, I blinked in wonder, my eyes finally squeezing shut as the most exquisite bliss swept me up in its arms, delivering a peace so profound it obliterated everything but the brutal thrusts of the man between my thighs.

"My girl," he grunted, his hands like steel, hips jerking to a stop as he glued his pelvis to mine, curled over my back, and emptied himself inside me. "Wren, my Wren, my Tweet, my love."

Soft lips caressed the back of my neck as he slowly lifted off of me.

Unable to move or speak, I simply waited.

His fingers pulled at the knot around my wrists, then massaged my arms. His hand slipped between us, holding the condom as he pulled out and pulled me upright.

Drawing back the covers, he nudged me forward. "Get in bed. I'll be back in a minute."

True to his word, within a minute, he climbed in the other side and lay facing me.

I could barely open my eyes, and wondered how soon it would be before I'd be able to walk or move. "Wow."

His eyes searched mine. "You okay?"

I nodded weakly. "So," my voice hoarse, I rasped. "I guess it's no more Mr. Nice Guy."

Laughing, he brought my wrist to his mouth and kissed the faint mark left by my blouse. "I'll bring out the boy-next-door now and then if it pleases you. I'll even let you torture him."

My eyes blinked open, my spine straightened, my brain lit up at the thought.

He chuckled. "You like that idea."

My eyes darted back and forth, thinking hard. To take control of his pleasure and mine? My entire body undulated as a shudder worked its way through me.

"I'll take that as a yes," he murmured, then sighed, deeply satisfied. Trailing his hand over my shoulder and down my back, he grabbed a handful of my ass and pulled me closer. "Our bodies were made for pleasure, Wren, not shame. Especially this gorgeous body. And I'm going to deliver it."

I sighed happily. With Max by my side, I could handle anything.

I spoke too soon.

31

Not With Me

B ridge bumped my hip with hers on her way through the kitchen. "Hello, gorgeous. You good?"

I untied my apron from around my waist and hung it on the hook. "Yup!' I chirped.

"You seem a lot better than you did on Thursday night. Did you sort it out?"

"Yes. Susie gave me Saturday mornings back and Rachel hired me to take the art class on my own. Between both, I can cover Aaron's brakes. I'll worry about the insurance if and when I need to."

"Good plan." She paused on her way back out to the dining room with her tray. "You know, if you're stuck, I can always spot you."

My face flushed as I opened my mouth to protest.

"Don't," Bridge warned. "There was a time I was so destitute I had nowhere to *sleep*. Someone helped me. I would only be paying it forward."

I searched her eyes. "You don't feel sorry for me."

She shook her head, then laughed and inched her head back and forth. "Only as sorry as I felt for myself."

I was still laughing when we bustled back out to the dining room.

Bridge wagged her eyebrows. "Don't look now, but tall, dark, and dimpled just walked in."

Max stood at the entrance, his smile warm, his gaze a sweet caress.

My own smile spread so wide it stretched my cheeks.

"Gag," Bridge mock complained, then cocked her eyebrow. "Are you going to be back for the dinner shift?"

I nodded. "Just having a quick coffee with Max before heading home for a bit. Susie is taking Audrey to the bookstore after school. I'll be back in a couple of hours."

Susie amazed me. In the short time she began looking after Audrey after school, she'd managed to open her world. For some reason, where I'd failed to coax Audrey out of her comfort zone, Susie succeeded.

"Hi," I stopped in front of Max and grinned up at him.

He eyed me lazily, his smile knowing.

A mental picture of Saturday night crossed my mind and flushed my cheeks.

His eyes lit as that damned dimple flashed. "You're thinking about naughty things."

I laughed. "I am."

Interlacing his fingers with mine, he tugged me toward the door.

"You want to walk?"

I looked up at the sky. Bright blue, sun shining. "We could walk down to the beach and back?"

"I've got time for that," he agreed.

Down by the beach, it was considerably colder, and the waves were wild. "I love that."

"The waves?"

"Yes. Wild and free. Uninhibited. Unapologetic. I wish—" I stopped abruptly.

"You wish," he prodded.

"I wish I could live like that."

Squeezing my hand, he reminded me, "You were wild and free last night."

Leaning close to hide my face in his arm, I admitted, "It felt good, but it didn't come easy."

Putting his arm around my shoulders, he pressed his mouth to the top of my head. "Nothing good does."

"So...practice?" I teased.

He grinned down at me. "As much as you want."

By the time he dropped me off at my door and jogged off to make his next appointment, my feet barely skimmed the earth.

It took me a minute to identify the energy rushing through me. When I did, I laughed. It was happiness. I was happy.

Humming under my breath, I practically skipped up the stairs to my door.

Swinging the door open, I jumped in surprise. "Aaron! I didn't know you were home!"

He sat on the couch, his cell phone face down on the coffee table in front of him with his elbows resting on his splayed knees. His head hung down and seemed to drop further as I watched.

"Aaron?" I froze in the doorway, alarm at his position slamming me back to earth and sending adrenaline coursing through my veins.

He grasped his hair in both fists, his despair snapping me out of my frozen state.

I slammed the door closed and rushed to the couch, my arms clasped around him before my ass hit the cushion. "What's wrong? Did something happen? Is it school?"

He raised his chin to look at me.

Eyes rimmed red and filled with regret, he stared back at me.

"Mom," he rasped, his voice breaking. "I'm sorry."

My grip on his arms tightened, fear wrapping her icy fingers around my throat. "Why? What happened?" I shook him slightly. "Tell me what's going on!"

"Nadine's pregnant."

My hold on him slackened immediately. My hands dropped to lightly clasp his upper arms as shock swept away the fear with all the force of a bitter gale wind.

Relief that no one had died, that he wasn't deathly ill or going to jail, all three of which possibilities ran through my mind at his distress, warred with dismay.

The voice in my head was not my own.

So, history repeats itself.

"I—" My voice cracked as my grip on his arms tightened.

My boy. My sweet boy.

I wanted to throttle him.

At least my kid made it to third year.

I couldn't find any words of my own.

"I need a minute," I gritted out between my teeth.

I stood up slowly, as if I'd aged forty years in the space of a handful of seconds. Two steps away from the couch, my hands came up to cover my mouth as I stared unseeing into a future that once again veered so sharply to the left it was impossible to plan for what might come next.

I hope you're happy with the example you set.

Turning my back on him did not ease the weight of his devastation on my shoulders. I closed my eyes, the walls in my mind crumbling around a memory better left buried.

You've ruined your whole life.

Again, I stuttered. "I- I need a minute." I swiftly crossed to my bedroom, leaving my son sitting on the couch. Alone.

Bending over, I braced my palms against the mattress and forced myself to breathe deep; in through my nose and out through my mouth.

Five things I could see. My bed. The flash of sunlight reflecting off the streetlight outside. The clay ring holder Aaron made for me in kindergarten. The paperback Max leant me on the bedside table. Audrey's crystal on the windowsill.

Memories better left buried battered at the door in my mind.

Standing outside in the cold, staring at my parents' front door, my disbelief growing with every second my dad failed to change his mind.

Alone in the middle of the driveway, the wind whipping about my legs, my mom's pale face like a specter peering through her bedroom window.

Max. Oh, God, Max.

Dan and Lou.

The cabin.

Screaming into a pillow that wasn't my own.

The darkness of those early days.

I swallowed bile. My father's voice berated me still.

He's ruined his whole life.

No. Every atom inside me screamed it. No, he fucking hasn't.

I rushed back into the family room to find Aaron in much the same position except now both his hands covered his face. His body trembled.

No.

This was my house.

My kid.

And this, this I would not have.

I thought about that tiny glass jar containing my very last fuck to give and realized even this wasn't worth it. I didn't care what my father thought. Only Aaron's heart mattered. And that, that I'd always had.

I rushed to the couch, the sound of my hurried footsteps snapping his neck up in alarm.

Sitting down beside him, I determined he would not walk away from this conversation alone.

Like I did.

He met my eyes, his reflecting a wariness I hadn't seen since he sent that baseball careening through the windshield of his teacher's car.

I recognized the feeling.

And it wasn't one I wanted him to ever have. Not with me.

Not ever with me.

He crumpled and reached for me. "I'm sorry, Mom. I'm so fucking sorry."

My heart imploded, collapsing in on itself as I pulled his head down onto my shoulder. Tunneling my fingers into his tawny hair, I lightly scratched his scalp and rocked him the way I used to when he was just a little guy.

When it was just me and him against the world.

Turning his face into my neck, his fingers digging into my sides, he cried. And my heart broke exactly the way it had every other time he hurt. I'd held him through skinned knees, a broken wrist, his first heartbreak, and the pain of being cut from the team.

And, no matter how it broke me, I'd hold him through this as well.

"My beautiful boy," I whispered. "You're going to make yourself sick."

He drew back and plastered his hands over his face, his breath releasing with a shudder.

"Deep breath, son," I murmured.

Dragging his hands down his ravaged face, mouth drawn into a deep frown, he looked at me.

"I fucked up."

I offered him a smile and shrugged one shoulder. "It's not ideal."

He snorted but his mouth quirked up at the corners with a hint of humor at my understatement.

I bumped his shoulder with mine. "And to think last week our biggest worry was the brakes on your car."

He met my eyes, and that hint of a smile bloomed into a laugh.

It was watery.

But it was there.

32

Cabbage Patch

We had one day to pull it together.

One day to let the news sink in before taking the next step, and we spent that day together. Max, me, Audrey, Aaron, and a red-eyed Nadine ordered pizza and watched movies. Nadine, who was normally shy and held herself aloof from Aaron in my presence, curled up in his lap on the chair, her face tucked against his chest, her hand fisted in his shirt.

Knowing her fear, feeling my own anew, I could barely breathe.

When Max questioned me, I asked him to give me a day. Aaron had asked me to hold off on telling Max until they told Nadine's parents. Max being Max told me to come to him when I was ready.

Sunday morning passed in a blur. Knowing Aaron was with Nadine at her family's home telling her parents had me wearing a path through my wood floors.

I pressed my palms together and raised my face to the heavens. "Please, please, please…"

I had no words, but I didn't need them. He knew my heart.

Then two phone calls came in one after the other.

The first a warning.

The second a summons.

I called Max who was out for breakfast with Gabe and Julian and asked if he could come home.

His knock barely brushed the door before I swung it open on his surprised face. "Max."

Though I'd coached myself to be cool and collected, I threw myself into his arms and clung to his shirt.

Enfolding me against his chest, he walked us inside and kicked the door shut with his heel. His big hands ran up and down my back roughly even as his mouth dipped to press against my crown. "What's wrong, Wrennie? What is it?"

"Nadine is pregnant."

Max's spine stiffened then he curled around me tighter.

Somehow saying the words out loud to Max made it both better and worse. It halved the burden. It brought the issue out into the light and burned the shadows from its edges.

But it exhumed memories better left buried.

"Fuck."

I huffed out a bitter laugh. "Believe it or not, that's not the worst of it. My father knows and he's called a 'family' meeting." Putting invisible air quotes around family allowed me to use the word without feeling like a total hypocrite. Because there was nothing remotely family-like about those gatherings.

He drew back slightly and searched my eyes. "Want me to go with you?"

"No." I shook my head vehemently.

The thought of Max witnessing the way my father treated me filled me with shame. Halfway through his tirade later that day, I wished I'd risked it.

He ran his hand over my hair and cupped the back of my head. "How about I stay here with Audrey?"

"Yes," I breathed, my shoulders sagging. Closing my eyes, I rested against his chest.

No matter what, it would be okay. I chanted it to myself, over and over again, and I repeated it as Aaron drove us to my parents' house. I declared it aloud, squeezing Aaron's hand as we made our way up the path to their front door. And I held it close even as I braced myself for what was to come.

My mother sat at the table with her eyes downcast, a crumpled tissue twisted between her fingers in her lap.

My father sat beside her at the head of the table with me on his left. Aaron sat directly in front of him. He barely glanced at Aaron but had placed him in the perfect position to bear witness to everything that was to come, everything I'd tried to shield him from.

I kept a tight grip on Aaron's thigh under the table to keep him steady.

We were only ten minutes in, and experience told me my father was only warming up. If I kept my mouth shut, we'd escape unscathed.

Mostly.

My eyes fell to the scratch on the table in front of me. I smirked. The one blemish in their otherwise perfect lives.

"All these years, your mother and I have tried to help but you continue to foolishly go your own selfish way. I was beginning to think you'd finally grown up, but no. Now you're going on business trips and traipsing around with that Brevard boy." He sneered. "That family is a mess, and they've drawn you down right alongside them."

He always lumped the Brevards and Bennetts together and I never missed the opportunity to set him straight.

"Max is a Brevard. And the Bennetts are good people."

My father ranted, "Bennetts, Brevards, what does it matter? That family is so tangled up they're practically incestuous."

I saw red. "That family took me in when this family made me homeless."

Aaron gasped, "Homeless?"

I winced at my involuntary admission. Now that the cat was out of the bag, it was long past time I gave them the credit they were due. "They looked after me when you wouldn't."

"That family interfered in our family business," he raged.

That family made me theirs when I had nothing to offer in return.

That family showed me what it was to be a family.

My eyes dropped to the table and that one blemish. If the table represented our family, that blemish was the only thing that was real. Everything else had been sanded down, stained, and varnished into non-existence.

Hard to do that with a baby.

I lifted my chin and met his furious gaze with one of my own. "The Bennetts are a beautiful family, and Max Brevard is a good man, the best man I know," I gritted through my teeth.

He could say whatever he wanted about me, but Max was off-limits.

"A good man?" His eyes narrowed as he went in for the kill. "A good man doesn't shack up with a vulnerable single mother. He's got a PhD. What do you think he's doing with a woman who works at a diner? And a good mother doesn't neglect her children for the sake of art classes and dating. Maybe if you devoted less energy to clothes and hair and make-up, Audrey wouldn't be in the state she's in."

Aaron spoke up, his voice hard. "Grandpa—"

I squeezed. Hard. Aaron's thigh fairly vibrated beneath my palm.

My emotions shut down, saving me from processing my father's words, in favor of getting Aaron out of there before things got worse.

I stood and indicated for Aaron to do the same.

But Aaron didn't move.

Drawing on all my experience in remaining calm in the face of Audrey's meltdowns, I faced my father and spoke quietly and succinctly. "This meeting has not been productive in any way. You called us here so you could belittle me. We're leaving and I hope we can pick this up when you've had a chance to digest the news and can discuss it calmly."

It was then my father's attention swung to Aaron. "I'm disappointed, but I don't blame you. Not entirely." Tossing a dismissive hand in my direction, he continued. "She should never have been allowed to raise you."

I stumbled under the force of his words.

Allowed to raise him?

What did that mean? Shame nipped at my heels, herding me toward the door to escape. I pushed my father's malicious words to the back of my mind. Reaching for Aaron, I cupped my hand around his shoulder, urging him to come with me.

With my back turned, my father buried his blade. "I told you back then, Lorraine, but you wouldn't listen. We should have sued for custody the day Aaron was born. It's too late for him, but we can still take Audrey. Renata is not fit to be a mother."

Like a bomb going off inside a building, there was a brief moment suspended in time between detonation and destruction where the building remained standing, the bricks and mortar of its foundation frozen in disbelief. My entire body absorbed the blow. The breath left my lungs, my blood thundered in my ears, and adrenalin pumped through my limbs as my stomach threatened to empty its contents in favor of survival.

I was that building.

And with those words, my foundation imploded.

My mother whispered brokenly, "Robert, no, that's not right—"

Aaron flew to his feet, his chair crashing to the floor behind him.

Both of my parents stared at him agape. My mother began to cry in earnest while the light in my father's eyes told me he relished the fight to come.

Aaron's voice trembled. "Do not talk to her like that."

"It's okay—" I began, reeling from my father's revelation but anxious to get Aaron away from my father before he turned his vitriol on my son.

Sneering in my direction, my father accused him, "She put you up to this. These past few months I've sensed a change in you. She never taught you respect because she never had any."

I narrowed my eyes. If he wanted a fight, I'd give him one.

But Aaron beat me to it.

Facing down his grandfather, he pointed a shaking finger at me. "*She*," he stressed, "didn't put me up to anything. *She* earned this. Because *she* has always been there for me. She gives me everything she has with no strings attached. She is everything I want to be for my kids. She has *all* my respect because *she* taught me how to love."

Aaron's impassioned words knocked the stuffing out of me.

My father stood, drawing himself up to his full height. "Then I guess you don't need me anymore."

Aaron's eyebrows flew up as his hand flew out to point at me. "When I have her? Who's everything you're not? No. I don't need you." His jaw hardened as he lifted his chin.

Looking at my son, for the first time, I could not see the boy for the man. My heart exploded with pride and grief. Pride because I had raised that man. Grief because he was poised to leave me to begin his own life.

Glaring at me, my father demanded, "Are you going to let him speak to me like this?"

Looking from my son to my father, everything became clear. My father was not even half the man my son already was.

He would never love me.

I would never be good enough. There was nothing I could do to make up for embarrassing him. And my children did not deserve to see their mother mistreated.

Worse, it would only take one mistake for Aaron or Audrey to become his next target.

Meeting my mother's eyes, I read her plea. Her example, the one I'd followed all my life, was her choice.

This was mine.

I shook my head. "No. You're absolutely right."

Turning to my son, I held out my hand for him to take. "I'm sorry. I'm sorry you feel the need to protect me." Aaron stepped forward and grasped my hand like it was his lifeline.

My mother's heart thumped in my chest.

There he is.

I met his hazel eyes and waited to be sure I had his attention. "You are the first man who ever stepped up for me, and you've done it time and time again. I'm so damn proud of the man you've become I could burst. However, this, tonight, should never have been necessary."

We'd come full circle.

The man who raised me on one side.

The man I raised on the other.

Turning back to my father, I made a long overdue decision. "We don't need the strings and shame and guilt that come with your gifts."

He broke as the icy control he'd wielded over me cracked. Face red, that ugly vein on the side of his standing out in stark relief as spittle flew from his lips, he screamed, "You disgraced this family! You could have done anything with your life, but you wasted it working in a cheap diner for minimum wage."

The room spun, leaving me standing outside my body. Every vicious word he hurled echoed my most secret of fears.

I watched the me of yesterday war with the me of today.

"Robert!" My mother gasped and stared up at him, horrified.

My life was not a waste.

Beginning in my organs and traveling outward to the tips of my fingers, my body began to shake.

Maybe I could have been anything, but I chose to be a mother.

Being a mother was *something*.

That something was *my choice*.

I looked at my son, my beautiful boy. He was here with me because I wanted him, and I chose to keep him. Knowing the repercussions, I chose him.

My heartrate slowed. I would always choose him.

That diner gave me the means, and the flexibility I required, to support my family. And Susie gave me the family and support I craved when my family would barely speak to me.

The truth settled over me with a sense of calm.

I faced my father, armed with truth, not anger. "My pregnancy was either a blessing or a curse. It can't be both. And Aaron is a blessing. He's always been a blessing."

Silent tears streamed down my mother's ravaged face as she watched Aaron.

I felt sorry for her.

But I felt sorrier for me.

Because I deserved better.

And so did my children.

I stood and quietly gathered my coat and purse, edging Aaron toward the door with a gentle hand to his back.

My father continued to rant, but my ears were immune until he threatened, "Expect a call from my lawyer."

My skin finally split under the pressure.

Spinning around, I lashed out. "Not once have you given me credit."

He laughed incredulously. "For what?"

"Wrennie, wait—" Using my childhood nickname, my mother was still attempting damage control. Even now, she could not accept we were long past saving.

"Aaron didn't grow up in a cabbage patch! Let's compare the results of our parenting, shall we?" Taking a single step forward, I met my father's eyes, satisfied to witness the briefest flinch as he braced himself for my truth. "My child is well-adjusted and knows his worth. He knows I'm there for him for whatever he needs. For years yours hung by a fucking thread unable to ask her parents for anything for fear of being belittled. You tell me who's the better parent."

33

Crazy Wonderfuls

Max stayed late and spent most of that time holed up in Aaron's room talking things over with him.

I didn't know how I felt about it at first.

Max cupped my face in his hands, his dark eyes as serious as I'd ever seen them. "Can you trust me with him? Trust me to listen and give him a shoulder to lean on? Give you a shoulder to lean on?"

My anxiety dissipated. This is what I'd dreamed of having all along. The fact Max was willing to talk to Aaron was a gift. That Aaron wanted to talk to Max was a miracle.

"Okay. But don't go home afterwards. Come to my room. Stay with me tonight. I need you, too."

By the time he came to bed, it was closing in on three o'clock. "Is he okay?"

He dropped his pants and yanked off his sweater, slipping into bed in his boxers and a t-shirt. "He's better."

"Is there anything I should know?"

He shook his head. "Just that he loves you. So much. You've done a helluva job with him."

I swallowed my sob and dove onto his chest.

He cupped the back of my head with one hand and curled around me. "It will be okay, Wren. I promise."

I nodded against his wide chest. Was it wide enough to hold me? Hold us?

"Last night was the first time I truly stood up to him. The last time he went after me, when he was pissed about my hair and new clothes, my knees were quaking." I huffed out a wet laugh. "Not that they weren't shaking last night, but I settled somehow, more angry than afraid. Free in a way."

His chest hummed beneath my cheek; his other hand stroked my hair back from my face. "You were defending your cub."

"I'm so angry with myself for not standing up to him sooner. I don't understand why he still affects me the way he does."

"You couldn't. He made his home under your skin before your brain understood you were a separate being. And, Tweet, he threw you out of the house."

"Yeah, but it's not like he can throw me out of my apartment."

Max pressed a kiss to my forehead. "It doesn't matter. He threatened your most basic of human needs for shelter and food when he did that. That's a wound that cuts deep. Twenty-year-old you is still standing on the driveway, and she is triggered every time he gets upset with you."

My hand twisted in his t-shirt. I didn't fight it this time when the memories surfaced. "It still hurts to remember that night."

"It was trauma. We tend to carry it with us." He tucked me closer.

Trauma?

"I barely made it through the front door, Max," I whispered, my voice cracking.

I sat at my parents' kitchen table with my hands twisting in my lap exactly the way my mother's hands had. This was not how I wanted to break the news to them. The suitcase that I brought back from university sat by the front door. I'd barely made it across the threshold before my parents corralled me into the kitchen. The sharp scent of autumn drifted in through the open windows, the faintest beginnings of a wintry bite in the air.

Dad sat at the head of the table as always, my mom on his right.

His brows low, he demanded, "What happened? Why are you here? Did you drop out?"

I sucked in a breath, hoping I wouldn't cry, but I failed.

"Oh, God, Renata," my mom gasped, reaching for me across the table. "Are you okay? What happened?"

My voice barely a whisper, I clung to her fingers and confessed, "I'm pregnant."

"What?" my father growled. His head dropped like an angry bull preparing to trample down everything in its path. His cheeks suffused with red as the thick vein on the side of his head began to pulse.

I tucked my chin into my chest, my eyes glued to the scratch I made years before in the shiny wood. My breath shuddered in and out.

My mother's hands went cold, stiffening as her fingers uncurled from mine and left me grasping at air.

Enraged, my father demanded, "Who's the father? Why isn't he here?" The weight of his fury filled the room.

I shook my head and tucked my chin to my chest, unused to defying him. "He doesn't want anything to do with us." My hands remained on the table, palms up, empty.

He huffed out an incredulous laugh and sat back in his chair. "What does that have to do with anything? He'll meet his obligations."

I winced and shook my head.

"Renata," he warned harshly. "I want a name."

"No," I whispered, drawing my empty hands down into my lap. "I don't want to be with someone who doesn't want me."

"He wanted you enough to plant a baby inside you."

Mom gasped. "Robert!"

In my peripheral vision, I saw him shake his head. His glare sliced me open. Exposing me. Leaving me cold, alone, and ashamed.

"Fine. If you won't give me a name, you need to leave. You want to do it your way? Do it your way. But you won't be doing it here."

Leave?

My head snapped up to look at him as my mouth dropped open. I'd counted on his fury. The possibility of him throwing me out somehow never factored.

The look on his face assured me I hadn't misheard.

My stomach heaved as the bottom dropped out of my world. "Daddy, please!"

Tears streamed down my face, a mirror of my mother sitting across from me. I hadn't called my father 'daddy' since I was twelve, the word simply bounced off the walls and fell to the floor, unheard.

My mother interrupted, her voice cajoling, "Robert—"

He cut her off sharply and faced me, his face no longer suffused with red, but blank. "You got yourself pregnant and threw away your future. You won't give me his name so I can make this right. You've embarrassed and disgraced us, Renata. You made your bed." His eyes hardened, his regard no longer hot with anger but icy cold. "You lie in it."

I sobbed in shock. They were strict, and his standards were high, but I never dreamed he'd throw me out. "Dad," I whispered brokenly. "Where am I supposed to go?"

"You should have thought about that before you jumped into bed."

"Robert, this is not the way—"

"Go upstairs, Lorraine."

The panic lacing through her voice leant me hope.

"Robert, no, this--."

My breath wheezed in and out of my lungs.

She was standing up to him this time. She'd make it right. "We can't—"

For the first time ever, my father raised his voice to my mom. "Go upstairs, Lorraine!"

I stood from the table, my voice shaking. "It's okay, Mom. I'll go outside and wait."

"I won't change my mind," my father replied, his voice steel.

With a sob, my mother pushed back from the table and ran upstairs.

Standing, my father turned his back on me in dismissal as he left the kitchen. He turned back only once. "Leave your housekey on the table."

My hands shook so badly, I could barely get my key off the ring.

Dazed and in shock, I pulled up the handle of my suitcase and dragged it back out onto the front porch. Cringing at the thought that someone might drive by the house and see me, I stood facing the closed door. Anyone passing by would think I'd just gotten home. I prayed for darkness to fall and hide me from their judgment.

The chill in the air crept up my legs as the temperature dropped. One by one the streetlights came to life as my hope sputtered out.

I didn't know how much time had passed before the sound of the deadbolt sliding home woke me from my stupor with the force of a thunderbolt.

My eyes sprang to the peephole. My voice hoarse, I called, "Dad?"

I raised my hand to pound on the door, but a single shred of pride remained. Real fear opened my eyes and steeled my spine. I swallowed the lump in my throat and backed away from the door. It would soon be dark, and it was a long walk to town. All my friends had left for university. And I needed to find a place to stay.

Halfway down the driveway, I turned to look back.

My mom's pale visage looked down at me from the second-story window.

Even from where I stood, I could see her tears.

I raised my hand, my face crumpling on her name. "Mom..."

Her panicked gaze swung away from me to look down the street. I could almost feel the breath leave her body as she sagged against the window.

Following the line of her sight, I tracked the SUV as it came to a stop at the side of the road.

Dan and Lou Bennett, the owners of The Sage Ridge Resort where my mom used to work, jumped out and rushed over to me. I'd known them both since I was a child.

Lou held out her hands for mine and gently pulled me forward.

Dan, a big bear of a man who looked fiercer by far than my father but lacked his bite, grabbed my case. "All right, Wrennie? We'll get you set up in a flash. You're all right, darlin'."

I blinked and found myself in the back of their car, Lou belted into the middle seat beside me, her warm hands cupped around mine that were like ice. I looked up at my mother's bedroom window.

She was gone.

The violent chattering of my teeth brought me back to the present.

"Easy, Sweetheart. Easy," Max murmured.

My body rattled like a storm trapped in a bottle.

"It was a long time ago. You're safe."

I nodded against his chest, my breath coming in harsh pants.

"And you're the one who made you safe. You kept Aaron safe. You keep Audrey safe. You're stronger than he gave you credit for."

"I am," I breathed. Telling Max lanced the wound. I closed my eyes. "I'm sorry. I don't know why all this stuff is coming up, but I shouldn't be dumping it on you."

He stroked my hair back at my temples, the rhythmic caress calming me. "No, Tweet. It's normal and healthy. A lot healthier than keeping it locked inside. Our brains bury our trauma until it's safe enough to heal. You've been in survival mode all these years."

"I don't have trauma, Max. Not like other people," I corrected him.

His hand froze in my hair for a moment before continuing. His voice was soft, almost careful. "Abandonment, getting kicked out of your house, your father shaming you, that's trauma."

I let his words sink in.

"Having a child with special needs meant staying vigilant, never letting your guard down. The fact that you're able to voice some of it now means you feel safe enough to begin your healing process." Holding me closer, his hand moved to tenderly cup the back of my head as he whispered fervently, "I'm so here for that."

The rest of the tension drained from my body.

He pressed his mouth against my crown as his hands tangled in my hair. "You've taken every bit of shit life threw at you and polished it into a fucking diamond. Scraps of nothing and you made something so fucking beautiful."

I took a deep breath, loosened my grip on his shirt, and exhaled. "You're a diamond, Max. My children are diamonds. Life has given me diamonds, too."

"We'll see about getting you more of those."

I huffed out a laugh. "That's the first time I've ever told anybody about that night."

"That's the first step in dismantling its power over you. Twenty-year-old you would be fucking astounded by thirty-nine-year-old you. If she could have seen into the future, her hope would have flared brighter than the sun."

"Yeah," I breathed, a quiet pride seeping into my bones. "Yeah."

His arms wrapped around me like a vice. "Sleep, Tweet. Morning's coming early tomorrow."

The next thing I heard was Audrey's voice.

"Hello, my Max. Do you like rainbows?"

I cracked one eye open. I lay on my side facing Max who was sprawled out on his back. My leg thrown over his pinned him to the bed, his hand splayed across my thigh pinned me in place.

Audrey stood beside the bed, her crystal dangling from her hand, casting rainbows across Max's sleepy face.

Max answered, his voice groggy with sleep. "Who doesn't like a rainbow?"

"I don't know. Who doesn't like a rainbow?"

He chuckled and folded his free arm under his head, his sleepy gaze on her face. "I don't know anyone who doesn't like rainbows. Are they your favorite thing?"

"No. Mom is my favorite thing. Are they your favorite thing?"

"No. Your mom is my favorite thing."

Her eyes snapped up to his to assess him before skittering away. "We both love Mom."

I froze.

Max answered easily, "Yup. We both love Mom."

I swallowed.

"I'm going to go eat my cereal now."

Audrey left the room.

I lay still.

Max chuckled. "Are you freaking out?"

I scrunched my eyes shut. "It's just, I don't want you to think-- I don't know what to say..." I hazarded a peek at his face, shrugged one shoulder, and smiled awkwardly.

Folding his arm under his head, he turned to me and suggested softly, "You could say you love me too."

"Isn't it too soon?"

He grimaced. "Two decades in the making is too soon?"

I snorted out a laugh and dipped my chin. "Max..."

"It's okay if you're not there yet, Tweet."

My head snapped up. "No, Max. That's not it. The truth is I never stopped loving you."

His face went blank, then his arm whipped out from behind his head to pull me closer as he turned to his side.

I stopped him with a firm palm to his chest. "Loving you has never been in question, Max," I whispered, my throat tight.

"Then what is in question, Wren?"

"I have kids—"

Grasping the back of my neck, he squeezed. "I'm in this, Wren. I want this with you. All of it. Your love, your trust, your life, your crazy wonderful kids, and all the baggage that comes with you from your asshole of a father. I want it all."

"But—"

"I am not an uneducated man. I probably understand the wounds you carry better than you do. I know what I'm getting into, Tweet. I know. And I want it."

I tried to temper my hope because hope inevitably led to disappointment. And pain. But it kept rising to the surface.

Everything I dreamed of waited for me in the shelter of Max's arms.

"Are you sure?"

He dipped his chin firmly. "I've never been more sure of anything in my life."

I dipped my chin and studied him. "You want me."

"I do."

"And all my crazy—"

"And all your crazy wonderful." He sighed. "Wren, I'm going to make it my purpose in life to lay all the evidence of your worthiness at your feet. You gave me a reason to believe. I'm going to do the same for you."

34

Unleashed

The altercation with my father and the subsequent fallout had me crawling into work Monday morning. Max stayed with me again on Monday night, and then by unspoken agreement, he packed a bag and stayed the rest of the week. And much of that time he spent in deep conversation with Aaron.

For the first time in his life, I was not Aaron's go-to. My jealousy caught me by surprise. Wasn't this what I'd always wanted? A father figure in his life? Someone he could depend on?

The tiniest of doubts niggled at the back of my brain. Could he depend on Max? Long term?

By the time Saturday rolled around, I was more than grateful. Because with every conversation they had, Aaron stood just that little bit taller.

Saturday morning, I worked at Susie Q's. In the afternoon, Audrey came with me to Artitude where I taught my class. Being back in the art room energized me and reminded me of who I used to be before I lived to make myself a smaller target.

Max met us at home with chocolate croissants and cheese buns to hold us over until dinner, then he and Aaron left to take a walk.

Nadine landed at our house almost every day, only going home to sleep. Even the nights Aaron worked, Nadine curled up on our couch, built Lego with Audrey, or puttered around in my kitchen. Despite the tension, Nadine wanted to stay with her parents for the time being and give them a chance to come to terms with her pregnancy. Only now she refused to stay away from Aaron.

She handed me the oven mitts as I bent to take the cupcakes I was making for Dan and Lou's cookout out of the oven.

"I told them I'd live at home for now if they wanted me but wouldn't be treated like a child any longer." She paused. "They were furious." She held her hands up in exasperation. "I mean, look at me! I'm twenty years old and pregnant. I'm trying to determine if I can be a mom or build a life with my boyfriend and they think that grounding me is appropriate?" She shook her head. "Like it or not, I'm an adult making adult decisions and adult mistakes. And they are mine to make."

"They are." I set the tray on the cooling rack on the counter.

"And I'm allowed to make mistakes."

I spun at the quiver in her voice and took her into my arms. "You are." Stroking her hair back from her face, I pressed a light kiss to her forehead. "I'm here for both of you whatever you decide, but sometimes mistakes are blessings in disguise."

She wrapped her arms around my waist. "Aaron could never be a mistake."

"Never," I agreed. "But you two have to make your own decisions."

"He wants to keep the baby," she confessed.

I tamped down the joy in my gut. I wanted them to keep the baby, of course I did. My child's child? I wanted to welcome them into the world with joy and love and celebration. And I would support Aaron and Nadine in all the ways I had been denied.

But I held my tongue.

"He's so angry with my parents," she murmured. "I've never seen him like that before."

I closed my eyes. What I wouldn't have given to have had that. But this wasn't about me. I shook off the thought. "He loves you. It's difficult to see someone you love being treated poorly." I winced. "And my parents..."

"Yeah," she answered softly. "He told me. Um...are you angry with me?"

I drew back to look her in the eye and shook my head. "No."

She was little more than a child herself. Honey-blond hair pulled back in a French braid, big brown eyes in a heart-shaped face, and such a gentle spirit. Still. She'd proven to be stronger than I was already.

She pressed her lips together. "Disappointed?"

I tilted my head. "It's not what I would have planned for you guys. But I didn't plan on Aaron, and he's been the biggest blessing of my life." I took her hand in mine. "Sometimes God gives you what you need before you know you need it."

Not surprisingly, Aaron and Nadine elected to stay home from the cookout.

I winked at Aaron as we left. "Leave a sock on the door."

Nadine barked out a laugh, her cheeks flaming. Aaron groaned and covered his face. "Too soon, Momma."

Max laughed.

Audrey asked, "Why do we need to put a sock on the door?" Head tilted to the side, her bright yellow hat with its ridiculously large pom-pom perched on top of her head, she looked at me quizzically.

"That would be kind of weird, hm?"

"Very weird."

I reached out and tapped her pom-pom. "You don't need your hat, Bean. It's warm out."

Batting my hand away, she disagreed. "I like my hat. It's happy. And yellow."

Her pom-pom bopped along in front of us as we made our way to Max's SUV. "You're sure it's okay to put Brooklyn in your car?"

"Absolutely."

"We could take Aaron's car."

"Not necessary."

"I just don't want—"

Max halted and faced me, his eyebrow cocked. "Don't want what? Don't want me to ever take you and Audrey out?"

I frowned. "When you put it that way…"

Wrapping his arm around my shoulder, he moved us along. "Exactly."

"Cocky."

Squeezing me closer, he bent to my ear. "You said cock."

"Context, Max!"

The drive was short, the sun shining through the windshield. Dan had the door open before we made it up their front path. "How's my favorite girl?"

"I brought cupcakes."

Dan's eyebrows rose. "I'm impressed. Can I have one?"

"Only if you eat all your dinner." She gave him a once over. "You look like you eat your dinner."

Max snorted.

"Oh my gosh, Audrey..."

Dan boomed with laughter. "That I do, Audrey. That I do."

Moving aside, Dan welcomed all of us inside their hive of loveable chaos.

Walking straight to Lou, Audrey held the cupcake tray up proudly. "Me and Nadine decorated them. We're going to open our own bakery next year. Dean and the Bean. Or Bean and Dean. We haven't decided yet."

"Next year?" Max murmured beside me.

"She's ambitious. Ahead of her time. A real pioneer."

"That's child labor. I'll have to report you. Punish you."

"Will I like it?"

His dark eyes flashed. "I'll ensure it."

When Max's dad approached Audrey with a gentle smile, she turned to him and said, "Hi, Pops."

I laughed out loud. "I can't believe how comfortable she is."

Even Brooklyn, her service vest cast aside after the first five minutes, lay on her back under Dan's huge hand.

Max grinned. "There are no demands, no expectations. She can just be herself here. Maybe she can sense it."

I had never had that.

I wasn't even sure if I'd managed to give it to my children as focused as I was on maintaining peace with my parents.

Aaron would be a better parent than I was, just as I hoped I was a better parent than mine were. Our parents' ceiling should be our floor. And I hoped to God I'd given him a firm enough foundation.

The Bennetts and Brevards moved around one another with ease. There were no scripts save for the inside jokes. No harsh judgments. No tension.

When I got pregnant, I had nobody. Not even the father. And I had very little of what these families took as commonplace.

My children had very little of it.

With Max in my life, perhaps they would have more.

"Are you okay?" Max, coming up behind me, curled his palm around my hip and murmured in my ear.

"I think so. It's disconcerting."

"What is?"

I shrugged. "Just the difference between your family life and how you grew up compared to mine." I huffed. "Even with Aaron and Nadine. I'm so proud of him for standing with her and standing up to her parents. It's just bringing up a lot of stuff for me."

Looping his arms around me, he eased me back against his chest. "Of course it is. How could it be otherwise?"

"I don't know what to do with all these feelings."

"You allow yourself to feel them. You don't judge yourself for feeling them. And let them go."

I smiled and turned my face to nuzzle my forehead against his chin. "Is that your professional advice?"

Chuckling, he answered, "It is, actually."

"Want to play doctor later?" I was insatiable. It was difficult to be quiet and we ended up on the floor more often than not because the damn bed creaked, but I couldn't get enough. The night before I tied his wrists, rode him to orgasm, then hopped off and took him down my throat.

Everything I'd ever thought about, read about, or watched, I wanted to try. And all those books I'd shied away from? I was devouring them.

Squeezing me, he chuckled darkly in my ear. "I've unleashed a beast."

Oh, God. Was it too much? Was I too much? Purposefully, I made my voice light. "Are you complaining?"

"Never. It's been the privilege of my life seeing you reclaim your whole self these past couple of months."

"I really have, haven't I?"

School, art, standing up to my parents, Max, enjoying sex, celebrating it even, never mind Aaron's father, Nadine's pregnancy, Brooklyn's surgery, Aaron's brakes, car insurance…

"Easy, sweetheart." He chuckled softly, his hands lightly caressing my stomach. "The story isn't over yet."

I blew out a breath and laughed. "I was beginning to spiral there."

"Yes, well, you've got a lot going on. But you're not alone, Wren. As long as I'm alive, you'll never be alone again."

"Is that a promise?" I asked, my voice husky with unshed tears.

"It's a fucking sacred vow."

Later, much later when dinner was finished, after Audrey told Noelle her baby was loud and annoying, when Hawkley laughed, Harley agreed, and Daire found her a quiet corner away from the hustle and bustle, I sat down with Harley and Noelle.

Audrey's bright yellow pom-pom was just visible over the back of the chair behind which Daire had made her a nest.

Harley handed me a wine cooler. "Drink this for me. I need the vicarious enjoyment. At least I'm not the only one suffering," she teased Noelle.

"Why can't you drink, Noelle?" I asked.

"She's breastfeeding," Harley answered.

Noelle laughed and sat down, placing a plate with cheese and fruit between us, wagging her eyebrows. "Yup! Breastfeeding Hawkley's enormous baby," she paused, "and pregnant with number two."

Harley froze in place, slowly turning her head to look at Noelle. "You're pregnant?" she whispered, her face breaking into a huge smile before squealing, "You're pregnant!"

Noelle laughed out loud. "Yup! We just told Pops and Max. I was going to tell Lou and Dan after telling you two but you kind of just announced it to everybody!"

Harley threw her arms around Noelle, tears in both their eyes. Then, much to my joy, they opened their arms and drew me in as well.

After Lou and Dan moved in to claim their hugs, I asked, "How far along are you?"

"Just passed 14 weeks. I'm due November 3rd." Noelle smiled and cupped a gentle palm over her growing mound.

"I'm surprised Hunter's still nursing," Harley mused. "I thought most babies went off the breast if mom got pregnant."

Noelle smiled evilly. "What can I say? He's a boob man like his father."

"Stop," Harley moaned, covering her ears, "unless you want me to start asking Wren questions about your brother?"

Noelle smirked. "Wren's too shy to answer. I think I'm safe."

"Oh, I don't know," I teased, caught up in the wonder that I had a group of girls to banter with. "Max is bringing out my sense of adventure. Last night we—"

Noelle's hands flew up. "Mercy! Mercy! I'll never say another word!"

"Vindication tastes sweet," Harley stated smugly before tilting her head to study me. "How are things going with you? We haven't had a chance to catch up lately."

I twisted my mouth to the side, then said, "We're all meeting up with Aaron's birth father tomorrow."

Harley whistled.

"Wow." Noelle nodded her head a few times. "How do you feel about that?"

I scrunched my nose, then closed my eyes in resignation before confessing. "I'm not even sure I remember what he looks like."

"And? It was almost twenty years ago." Harley pulled a few grapes off the vine and offered them to me.

Taking some, I admitted, "I feel weird about it." I rolled my eyes. "Like I'm loose."

Noelle popped a cube of cheese in her mouth. "I slept with Hawkley the day after I returned to Sage Ridge after not speaking to him for ten years. And got pregnant."

"I slept with Daire before our first official date."

My eyes darted back and forth between them.

Noelle wagged her eyebrows.

Harley tipped her head in her husband's direction then looked back at me, her eyes wide. "I mean, can you blame me?'

"Well," I paused, letting go of the self-judgment, then smiled, the memory of Max tying my arms behind my back warming my cheeks. "Aren't we just a bunch of dirty sluts."

35

Push

Waking up wrapped up in Max on Sunday morning brought a smile to my lips before I even opened my eyes. Eight weeks ago today, he drove me up to Moose Lake and kissed me for the first time in almost twenty years.

"Good morning, Tweet." His sleepy voice opened up something warm and safe inside me.

"Good morning, Max," I practically purred.

He chuckled warmly. "What are you thinking so hard about? I smell smoke."

I laughed and tucked myself tighter into his chest. "Eight weeks ago today, you drove me up to Moose Lake. Since then, my life has turned completely upside down."

"It has. A lot of change in a very short time. You must feel like you're spinning."

"I am," I agreed. "I've talked about the past more than I ever have. That's been healing but it's also brought up more stuff."

"Like what?"

"I'm angry, Max," I admitted. "I should have had an Aaron beside me when I got pregnant. I should have had a mom beside me. My children should have been celebrated and welcomed rather than one being considered a mistake and the other an object of pity."

"Ouch."

"Yes! Ouch!" My voice trembled. "I never stood up for myself. Not once. I just let him walk all over me all these years. I've been a doormat. And that's precisely what my mother has asked me to be, time and time again."

"Did she email you again?"

"Yes," I sighed. "I wrote her back and told her I wasn't going to try talking to him again without some assurance that he would be supportive."

"Good boundary."

"Why, thank you, Doctor," I teased.

Dropping his hand, he smacked me lightly on my bum. "Why did you let him walk all over you?"

His question immediately put me on the defensive. "What do you mean 'why'?" I asked irritably.

"Why did you make yourself a doormat. You must have had a reason."

My mouth, which had been open and ready with my retort, snapped shut. After a moment, I answered, "To make sure Aaron and Audrey got what they needed." I paused. "But I should have been able to provide what they needed!"

"First of all, nobody does it alone. Second of all, you did. What you couldn't give them, you got for them."

Uncomfortable with his undeserved praise, I teased, "There's also so much good stuff. Like you. And finishing my diploma. Getting more hours at Susie's. The girls. I love being with those girls. I've always loved Harley, but having Noelle, Shae, and Bridge now, too? That's a dream."

No matter how I tried to focus on the positive, I worried about the rest. My relationship with my parents had officially tanked. All those years toeing the line for nothing.

"You're deflecting. You're allowed to be pissed, or worried, or happy, or any other fucking feeling you're having. What else is on your mind?"

"God, Max. Are you a mind reader?"

"You're huffing and puffing like The Little Engine That Could. It's not hard to figure you out."

I laughed. He always made everything better. "The fight with my parents was truly awful," I murmured, then winced with the guilt of my next statement. "And I don't know how I truly feel about Aaron having a baby."

"I imagine you've got lots of feelings. If anyone knows how tough this road is, it's you."

"Hm," I hummed noncommittedly.

"I've been thinking about something I'd like you to consider. Where would your children be without Dan and Lou? Rachel? Anita? Harley?"

"Why?"

"Your dad wasn't the only one helping you."

"I know," I snapped. "That's the problem."

"Is it? Those people are in your life because they want to be. They care about you. When you care about someone, you want to ease their way. It's not a matter of charity, it's just love."

"Love comes with strings, Max. Charity doesn't."

To his credit, he allowed the silence between us to amplify my words until even I could not miss the insanity of my reasoning.

"That's insane," I muttered.

Laughing, he pulled me close. "I wouldn't go that far."

"Professionally speaking?"

"Of course," he murmured. "But maybe because you learned that some people's love comes with strings at such a young age, it's colored your perception of the other people in your life."

It was possible. Of course, it was.

"And maybe, the people who choose to be in your life receive just as much from you as you do from them."

I snorted my objection. "Max, really. What do I have to offer? I'm always on the receiving end."

"Who does Susie talk to when Quinn's not here? How about the joy you give Anita? And Rachel? The baking you do for the shelters? And the school? The graphic design work you've done over the years and never taken a penny for it?"

"I'm not a professional," I murmured my excuse. "It didn't seem right to charge people. Besides, most of them were just starting out with their businesses and couldn't afford a real designer."

"That's giving, Wren. You give. A lot. I think what bothers you is when you don't pay back or even the scales. Evening the scales is not giving. It's not generous. It's keeping people at a distance."

"That's not fair, Max," I protested. "We're supposed to reciprocate."

"Or pay it forward," he suggested softly. "How would you like it if the women at the shelter insisted on paying you for your baking? Or if the shelter refused to accept your donated graphic design work?"

"Bad."

"Yeah."

My mind hopped from one thing to the other to the next. "Rachel offered me a permanent part-time job at Artitude."

"That's fantastic!"

My chest tightened like a rubber band. "I can't take it. After Susie went through all that trouble to help me get my diploma? She looks after Audrey, for free, so I can work her hours. How can I leave her?" I shook my head. "I can't."

"She wouldn't want that. Susie's help didn't come with strings. Neither does her love."

"Hm," I hummed. Normally, I'd agree, I wanted to believe him, but Max didn't know about Susie's knees and just how badly she needed help.

Susie's steady presence had anchored me for years. I couldn't leave her high and dry. But maybe, just maybe, I could do both.

"How are you feeling about meeting Aaron's father today?"

I covered my eyes with my hand and whispered harshly, "Max, I barely remember what he looks like. I don't even know if I'll recognize him. What does that make me?"

"Someone who doesn't have a photographic memory?"

I snorted out a laugh. "I'm serious."

"So am I. Do you think I remember the face of every woman I've slept with?"

Lunging at him, I covered his eyes with one hand, his mouth with the other. "No! Don't you dare!"

Laughing, he bit my palm lightly. "I have no interest in anyone else, not even in my memory. It's only you for me. It's only ever been you."

"It's always been you for me, too, Max. I love you."

Grabbing me, he rolled me onto my back. "Finally, she says it!"

"What do you mean?" I cried. "I've said it!"

He shook his head and mocked me, "I feel the same, Max," is what you said."

I thought back. "My God, you're right."

Pushing him off me, I got up on my knees and smacked a kiss on his lips, then his chin, followed by his cheeks, forehead, nose, and finally returned to his smiling mouth, declaring my love for him in the pause between each one.

"I think he knows, Momma. My Max, would you like a waffle cone?"

Audrey's voice froze me in my tracks.

Max grinned up at me, his dimple deeper than I'd ever seen it as I looked down at him with big eyes. "I'll take her to Anita's and the hardware store. We need a lock for that door."

36

Crooked

While Max took Audrey for a waffle cone, Aaron and I walked to Susie Q's.

I suggested we meet Kian at home, but Aaron preferred to meet at Susie Q's. That way, if it got to be too much for him, he could escape without leaving me to deal with an unexpected houseguest.

When we walked in, Susie tipped her chin in the direction of the lunchroom, indicating that Kian had already arrived. "They're waiting for you in the lunchroom."

Aaron and I looked at each other, twin expressions of surprise on our faces as he mouthed, "They?"

As soon as I pushed the door open, Kian pushed back his chair and jumped to his feet.

"Hi." He stood stock-still, barely sparing me a glance as his eyes devoured our son. "Aaron," he practically wheezed. "I'm so happy to finally meet you."

"Hey," Aaron replied, his eyes skittering to the small boy staring up at him unabashedly. Choosing the chair furthest away from Kian, he sat down.

Kian blew out a breath and took his seat. "You look exactly like my brother," he blurted.

Aaron's eyebrows rose. "You have a brother?"

Kian offered a crooked smile, the same one Aaron flashed almost daily. "I have two brothers and three sisters."

"Whoa," Aaron huffed out a laugh. "Big family." Nodding to the child who'd yet to take his eyes off him, Aaron asked, "Who's this big guy?"

Kian said, "This is Isaiah," at the same time as Isaiah declared, "I'm your brother from another mother."

Kian rubbed a rough hand over his head. "Isaiah, I thought we agreed we wouldn't say that."

Isaiah had the good grace to look chagrined. "Sorry, Dad. It's just that I practiced it so much it kind of just slipped out."

Aaron's lips tipped up into a wry grin. "Words have a way of doing that," Aaron murmured softly, then held out his fist. "Fist bump?"

Eyes widening, Isaiah butted his fist against Aaron's. "I totally knew you'd be cool."

My eyes burned.

When Isaiah turned to me, I held my breath. He cocked his head to the side. "Are you the other mother?"

Utterly enchanted, I barked out a watery laugh. "Yes. I'm Wren."

I held out my hand and he shook it solemnly. "I'm sorry for your loss."

Kian groaned and scrunched his nose. "I swear to God I tried to prepare him for this meeting."

I smiled at Isaiah. "He's wonderful."

I'd yet to really look at Kian, but I couldn't avoid it any longer. When I did, it was to find him staring back at me, his sad, hazel eyes an exact replica of those I'd smiled into every day for nineteen years.

Inhaling deeply, he spoke. "First of all, Wren, I'm so very sorry I wasn't there for you."

Before I could answer, Aaron cut in. "It was hard for her. My grandparents were dicks. Did you even try to find us?"

He winced then nodded slowly. "I'm ashamed to say it took almost two years to seek you out. By that time, you were smoke."

"Did you try?" Aaron pushed.

Kian nodded. "I hired a private investigator. I went to every alumni reunion. I looked up everyone I could think of from my time at university, but nobody could tell me anything. I even posted on Facebook. Walking away from you that day is my biggest regret."

Aaron continued, hammering away in a way I did not expect. "Why did you do the ancestry test?"

He smiled wryly. "Hope. A plea to the universe, I guess."

"I did mine as a dare to the universe," Aaron confessed. At Aaron's grin, a look of wonder and adoration settled over Kian's face. His Adam's apple bobbed once in his throat before he managed to smile back.

Aaron's smile faded. "Where's Isaiah's mother?"

Kian nodded, perhaps expecting this question. "My wife died when Isaiah was two. I've raised him alone since." Again, he turned to me. "I know how hard it is to raise a young child alone, but I had the benefit of a great job and my parents have been wonderful." He shook his head. "I know I can't ever make it up to you, but—"

I cut him off. "It's okay. You lost more than I did. I could have tried again, for Aaron's sake, but I was afraid. I'm sorry."

Kian winced. "You have nothing to be sorry about, Wren. I wouldn't have tried again if I were you either."

"It's all in the past, now." I dropped my eyes, the weight of his regret almost as heavy as my own.

At that, Kian focused on Aaron entirely. Peppered with entertaining comments from Isaiah, their conversation flowed easily from one topic to the next while I snuck off a quick text to Max to give him a triple thumbs-up.

My head shot up at Kian's next question. "Do you have anyone special in your life?"

Aaron cleared his throat, shooting me a quick glance before answering. "I do. In fact, we just recently found out we're expecting a baby."

I stared at Kian, mesmerized, as he scrunched his nose and rubbed a rough hand over his head exactly the way Aaron did when flustered. "I don't want to push..." He shook his head and smiled ruefully. "There's just so much I want to do, offer, make up for..." he petered off then seemed to steel himself. "When I finally got my head on straight, I calculated what I would have been paying in child support all these years and put it away every month. It's yours." His look encompassed me as well. "Both of yours to do with whatever you will."

Aaron's mouth dropped open; his brow lowered. "I don't want your money."

Kian winced. "It's not mine. It's yours. Or your mother's. And it makes up for nothing. I'd like to stick around, see you again, get to know you better if you're open to it, but there are no strings attached to the money."

"Why didn't you just send it then? Why push to meet me?"

Kian flushed. "If you hadn't agreed to a meeting, I would have sent it to your mom. It would have been yours either way."

It was a noble gesture, but if Aaron didn't want it, I'd never take it.

Isaiah's nose scrunched as he peered up at Aaron, and I just about died at the sweetness of it all. "Are you mad at my dad?"

Aaron's gaze flicked to his half-brother.

His half-brother!

"A bit," he answered honestly, then met Kian's eyes with a small smile. "But not as much as I was."

"He makes me mad sometimes, too," Isaiah offered eagerly, the blue eyes he must have inherited from his mother blowing wide. "But he makes great pancakes and he's the best Lego builder on *earth*."

Aaron smiled down at him, slightly bemused by his very existence. "You like Lego, buddy?"

"Yup," Isaiah small mouth popped on the 'P'.

"Me too," Aaron admitted, his eyes darting up to Kian's for a split second. "Maybe your dad can buy a kit and we'll build it together."

I couldn't see Kian clearly through the blur of my tears, but I heard his clearly in the thickening of his voice when he assured Aaron he would do just that.

When they left, Aaron dropped his mouth to the top of my head and held it there for several seconds before walking them out.

I sat at the table by myself. Deflated? Elated? Maybe a combination of both. The anticipation and accompanying anxiety had dissipated, and I was delighted at how well they got along, but there was a sadness overlying all of it. Sadness for Aaron. Sadness for me. And now, sadness for Kian and Isaiah for what they missed.

And lost.

Three uncles. Two aunts. Grandparents who were chomping at the bit to meet Aaron.

He could have had it all, all these years, if I'd only tried.

When the door opened, I plastered a smile on my face as I turned.

"It's just me, doll." Susie bustled in. "How did it go? Are you okay?" She shook her head and laughed. "The three of them walking out together...there's no denying they're related!"

I huffed out a small laugh. My heart thudded in my chest at the conversation I needed to have with Susie.

There's no time like the present.

"Susie, do you think we could talk about moving my hours around a little bit?"

She raised her eyebrows. "What do you mean?"

"It's just that Rachel offered me a part-time position at Artitude, and you know art has always been my passion." I closed my eyes for a second, twisting my hands together as I searched for the right words. "I don't want you to think I'm not grateful after everything you've done for me—"

Susie's face paled. "Wren, doll, I would never want you to stay out of guilt." She reached for my hand and squeezed tightly. "You need to follow your own path." She shook her head and tutted. "Anything I did for you, I did with my whole heart. There are no strings attached." She flung her arms wide. "Susie Q's was my dream. I want you to find yours."

I sniffed and ducked my chin as my eyes began to burn. "I'll still be here part-time."

Bridge threw the door open with a wide grin. Looking between us, she cocked an eyebrow and snarked, "Who died?"

I winced, and Bridge slapped her palm over her mouth. "Oh my God. Did somebody die?"

Susie rolled her eyes. "One day you're going to put your foot in it so hard you'll chip a tooth on your kneecap." Herding Bridge out of the breakroom, she continued, "I've got a proposition for you."

37

The Damnedest Thing

"You were quiet on the way up."

Dappled sunlight danced across the front yard of the cabin as a light wind rustled the leaves over head.

Max and I emptied the SUV while Audrey poked around inside the cabin. Contrary to my expectations, Audrey handled the news about Brooklyn's surgery well and was excited to drive up to Moose Lake, especially knowing that's where I stayed when I went to school. Hanging out with Rachel and Susie had given her a much-needed boost in confidence, and she was so much more willing to explore the world around her.

My voice shook. "I got an email from my father's lawyer requesting a meeting, and another one from my mom asking me to reach out to my father again."

Max set the grocery bag down on the front step, strode to my side, and tipped my chin up to face him.

"I'll hire you the best lawyer, Tweet. You are not alone."

I held his gaze, both thankful I had him and embarrassed I needed him. "It sucks."

He looped his arms around my waist. "That's the understatement of the year. Did you answer your mom?"

I twisted my lips to the side. "I forwarded the lawyer's email to her and told her we can't speak or see one another until this issue is resolved."

"Good for you."

"I feel bad. She always gets caught between us. It's not fair."

He shook his head. "That's her battle, not yours."

I nodded and laid my head on his chest.

"Can you put it out of your head for now? I promise, we'll deal with everything when we get back, and we'll deal with it together."

With Max in my corner, I couldn't lose. And I refused to allow my father to steal this mini vacation away from me and Max and Audrey.

After breakfast, Max passed Audrey a gift bag and explained, "This is to document our adventures this weekend."

Inside was a polaroid camera, a ton of film, and an album to organize her photographs. Audrey stared at the gift then moved to Max. Leaning against his shoulder, her version of a hug, she said, "I like it, my Max."

Max's face softened with pleasure. "You want to go out and see what we can find?"

We spent the afternoon traipsing along the trails, stopping every so often for Audrey to take pictures. When we reached the shore of the small lake, Audrey refused to budge for over an hour, utterly enthralled with the ducks. When we got back, Audrey showed us each photograph as she put them into the album. After dinner, Max built a fire in the pit, and we gorged ourselves on toasted marshmallows, promising Audrey we'd go back to see the ducks again tomorrow.

Aaron sent pictures of Brooklyn being her sweet, goofy self, assuring me there had been no ill effects from her surgery.

My mother emailed me back and promised to rectify the lawyer situation.

And when bedtime rolled around, Audrey dropped like a rock.

Max took me by the hand and led me into the master bedroom. By the time he was done with me, I dropped too.

I woke up to a nightmare.

It pressed down on me from all sides as I ran through the cabin again and again.

"Max!" I screamed. "Max, she's gone!"

The air wheezed in and out of my lungs. Dropping to my knees, the seams of the wood floor bit into my flesh as I looked under the beds. Running from room to room, I whipped back curtains, flung open the closet doors, and in a state of utter terror, darted out the back door.

Max careened out the door behind me, scanning the forest behind me. Grasping me by my upper arms, he pulled me around to face him. "Was the back door open? Did she leave out the back door?"

"Y-y-yes," I stuttered, my eyes wide. The sun was just beginning to peek over the horizon. "Oh, God! I don't know how long she's been gone! Max, she could be anywhere!"

"We'll find her, Tweet." Dipping his knees, he faced me head-on. "Is her new coat gone? The bright pink one?"

"I think so. Yes. And her rubber boots are gone."

"What about her hat?"

"I don't know," I yelled.

"Get your shoes on and grab a sweater."

I looked down at my stockinged feet. "I don't need—"

"Now, Wren," he commanded.

Three minutes later, closing the back door of the cabin behind us, Max held his cell phone to his ear. "Every neighbor, every resident who's here, tell them to be on alert but not to call out to her or alarm her in any way. Yellow rubber boots, bright pink jacket. She may or may not be wearing a yellow knit hat with a pom-pom on top."

Crashing through the brush, the branches hitting me in the face, I screamed Audrey's name. "Audrey! Audrey, answer mommy!"

"Wren, Wren," Max spoke sharply. "You told me she gets scared if she hears yelling."

I sobbed. "This can't be happening, Max."

"It's not, Wren. I promise with everything I am it's fucking not. Take a deep breath. Be the mother she needs you to be."

My breath whistled in and out as his words penetrated my panic.

I sucked in a deeper breath, then blew it out again.

"That's right," he soothed. "She hasn't been gone that long. We don't want to scare her, okay?"

Max's cell rang and he stabbed the screen to accept the call. "Max here." I continued walking along the hiking trail going into the forest.

"Thanks. Keep me posted."

"Who was that?" My eyes scanned the area in front of me then returned only to scan again.

Stay calm, stay calm, stay calm.

"Our closest neighbor. The phone tree is activated. Anyone who's here will be sitting outside their residence or walking the trails behind their houses to watch out for her."

I nodded.

"It's early in the day. She can't have left that long ago. We'll find her, Wren. Talk to her."

Stay calm, stay calm, stay calm.

I squirrel darted in front of me on the path and I screamed.

Max spun me around in his arms and clutched me to his chest, his arms bands of iron around my back. His body trembled. "Breathe," he demanded. "Breathe, dammit."

I pulled in his scent. Nodded my head. And pushed back against his chest. "Okay. I'm okay."

Please, God. Please, oh please, oh please.

For two hours we combed through the woods, passing Max's neighbors or catching glimpses of them on another trail through the thick leaves of the forest.

There were so many.

And she was so small.

I bit back my sob.

My breath rasped in and out.

My jaw ached.

My eyes stung.

Every time Max's phone rang, my heart leapt with hope. Every time he hung up, I fought to remain standing under an ever-swelling mountain of despair. I pushed through, barely blinking as I swung my gaze back and forth.

Finally, when the sun reached its peak in the sky, Max received a text. The blood drained from his face as he read the message, then looking at me, he nodded. "We've got her. She's safe."

Without waiting for me, he took off running, backtracking to a path we'd bypassed earlier.

"Where is she?" I gasped, my legs pumping to keep up with him.

"We'll be there in ten minutes. She's safe. Unhurt. And she's not scared." He glanced down at his cell phone and slowed his pace. "She's playing with a litter of puppies. As far as she's concerned, she went for a walk." Stopping entirely, he turned to me. "We've got to be calm, or this will be traumatizing for her."

I halted in place, covered my face with my hands, and sobbed in relief.

Max's body crashed into mine as he lifted me in his arms, held me against his chest, and squeezed the breath from my lungs.

True to his word, a few minutes later I heard her voice.

Looking at me over his shoulder, eyes intent, he asked, "Are you ready?"

Gathering the ends of my frayed nerves, I nodded.

Stepping into the clearing, Max greeted her. "Hello, Bean."

"Hello, my Max," Audrey replied easily. She sat on the ground, a litter of roly-poly puppies climbing over her legs. Dappled sunlight dotted the ground. She was a picture. A perfect picture.

I forced myself to take a deep breath.

She's okay.

Sweat broke out on my forehead and ran down my face. I swiped my face with my sleeve, grateful for the sweat that masked my tears.

"What have you got there?" Max cast a concerned glance in my direction.

I nodded and forced a small smile, but couldn't speak past the sob caught in my throat.

"Puppies. Lots of them. This one pooped." Audrey glanced up at Max without a care in the world. "And it stinks."

I reached out a hand and braced it against the papery bark of a birch tree.

Three things I can see...

The elderly gentleman behind her chuckled and shook his head. "Was the damnedest thing." Pointing up to his kitchen window, he continued, "I was washing up the dishes after makin' breakfast for the missus, looked out the window, and saw this little bit of a thing sittin' in my boat."

All the breath in my body left my lungs in one explosive exhale. My chest tightened painfully as my eyes followed the line of his finger to the small rowboat rocking gently in the waves, doing its utter best to escape the meager stake tying it to the shore.

Saliva pooled in my mouth. I swallowed rapidly, fighting back the nausea.

From the corner of my eye, I saw Max's hand reach back for mine, his face aghast.

Yes, it was just that close.

I backed up, a wave of dizziness sending the world spinning.

The gentleman chuckled again. "I know the text said not to alarm her, but I didn't think you'd want her to sail away so I invited her to take pictures of my puppies instead of the ducks she'd been chasing." He turned his attention to Audrey. "Did you get any good ones, young lady?"

I followed Max's horrified gaze to the Polaroid camera sitting next to her on the ground.

At the reminder, Audrey pointed out the ducks swimming in a haphazard line across the water. "Look." She smiled joyfully. "Ducks."

Drowning is among the leading causes of death for people with autism.

Like a brightly lit ticker-tock, the terrifying statistic raced across my brain.

Max caught my gaze, his eyes anguished, an apology he didn't owe etched into every line on his face.

I smiled at him weakly as bile stung my throat and the back of my tongue. I swallowed it down but my mouth filled again with bitter saliva. I turned my head away, needing a moment, just a moment, to wrestle what might have been back into submission but the water pulled my gaze like a magnet. That same water that had filled me with peace the day before, now shattered it, proving peace to be nothing more than an illusion.

There was no rest.

Heart thundering in my chest, I backed away slowly, turned into the forest, and quietly wretched into the bush.

My hand shook as I wiped the back of it across my mouth.

Max's firm hand landed on the small of my back. He turned me into his chest and held me tight. Stale sex, sweat, and the acrid smell of fear hit my nostrils and filled me with shame.

Won't a boyfriend be a distraction?

Thank God for Max. He got both of us back to the cabin and kept Audrey occupied for the afternoon while I pulled myself together. We had another campfire and roasted hot dogs for dinner and smores for dessert which thrilled Audrey.

I slept with Audrey that night with several toys piled in front of the closed door. If she got up, I'd hear her.

When I opened the door the next morning, I nearly tripped over Max.

"What are you doing?"

Rubbing a hand over his drawn face, he pushed the sleeping bag down and sat up. "Playing guard dog. Thank God you have Brooklyn. I don't know how you survived the early years when she was doing that all the time."

Looking back caused me to shudder. I closed my eyes at the memory of her running into traffic, walking through the cornfield, hiding in public spaces when she needed to escape. "I honestly don't know."

"Are you okay?"

I watched him get to his feet and swallowed my standard reply in exchange for honesty. "No."

"It wasn't your fault, Wren. It was an accident. If anything, blame me. I thought about getting a portable alarm for the door, I just never got around to it."

"That's just it, Max. I should have thought about and bought the alarm, not you. She's my kid. I know very well what she's capable of. I failed to protect her and very nearly lost her."

"Wren," he interrupted sharply.

I held up my palm with a shudder. "I can't, Max. Not right now. I just want to go home."

Disappointed that I refused her request to see the ducks one more time, it took a while to get Audrey packed up and into Max's truck. It would have been easier to have just taken her, but what had been an exciting adventure upon arrival now fairly pulsed with danger. My entire body thrummed with pent up energy, the stress of Audrey's near miss permeating every muscle and tendon. Even my bones hurt. I wanted nothing more than to take her home where she was safe.

At home, I rubbed Brooklyn down and put her service vest on along with the double alarm on the door. I could finally relax my guard.

When Max pressed me to talk to him, I cracked and snapped, "Everything has happened so fast, Max! I need to catch my breath. I can't just rush into things all willy-nilly, someone will get hurt, and that someone will be Audrey." With that, I burst into tears.

Drawing me into his arms, he soothed me with his hands, his voice, and the warm, solid, strength of his body. "It's all right, Tweet. You have all the time in the world, and Audrey comes first. Always."

I nodded against his chest, soaking up comfort I didn't deserve after the way I treated him, and silently disagreed.

Clearly, my time had run out.

I asked him to leave and give me time to recuperate. The hours, made heavy by the thoughts in my head, crawled by without him. When Audrey finally yawned, I tucked her into her bed. I perched beside her, something I hadn't done in well over two years, traumatized but what might have been. Within minutes, sleep claimed her.

My hand smoothing her hair back from her forehead shook so violently I had to pull away. She was still so young, and oh so much younger on the inside.

She needed more than I could give her, yet I was all that stood between her and disaster.

The bitter truth, the one I'd failed time and time again to accept, made itself known.

My hope dissipated like the smoke from a dying ember.

Because my father was right.

I couldn't handle it all.

38

Her Mask

You never should have taken your eyes off her.

Leaving Audrey's room, I headed to the kitchen for a cup of tea but only made it as far as the couch. I folded my aching body down into its plushy, familiar, welcome and sat in the dark with my head in my hands.

I should have known that Audrey was an automatic flight risk without Brooklyn, but I'd grown complacent. Distracted. I was more interested in Max and the dreams he resurrected than looking after my daughter. She could very well have paid with her life and for what?

Love.

I shook my head. There was no room in my life for romance. I walked a tightrope every day to keep everything in balance. One false move and my house of cards toppled. I was crazy to think for even a second things could be different.

We're not meant to fight alone.

I inhaled a shuddering breath and closed my eyes. I couldn't afford to place my hope in that.

When Max called, I pleaded fatigue. It was selfish to string him along. But even after having faced the terrifying consequences of spreading myself too thin, I still couldn't fathom letting him go.

And I had to. This life that had been mine for so short a time was ripe with risks I could ill afford.

And yet, I was trapped. Because I no longer had my parents and I couldn't do it by myself. If Max walked away...

My mind spun, a thousand disjointed thoughts fighting for supremacy. I looked up, my gaze drawn as if by a magnet to the delicate glass hearts hanging in the window. Made by my own hands the summer I spent with Max, there were eight in total, one for every week we were together.

I closed my eyes, remembering him looking at them the first time he came here.

Did he remember the way I did?

Did he remember the blue and gold one was for the night at Carousel Park?

Or that the seafoam green one represented the days we spent on the beach?

The fuchsia one I made after he kissed me for the first time?

My lips thinned and my jaw clenched; my teeth gritting together harshly. Heat mottled my cheeks and raced across my chest as my breathing accelerated. My last glass project, my last *art* project. When I dared to ask my mom to babysit Aaron while I took an art class, my father flew off the handle.

Anger, that fearsome demon, raged and billowed, burning me alive from the inside. It burned dark and extinguished the light, its blackened clouds suffocating everything it touched. It was the kind of anger that made me want to tear into my own skin to escape its stranglehold.

I stood, rolled out my neck, and shook my hands out as I exhaled harshly. This kind of anger screeched about the unfairness of life, but life wasn't unfair. Life was simply a matter of cause and effect. Better to accept the consequences of my actions because this kind of anger never got me anywhere.

I swallowed it, like I always did, forcing it deep down where it singed the lining of my stomach before turning into a lead weight.

I paced back and forth, thoughts of Max rushing in to fill the void left by the anger I repressed. Max and his beautiful face which reflected all his moods, dark with concern, soft with empathy, tight with passion, and alight with laughter. Max who offered me the brass ring, everything I ever wanted, but it dangled just beyond my reach.

We're not meant to fight alone.

And yet, hope persisted.

I pressed my palms to my face and worked to steady my breathing. It was all too much.

My father's lawyer, Nadine's pregnancy, Aaron's car insurance, and most definitely his car payments.

The addition of Kian and Isaiah to our lives, while necessary and maybe even good, carried its own brand of stress. How would they fit into our lives? Would they fit into our lives?

Working for Rachel was a dream but juggling those hours along with my hours at Susie Q's while researching health insurance and securing childcare made me want to rewind the clock by two months and keep my big mouth shut.

Because it wasn't until I finished that course that my life began to change.

And subsequently fall apart.

It struck me with the force of a heavy fist to my gut that we would no longer have my father's assistance in paying for Aaron's education. I hadn't even accounted for that.

If you've got time and money to be gallivanting all over the place it's time you stand on your own two feet.

As for Audrey, every time I remembered waking up in the cabin without her, I relived those terror-filled hours within the span of a handful of seconds.

If you're going to be pawning your parental responsibilities off on someone else, it better be worth it for the kids in the end.

I squeezed my eyes shut, my stomach roiling like that little boat bobbing gently in the waves of my worst nightmare.

Drowning is one of the leading causes of death for autistic children.

Gripping my hair, I stood in the middle of my family room with my eyes squeezed shut. My breath rasped in and out as the tight confines of my home closed in on me, the harsh sound shocking in the utter silence.

My head shot up as I drew in a quavering breath. I needed a distraction, something to block my mind from replaying the loop of Audrey's near disaster narrated by my father's voice.

His voice that always seemed to drown out everyone else's. Even my own. Especially my own.

Pushing my shoulders back, I opened my chest to fill my lungs only to have panic lick a path along my sternum. My eyes widened as the thoughts pummeled me. I gasped for a deeper breath, one that would calm me.

I can't keep it all together.

I'm on my own.

Aaron's going to lose everything.

I almost lost Audrey.

Blowing out short, harsh, breaths, I struggled to regain control. I jogged to my bedroom; it would not do for Aaron to find me in this state.

I flipped on the harsh overhead light and quietly closed and locked my bedroom door with the lock Max had so recently installed. I sobbed. There was even less to distract me here. Looking around wildly for something, anything, to keep me grounded, I spied my closet door.

I snorted out a bitter laugh as I pulled it open. My life was falling apart but my closet would finally get its shit together.

Dropping to my knees, I yanked out nineteen years' worth of bittersweet memories. School pictures, baby shoes, and kindergarten crafts. Favorite stuffed animals and the cowboy hat Aaron refused to relinquish, even to sleep, the year he turned six. Audrey's button box and Brooklyn's puppy collar.

I pushed away the memories attached to each and every one. If I allowed myself to remember, I'd lose what little hold I had left on my emotions.

If I started crying, I'd never stop.

Rising to my knees, I reached into the back of the closet and my hand landed on the lid of a large plastic container. I searched my mind to recall its contents then yanked my fingers away as if burned. Shock that I could have forgotten for even a second widened my eyes. Did that mean I could do it? Could I face those demons?

Hooking my fingers under the rim of the lid, I dragged the past out into the light. Though I drew a steadying breath before opening the lid, nothing could have prepared me for the onslaught of memories it unlocked.

Folded over the entire contents of the box lay a Sage Ridge fleece blanket, the same one that adorned every bed at the resort, including mine for the ten months I lived there.

I ran a trembling hand over its' worn and nubby surface.

I'd spent countless hours wrapped in that blanket, curled into the armchair beside the window in my tiny cabin. It kept me warm all through that long, bitter winter as I stared out, unseeing, wondering how I would make it on my own.

I laid my newborn son on that blanket and stretched out beside him, night after night, filled with equal parts wonder and terror as I watched him sleep.

Everywhere I went, I took that blanket with me for Aaron to lie on.

Dan's hearty laugh rang in my memory when he spotted me hauling it out of my bag when I brought Aaron up to the resort for our daily visit. "We might have one or two hundred extra blankets lying around, Wrennie! You don't have to bring the one from your bed!"

But I did. I claimed it, and it was mine. Mine and Aaron's.

Shockwaves of grief rocked me at the memory because while Dan still laughed, often, he never laughed like that anymore.

Back then, we still had Hunter. Dan had yet to shrink into himself. Lou had yet to shatter.

Lou's hugs had sustained me all those months and for all the years following. I remembered her face when my father proclaimed it was past time for me to return home. As if he wasn't the one who forced me to leave.

She offered me to stay as long as I wanted and asked me again to move into their house with them. I wanted. Desperately. But that would completely sever the relationship with my parents, I needed help with Aaron, and I couldn't further burden Lou and Dan.

Tears shone in her eyes as she folded the blanket off my bed and tucked it into one of my moving boxes. Tears that told me like nothing else how much she would miss us.

A tear rolled down my cheek.

That first night home, needing the warmth of Lou's love and acceptance, I had spread that blanket down on my mother's living room floor and laid Aaron down with his baby toys.

My father had sneered as if it sullied his floor. "Lorraine, can we not get a better blanket for this child rather than one that's been shared by God knows how many bodies?"

"Bastard," I spat as I swiped away my useless tears with the backs of my hands. "You took everything good, everything sweet, everything pure."

I had pretended not to care, or even hear, but later that night, I rolled it up and packed it away. Pulling it out now, I spread it over my lap and filled my hands with its softness, a softness I was so often denied, and drew a deep, cleansing breath.

I traced the edge of the Sage Ridge Resort icon with the tip of my finger. This was our beginning, and that beginning was steeped in warmth and family. It wasn't my family, but it taught me what kind of family I wanted us to be.

When my eyes returned to the box, my heart leaped up and lodged in my throat. Hunter's teddy bear stared up at me with glossy black button eyes.

Every atom of self-preservation I possessed urged me to slam the lid down on the box and shove it to the back of the closet. But I'd already come this far. I swallowed my trepidation. My hand shaking, I reached for its furry paw, freed it from the box, and cradled it in my lap.

I was only a few months pregnant when Hunter brought it. He had knocked and waved at me through the window of my tiny cabin until

I opened the door. With his signature wide smile, Hunter pulled the bear out from behind his back and presented it to me with a flourish.

"It's so cute," I exclaimed as I reached for it, forcing a little extra *enthusiasm into my voice. "I'm sure the baby will love it."*

He smiled but shook his head. *"I'll get him one when he's born. This one's for you, Wrennie."*

Wrennie.

A deeply seated grief, one I'd never allowed myself to acknowledge, pulled itself out by the roots and shook the dirt and debris of the past into my lap. Hugging Hunter's bear against my chest, I grappled for control. Back and forth, my breath sawed in and out like a bellows.

This one's for you, Wrennie.

The sweetest of gifts at a time when I believed I deserved nothing.

A gift meant to comfort a child when I was little more than a child myself and comfort was the one thing I sorely needed.

Dropping my chin to my chest, my heart ached. Where would I be now if I'd allowed Lou and Dan to enmesh me in their family like they'd offered?

Just as I had then, I shuddered at the thought. Because to be part of them, was to continually see Max and know he would never be mine.

I hugged Hunter's bear to my chest and mentally tumbled back in time to my tiny cabin. Once again, I stared out the window, watching Max lope across the parking lot with Hunter, Hawkley, Noelle, and Harley when he came home for Christmas break.

I could almost hear the laughter I saw on his face.

Not wanting him to catch sight of me, but loathe to tear my eyes away from him had me shifting back and forth until finally, I pressed my face up against the window until he turned the corner.

The sharp stab of loss pierced my heart and stole the breath from my body just as Aaron tumbled around inside me. I dropped to the floor and rocked back and forth, my arms wrapped tight around the child in my womb, gasping as the pain of losing Max refused to stay buried. I physically turned away from the past and the future I once dreamed of.

Climbing up onto my bed, I yanked the blanket to my chin. I curled into a ball and hugged Hunter's bear to my chest, barely able to breathe through the pain, as I cried myself to sleep.

The next morning, I dialed down the volume of my heart. I drowned its' cries under the noise of shame and responsibility. Later on, that all-encompassing love I held for my son, and then my daughter, buried those desires deeper still.

I carried that pain all the years between then and now and still it bled. I had never once allowed myself to grieve all I had lost. A tidal wave of images from the past battered my walls and they trembled under the onslaught.

Max laughing.

Aaron crying with ear infections, teething fevers, skinned knees, and a broken heart.

My father's disdainful looks filling my stomach with bile that rolled into a ball of fiery rage at the sight of my mother's ever-wringing hands.

Max in his car with another woman.

I gagged as the bile hit my throat, then sobbed as the slam of the screen door echoed through my heart, making me flinch even now.

Audrey's screaming meltdowns when the world became too fast, too loud, too much.

David leaving.

Aaron's naked toes on the icy concrete.

The sound, oh God, the sound of his grief as David drove away. I covered my ears and rocked but there was no escape from the past playing out in my head.

The shame of all my failures, my hands shaking with the desire to destroy something. Anything.

And every single day locked in the prison of Audrey's routine with no one to talk to, lean on, or confide in.

My heart's cries unspoken. Unheard. Unmet.

Until now when it refused to be silence. Now when there was nothing left of me save the shattering of my fragile glass heart as my grief crested.

My head rolled back, pain and rage a fiery maelstrom inside me. I opened my mouth wide, a silent scream aching to be set free. A gruff bark broke through, rolled me to my knees, and pressed my face into the soft plush of Hunter's bear to stifle the sound. His bear comforted me now as it comforted me then.

And I wept, keened from the broken heart of the girl who sat in that chair, alone in that tiny cabin, unable to mourn for herself.

Lost dreams. Lost faith. Lost woman.

My cries burst forth like a child's until, like a child's, they wrung out. Gradually, my breathing slowed, shuddering in and out, my brain foggy and spent.

Shifting onto my side, I burrowed under the blanket that represented all that was home and love and family, all the things I fought so hard to give to my children.

And all the things I'd accepted I would never have for myself.

The things that were now mine for the taking.

Where would I be without Dan and Lou? Or Susie? Where would I be without Harley?

It did not bear considering.

Where would I be without Max?

I knew where I would be without Max because I'd lived without him, without my dreams, for all my adult life, convinced I was worthy of neither.

I held my nubby, pilled, precious, blanket under my chin. I didn't know where or who I would have been without them. I barely knew who I was now.

Was I still the same girl curled up on the bed muting her heart to avoid the pain?

Or was I the woman willing to fight back against the past, to fight for my family, my dreams, and the man I loved?

Should I even consider it? Could I handle all of it? Would I still be able to give my children what they needed?

We're not meant to fight alone.

The peel of my cell phone snapped me out of my fog. I reached out and snatched it up before it woke Audrey. It vibrated in my hand as Max's name flashed across the screen.

I teetered on the edge of indecision.

It would be easier to go back to the way things were.

My lips curved in a tremulous smile. But when had I ever done things the easy way?

I stared at the screen, torn between the Wren I used to be and the Wren I wanted to be.

Picking up the call, I held it to my ear, terrified of making the wrong decision. I opened my mouth, but no sound escaped. I swallowed and tried again.

"Wren? Tweet?" Max's concerned voice broke the silence. "Are you okay?"

Max.

Max who I'd loved with every ounce of my tender, youthful heart.

Max whose loss I grieved in another man's arms.

Max who I watched move on with his life even as I moved on with mine.

Max who held my heart, who'd always held my heart.

"Max," I whispered, every bit of anguish in my heart permeating the sweet sound of his name.

"Wren." His voice guttural, he demanded, "Tell me you're safe."

"Safe," I hiccoughed.

"Okay, baby girl. Okay." Rustling sounds came from his side of the phone. "I'm on my way. Give me fifteen minutes to pack a bag. I'll call you from the car. I'm coming, my baby. I'm coming."

He heard my heart.

And answered.

At that moment, anger dropped her mask.

In her place, stood grief.

39

Dearest Max

Max didn't say a word as we picked our way through the mess on my floor to get to my bed. Once there, he lay down beside me, pulled me into the sanctuary of his chest, curled his big body around mine, and held me while I cried.

Finally spent, his shirt twisted up in my fist, I whispered, "I don't think I'm angry, Max. I think I'm sad. I'm so sad."

Palming the back of my head, he pressed his mouth to my crown. "Anger often disguises our more painful feelings. It's also our built-in red flag telling us something is wrong."

My thoughts turned inward, searching for my truth. I ignored the tears rolling down my face. Images flashed through my brain almost too fast to catch. "For so long, I wanted...more. But wanting more felt selfish. I didn't have the right to complain because I brought everything on myself."

Max stiffened. "What do you mean you brought everything on yourself?"

"I was the one who had too much to drink and slept with Kian. I'm the one who married David. I made those choices, those choices resulted in my kids, and my kids deserved everything I could give them. Even then, it was never enough. How could I even think to expend time, energy, or money on myself when I couldn't even meet their needs?"

His mouth pressed against the top of my head then he spoke against my hair. "Do you still think you didn't give enough?"

I thought about the car I couldn't afford for Aaron. All the times he slipped extra money into my bank account. The brand name clothes I couldn't afford, the school events I didn't make, the team sports I relied on other parents to get him to and back.

In a flash, I saw every letter or doctor's report advising me how to help Audrey progress. Pages and pages of recommendations and how little time I had left over to devote to any of them.

All the financial advantages they received from my parents.

Aaron bent over with laughter as Audrey pointed to the sign above The Beanery.

Audrey's face, smoothed of anxiety, as she burrowed into Brooklyn's fur.

Aaron holding Nadine on his lap, his face serene despite their situation.

Audrey's hand in mine. The yellow pom-pom on her hat. Lego builds on the table, crystals in the window, teenagers laughing about socks on the doorknobs.

I unfurled my fist from his shirt and splayed my palm over his heart. "I didn't give them everything, but I gave them the most important things. I wish I could have done more, but I did enough."

He exhaled slowly, his hands spreading wide over my back. "Good girl. Now tell me, what did you want for yourself?"

I sighed, the knots inside me beginning to loosen the more I talked. "I wanted everything I dreamed of having with you, and I wanted it with you. I wanted good friends to talk to, laugh with, and go out with. I wanted to finish my education to get a better job so I could get out from under my father's thumb. And I wanted to pursue my art again."

"And now that you have all that?"

My breath quickened as my chest heaved. I tried, and failed, to quell the sobs building in my chest. Because getting all of that brought my greatest nightmare to life. I dropped the ball and nearly lost Audrey.

"It took my attention away from Audrey and I nearly lost her."

"That sounds more like your dad's voice than yours. If your attention had been snagged by anything else, anything that you don't deem as for you, would you feel the same?"

My eyes darted back and forth as I weighed the validity of his statement. "He's been so spiteful and mean. Shouldn't he want me to succeed? Or maybe it's just that anything other than university isn't good enough."

"I don't know the man, but I know men like him. He wants control. And I think your success would invalidate his anger. He'd rather be right about you ruining your life than proven wrong by watching you succeed."

"That's sad," I murmured. He missed out on having a beautiful family life, one with grandchildren's birthday parties, summer barbecues, and the joy of Santa coming on Christmas morning. A life like Max and Harley had with their families.

"It is."

"For him, I mean," I corrected, not wanting him to think I was talking about myself.

"Sure. But it's sadder for you. You paid for his choices. Focus on your feelings, not his."

"Is it unfair that I'm most angry with my mother? How could she let him throw me out of the house?"

"You're allowed to be angry. You should be angry. Anger's job is to protect us. If you don't allow yourself to be angry, you're pulling the wires on your internal security system."

His validation cleared the way for compassion, and I murmured, "I think she did what she could. She had a terrible childhood. She was always working behind the scenes, trying to smooth things over and keep everything going. It must have been exhausting." My anger flared to life once more. "But to toss your child out like that? Pregnant?"

"Did you know it was your mother who called Dan and Lou to come get you?"

I jerked back. "No..." The word trailed off. "I thought it was you."

He shook his head and pulled back, his dark eyes warm and steady on mine. "I did call them. I wasn't sure when you were going home or how your dad would react to your pregnancy. I asked them to look out for you and told them I'd pay for a cabin if you needed a place to live."

The blood drained from my face. If Max paid for my cabin, my entire relationship with Dan and Lou was not what I thought it was. "You paid for my cabin?"

"No." He shook his head sharply. "They didn't want payment. And they already had you. Picked you up the day before. What I'm trying to tell you is your mom didn't just abandon you. She made sure you were looked after."

That wound had festered so long, it was not easily lanced. Knowing she called Lou didn't absolve her, but it eased the ache of abandonment. Because she never let me go. Not completely.

A memory long buried struggled to the surface. Boxes and boxes of new baby clothes, diapers, burp pads, and receiving blankets regularly showing up at my door. Other times it was shampoo, body lotion, nail polish, and pads. One delivery included my favorite perfume, which I thought at the time was a wonderful coincidence.

Lou swore she had nothing to do with them. I thought they were donations. Maybe they were. Or maybe they were from my mom.

Though my brain screamed at me to let this last piece of the puzzle go, my heart would not be appeased. "Max..." I paused, worrying my lips between my teeth before continuing. "Why did you break up with me? Was it something I did?" I swallowed, unsure if I wanted the answer to my next question. "Was there someone else?"

He answered immediately. "There was no one else. There have been other women, Tweet. I don't deny that."

I tensed at the admission though I knew, of course I knew. I shuddered as jealousy ripped through me.

"I'm sorry, Tweet. I knew this conversation would come up eventually and that it would be painful for both of us. The truth is no other woman ever held my heart. Not even the tiniest fraction of it.

"I broke up with you, purely and simply, because I was scared. I'd always struggled with feeling too much. My heart beat for you every second of every day until I couldn't tell where I ended, and you began.

"It all happened so fast. I figured a few months apart would tell me if what I was feeling was true. I didn't bank on everything that happened afterward. If I'd known, I never would have broken up with you.

"But Tweet, and I need you to hear this, with everything that came after, Hunter's accident, Noelle leaving, Dan and Lou falling apart, my mom's cancer, and how my dad reacted? I would not have been able to hold onto you through that. I would have torn us apart."

Half of me heard him, the other half was lost in the past. "I still can't hear the sound of a screen door slamming without thinking about that night," I murmured. Guilt suffused me as my brain fully processed his words. "I'm sorry, Max."

He rubbed his big palm down my back to close around my hip. "I hurt you."

I closed my eyes, prepared to move on. "It was a long time ago."

"But it still hurts, and it's going to hurt until we put it behind us. We can't do that until we bring it out into the light."

I scrunched my eyes shut, the sound of a slamming screen door echoing in my memory.

He nudged my temple with his nose and whispered, "Give it to me, Wren."

I struggled for a moment to find the right words while he patiently waited. "The worst part was the shock. I didn't expect you to break up with me."

I stepped back into my twenty-year-old heart and felt it break all over again. "There'd been no sign you were even thinking about it. You were the first person I ever opened up my heart to entirely, and I had no armor against you."

Max's arms tightened; his heart thudded in his chest under my hand. "Go on, Tweet."

"We were sitting on the couch. I knew something was bothering you, but I thought it was because we were leaving for school in a few days. I was just about to reassure you I only wanted you and then you told me you wanted to take a step back. I froze. You got up and walked away while I was still struggling to process what had just happened."

My cheeks burned at the memory. "I felt like a fool. The screen door slammed behind you, and I ran. I chased after you like a dog, Max."

My mind flitted to Aaron's toes on the concrete. How much it hurt. How easily I understood.

"And you didn't even look back. I don't know how long I stood there looking out, waiting for you to change your mind and come back to me, but it wasn't until my parents pulled in the driveway that I snapped out of it."

Max exhaled shakily. "I'm so sorry, Wren. You weren't the fool. I was. I'm so fucking sorry."

Now that I'd started, I couldn't stop. I didn't want to hurt him, but I wanted him to know. Needed him to know. Because if I was going to put my heart in his hands, he needed to understand that he had the power to crush it.

"I moved to university and cried for a month straight. Every night." I huffed out a short laugh. "Drove my roommate nuts until she started forcing me to go to parties with her." I shrugged on shoulder. "The rest is history."

He pulled in a deep breath and let it out slowly, triggering me to do the same. My body relaxed, molding sweetly to his. For the first time in my life, there was room in my life, room inside me, for me.

"It wasn't until Noelle told me you went home and cried that I stopped feeling like such a fool. I thought my love for you was one-sided."

He pressed his cheek to the top of my head and murmured, "It wasn't. You were just so much braver than I was."

Each word from his mouth formed a stitch to close the wound. The hurt was still there, perhaps in some way it always would be.

I'd lost too much and believed the worst of him and myself. But with only a few words and his open heart, the pain began to fade. To think all along I only needed to be heard.

"Thank you, Max," I breathed. "Thank you for hearing me."

"Always, Wren, always. We all, all of us, just want to be seen."

In his arms, I found peace. And I wanted to give that back to him in every way I could.

"You lost so much, Max. I'm so proud of you for taking the risk with me. Especially with everything I have going on, and how unsure I was, I'm so happy you took the risk."

He nodded against my head. "I brought something with me that I want to share with you. Are you okay for a minute if I go get it?"

I eased away from him, the cool air slipping between our bodies as I watched him inch his way across my bedroom. He glanced back at me and flashed me his dimple. "Organizing your closet?"

I laughed. "I told you it was worse than your spare room."

Chuckling softly, he eased my bedroom door open and padded down the hallway. When he came back, he shut it just as quietly and made his way back to the bed.

Sitting on the edge, he held up an envelope.

The envelope.

He handled it almost reverently, his long fingers caressing the edges as he turned it over in his hands. "Remember you asked me, on our way up to the cabin that first time, 'why now' and I told you one day I'd share?"

"Yes."

"One day is today." He turned the envelope around in his hands and took a deep breath. "This is the letter from my mother, the one she wrote me before she died."

"Oh my God," I breathed at the thought I'd finally get to read it. I pushed myself up to sit against the headboard.

"Indeed," he smiled though his eyes welled with tears. "It wasn't easy to read the first time. When I read it for the second time, just a few months ago, it hadn't gotten any easier. But I was finally ready for what she had to teach me. I'd like you to read it."

He held out the envelope to me, and I took it with trembling hands. The paper she wrote on, barely handled, was pristine.

I began reading. By the third line, tears streamed from my eyes.

By the last line, I was weeping.

Dearest Max,

I've heard it said a son is a mother's last love. And, oh God, how true that is. No one has ever or will ever hold my heart the way you do.

My love for you is endless. Eternal. And it's been the driving force behind every day of my life.

I was your first teacher.

I taught you to tell the truth, to make time for fun, and to set your boundaries.

I taught you when to give it your all and when not to sweat the small stuff. (Spoiler Alert: most of it is small stuff!)

I taught you to walk and how to tie your shoes.

How to hold a crayon and how to clean your room.

I taught you to dig deep and to know when to throw in the towel.

But even with all the things I taught you, you taught me more.

You made me a mom. And I learned more about life and love and even myself from you than anyone or anything else.

I'm grateful for every lesson, even this one that is so very hard to swallow, because it's given me one more thing to teach you. And I think it's something you need to hear.

Max, don't be afraid to love again.

I know it's scary, especially for someone like you who feels everything so much deeper than anyone else I know. And it must seem scarier still right now with everyone you've already lost, and what we're about to lose.

Love is scary.

But it's also beautiful.

Without love, there are no apples on the counter. There are no Halloween costumes, or dads who dress up like Santa. There are no Valentines or handwritten notes tucked into school lunch boxes. No stolen kisses. No inside secrets. No conversations contained within a solitary glance. No poetry in the curve of a smile.

My son, there is no greater purpose.

Love is breathtaking and life-affirming. It's soul-deep and as ethereal as a summer morning mist. It's the very thing that makes life worth living, the easiest way to break a heart, and the only way to mend it.

It makes the strongest man weak and the most stable of women insane.

It's infuriating and it's maddening.

But.

My beautiful boy.

There is no sweeter madness.

Love, Momma.

The sounds escaping my throat were primal.

Love and loss.

Hope and suffering.

Agony and ecstasy.

With shaking hands, I folded the paper carefully and slid it back inside its protective envelope. Placing it carefully on my bedside table, I turned and threw myself into his arms.

And just like he promised he would, he caught me.

40

Theories

M y mother met me at the front door before I had a chance to knock. As soon as I set foot in my parents' house, I began to shake.

I grew up in that house. I couldn't possibly count how many times I'd crossed that threshold. I couldn't pinpoint the day it stopped being a comfort, but it was sometime in my early teens.

Before that, I was the apple of my father's eye. At least I thought I was. But at some point, he began to find fault with everything I did.

Coming home pregnant and unattached at the age of twenty broke whatever tendrils of affection remained.

From his side.

I hung on a lot longer.

Even now, when the hope of reconciliation was dead, the little girl inside me grieved the loss of his love even while the woman prepared for battle.

Because even if my mother lost this fight, I would not. My children were the center of my world. While I couldn't say I deserved them, I was no less deserving of my children than any other mother. And I would not give them up.

Not for anything or anyone.

"It'll be okay," my mother reassured me. "Contrary to how it looks, I know how to handle my husband when it counts."

She took my hand in hers and led me to the kitchen where my father sat, a coffee and an open book on the table in front of him. His eyes darted back and forth between me and my mother.

I'd never been particularly adept at understanding him, but even I read the doubt and guilt written on his face.

Mom marched to the end of the table and set her purse down gently. She wasted no time. "Robert, you've always been a hard man. And in many ways, when things were tough for us, it was that strength that pulled us through."

"What's this about, Lorraine?" he demanded gruffly.

"I know you called the lawyer. Renata told me right after she tried to cut me out of her life."

"What?" he snapped, his furious gaze searing me as he stood up. "She has no right—"

My mother raised her voice for the first time since I could remember. "She has every right! She has every right to protect her children from your vitriol. This isn't strength, Robert! It's bitterness!"

He drew back, his mouth falling open, at her outburst. "Lorraine..."

"No." She dipped her chin and shook her head. "I've thought long and hard about this. I sought biblical counsel. I've tried, God how I've tried to barter peace in this family, but you have gone too far."

His eyebrows lowered, but before he could speak, she continued, her eyes shattered.

"I love you," she whispered. "I have always loved you, but I won't allow you to take me away from my daughter and my grandchildren."

"Your duty is to stand beside your husband," he stated gruffly, attempting to regain his equilibrium.

She shook her head. "I won't ever leave you, Robert. But I won't be held prisoner by your judgment and lack of forgiveness."

"Lack of...what are you talking about, woman?"

"You never forgave her for letting you down and embarrassing you in the church. But that church let us down. And I'm embarrassed by the way it treated our daughter. If she sinned, it was never against us. But we sinned against her. We let her down over and over and over again. The only people in this family who should be begging for forgiveness is us."

He sat down, all his bluster draining out of him in front of my astonished eyes. "Lorraine..."

My mother closed the space between them and sat down at the table in her usual place. She offered him her hand. "It doesn't have to be this way."

His hands remained on the table. "I have to do what I think is right," he muttered.

"Do you really think it's the right thing to do?" She ran her thumb over the back of his hand. "I won't support it. If you try to go through with a custody suit, I will testify to the truth. And the truth is, Renata is twice the parent to her children than you or I ever were to her. And she's done it on her own."

His eyes snapped to meet hers. "We helped."

She answered immediately. "Not nearly enough."

He slowly rose from the table, but not before giving my mother's hand a gentle squeeze.

He met my eyes, his anger momentarily banked. "I'll cancel the lawyer. I'm—" He dropped his eyes, shook his head, and left the room.

Chin dipped down, closing her eyes as she exhaled, my mother sat alone.

And I realized, that's all she'd ever been.

Later that night, wrapped in Max's arms, I confessed, "I don't understand him. I don't understand how he backed down so quickly. Or why he held onto that anger for so long."

Up and down my back, Max's fingers trailed. "Again, I don't know the man, but I have some theories based on our few encounters and what you've told me."

"Please."

"He backed down because the public exposure of your mom going against him was worse than any other outcome he could imagine. Your pregnancy with Aaron put him under the spotlight at his church. And he draws his worth and validation from the respect of others."

"You think it's that simple?"

"That and he's got some seriously strong narcissistic traits. He's not capable of taking responsibility, but he knows when to hedge his bets."

"My mother seemed so alone."

He sighed and pulled me closer. "She is."

"I'm proud of her and sad for her. And I'm still a little bit angry. She tiptoes around him and taught me to do the same. I don't want to live like that."

"Now that you see it, you don't have to. And Wren? Exorcising childhood demons is not a one-time endeavor. For any of us. The victory is in the battle, not the war."

41

Storytime

Licking the chocolate off my finger, I eyed the remaining chocolate croissants in the box and remembered Max's wicked smile when he set them on the table this morning. It was a wonder how good chocolate tasted when sucked off certain body parts.

"Have another one." Max grinned, the flash of his dimple reminding me how hard we laughed last night when I tried my hand at dirty talking.

I was less than...proficient.

"Pull my hair and tell me I'm pretty," I murmured for his ears only, my eyes crinkling.

His grin broadened into a wide smile, that damned dimple my complete ruin. I laughed out loud.

Sitting across from him at my tiny kitchen table, I realized it was no longer big enough for all of us. So much had changed in only two handfuls of weeks. I finished my diploma, increased my working hours, got a new job, stepped back into the art world I loved so much, and held the hand of the man I loved more than anything.

I traced my finger over the dents and scratches that told the story of my children's childhood like braille. We had reached the end of an era. Though there were still moments pregnant with disbelief, I was mostly ready.

Audrey knelt in front of the family room window, her quiet humming evidence to all within earshot of her good mood. Lined up according to size on the windowsill in front of her lay an assortment of Crystal prisms. Each had a tiny hole drilled through the top just large enough to pass a piece of fishing string. A white-washed branch, readied with tiny hooks, hung suspended from the window frame. Her first art project with Rachel, completed.

She'd been happily at it for over an hour. Every time she finished hanging them up, she twirled the crystals for a few minutes then promptly took them off again to rearrange into a better configuration.

Each time she held it up to the window, rainbows painted the walls.

Those fragile glass hearts drew my eye exactly as they always had, maybe more so now that I'd added two more. Only now they only ever filled me with light.

They had stood the test of time. Perhaps they were not so fragile after all.

Max followed my line of sight to the window. "You added another heart," he murmured. "Does it feel good to get back to your work?"

Every time he referred to my art as my work, my heart thrilled. He never dismissed it as a fanciful but useless hobby. He understood.

"I never thought I'd add another one; I thought our story was over," I admitted, meeting his serious gaze.

He covered my hand with his. "We're never going to be over."

I smiled, thinking of the hearts I would continue to add. "No. We're not."

Aaron and Nadine sat close together on the couch. Tempers were still running high at her house, and Aaron was no longer welcome. Nadine was running out of patience but continued to hold out hope that her parents would come around. She also knew she had a place with us. I would be her Lou.

But I hoped, for her sake, she wouldn't need me like that.

At least with Aaron by her side, she wouldn't have to deal with everything alone. Looking at them now, seeing just how young they were, brought home to me just how young I had been.

Just how alone.

And how well I did with a little help from my friends.

"When you're ready to move into my place, I think perhaps we should consider keeping this one for Aaron and Nadine."

My eyes flew to his. "You want us to move in with you?"

He nodded. "Tomorrow would be good. I want Aaron, too. And if Nadine is part of that package, I'm good with it. There's more than enough room for all of us. We can finish the basement into a separate apartment for them. And if they decide they want to make a go of it on their own, we could still help."

The thought of Aaron not living with me grieved my mother's heart. Was I ready for that? More importantly, was he?

Should I stay here, keep everything the same for the kids?

Was it okay to move forward?

I glanced at Aaron and Nadine. They were young, but they deserved their shot. My gaze slid to Audrey. She would struggle, but she would adjust. If there was anything I had learned in the past month, it was that she could adjust and be all the stronger for it.

I nodded slowly then met his gaze, warm, steady, and patient, on mine. "I think we could start planning for that."

His smile stole my breath. "I'll try not to push," he said, then huffed out a laugh. "But the sooner the better."

I smiled and ducked my head. Waking up every morning in Max's arms? Slipping into bed with him every night? Walking through life together? Yes. Looking back up at him, I grinned. "The sooner the better."

My eyes drifted around my apartment. Within these walls, I put my family back together. If walls could speak, they'd tell a tale of tears and trials, fights and fatigue, and most importantly, laughter and love.

"This could be a good beginning for them, Max," I agreed quietly.

I'd have to talk to Aaron to see if this was what he wanted. While they had decided to keep the baby, living together was an entirely different question.

With the way he felt about her, I was almost certain I knew the answer.

Smoothing my palm over the scarred surface of my table, I mused, "Maybe I should sand this down and revarnish it for them; make it new again."

"I'd be more inclined to varnish it exactly the way it is, preserve all these nicks and scratches that tell the story of your family."

"Aw, Max!" I teased to cover the blast of emotion his words elicited. "I had no idea you were such a romantic!"

Aaron and Nadine's laughter died. I twisted around to see what caused the sudden silence, but Max's voice drew my attention back to him.

"No?" He cocked an eyebrow and pushed his chair back. His long legs erased the distance between us he rounded the table to stand in front of me. Looking down at me, face serious, he cupped my cheek. "Then this is going to blow your mind."

He dropped to one knee.

I stared at him, my heart falling at his feet. "Max," I whispered.

"Is he asking now, Dean?"

"Shh, Bean. Yes," Nadine squeaked.

"Oh," I breathed, covering my mouth with my hands. "You have an audience," I advised, my voice shaking.

"Yes, well," he slanted a wry look in Aaron's direction, "when I asked Aaron for his blessing he got so excited I decided to make it a family affair."

Glancing up at Aaron, catching sight of his wide, crooked, grin, crumpled what was left of my composure into itty-bitty pieces.

I sniffed and drew in a shuddering breath before returning my attention to Max.

"Well…" I circled my wrist in the universal sign to get on with it, then laughed wetly at the incredulous look on Max's face.

His Adam's apple bobbed in his throat. "Renata Lewis, Wren, Tweet, no matter what name you go by, you are my love, my life, my happiness, my living dream, and I pray to God one day very soon you'll be my wife."

He offered me his hand. With no hesitation, I slid my palm across his.

And he closed his fingers around mine.

"Wren, in all the years I spent apart from you, I never truly lived. How could I when you are my life? You've held the key to my heart for over twenty years. And you're the only one to ever unlock it. Whether or not you give me yours, I will love you for the rest of my life to the best of my ability. Trust me, Wren. Trust me with your life, your children, and your precious heart, and I will give you all of me for eternity. Tweet, will you be my wife?"

I nodded vehemently, my vision rapidly blurring with tears.

"I'm going to need verbal confirmation," he murmured with a sweet smile.

I laughed. "Yes. It's a yes."

Aaron whooped, and Nadine laughed as Audrey praised, "Good job, my Max."

Sliding his hand into his pocket with a small grin, he withdrew a ring. "This was my mother's. If you'd prefer something different, I understand. But she and I would be honored if you wore this one."

There was no question. It could be a hideous bauble worthy of a gumball vending machine, and I'd wear it proudly.

Easing his grip on my fingers, he pushed the ring over my knuckle, kissed the back of my hand, and sprang to his feet. With a look of sheer, stark, relief on his face, he yanked me up from my chair and into his chest. "You've made me a happy, happy, man, Wren Lewis." He drew back and cocked an eyebrow. "Should I say Wren Brevard?"

"You should." I smiled up at him happily, wrapping my arms around his back. "You definitely should."

With his thumbs, he brushed the tears from my cheeks and leaned in to press his lips to mine. His hold on me tightened as his breath hitched in his throat.

Circling my arms around his neck, I pressed my lips to his and held him together until the tension eased from his large frame.

"I promise, Max," I murmured against his mouth. "Our story is only beginning."

Epilogue

Five Years Later

Audrey grabbed her bag and shot Max a grin before heading into the cabin. She'd beaten him at backgammon the night before and the cockiness from her hard-won victory hadn't quite worn off yet. Brooklyn, a little slower and officially retired, padded along at her heels.

Aaron's car, a row of tiny stuffed animals lining the back window, sat in the vehicle turn around.

"Kids are here," I murmured.

Max's hand came to my hip as he leaned in, eyes soft. "Brace yourself, beautiful."

I laughed as he picked up my left hand and kissed the double diamond band that embraced his mother's ring. "Happy five years, Tweet."

"Happy five years, Max." I smiled and tipped my chin up to receive his kiss, something that even now, after five years, never failed to thrill me. "I don't know how I'm going to last for five days without my favorite appendage," I murmured. "You make it too hard to be quiet."

His eyes lit up. "You make it hard period."

I laughed. "Juvenile."

He wagged his eyebrows then slanted me a sly look. "I won't let you suffer. It wouldn't be the first time I stuffed your panties in your mouth to keep you quiet."

I dropped my forehead to his chest. That good girl upbringing still brought a flush to my cheeks, but oh, man, was it ever fun to shed it. "That was a good night."

"We've had a lot of good nights."

"Hm," I hummed.

"Bean!" rang out from inside the cabin as Audrey opened the door.

Tipping my head back, I smiled up at him.

Chuckling, he put his arm around my shoulders and tugged me close as we headed for the door.

As soon as I cleared the doorway, Aaron loped over to me, hazel eyes smiling as he wrapped his strong arms around me and lifted me off my feet. "Hey, Momma."

"Hi, baby. How's my beautiful boy?" I murmured, hugging him tight. I squeezed my eyes shut to keep the tears in. In the past two years, his shoulders had broadened, his chest had thickened, and he put on the pounds to fill out his six-foot, two-inch frame.

Five years ago, he was already a man. But now he looked the part. "How's the family?"

He drew back and assessed me then gave me a knowing grin. "We're good, Momma."

With support from me, Max, Kian, and my mother, Aaron continued at school full time and got his Bachelor of Social Work. Going back for an additional year secured his Masters.

"Everyone is good, Momma. Great, actually."

"Did you enjoy your year abroad?"

He shook his head in amazement. "It was incredible. Nadine was incredible. I've never seen anyone work as hard as she did."

Pushing Aaron out of the way, Nadine wedged her way in. "Hey, Wren." Throwing herself into my arms, she squeezed the life out of me.

I laughed out loud. "Well, there's quite a bit more of you than there was last time I saw you," I teased.

She drew back, laughing, as she palmed her stomach. "Three months to go."

"Are you excited?"

She wagged her head back and forth chuckling. "Thalia's keeping me on my toes as it is. I'm grateful she'll be in school when this one comes."

"Have you registered her anywhere?" I prodded.

After finding out she was pregnant, Nadine finished her semester and then took a year off with baby Thalia. At the end of the year, she did an about face and changed her education plan completely. With respect to her parents, she said, "I've already pissed them off, I may as well do what I want", and apprenticed under the chef at Ayana's in nearby Mistlevale.

When she earned the opportunity to study in France, Aaron packed up and went with her. The day he told me they were leaving, he said, "She's waited for her turn, and I'm going to make sure she gets it."

I've never been prouder. Or maybe I have. He's made me beam so many times I've lost track.

Two weeks ago, they came back and had been taking some time at the cabin to decide where they were going to settle. I didn't fool myself into thinking Sage Ridge would be able to offer them both what they needed, but I hoped against hope they would be close, or at least, closer.

I sighed happily as I looked her over. "You look good, sweetheart."

"Thank you, Wren." Her face sobered as she stepped closer. "You know what you mean to me, don't you?"

I smiled, the truth shining in my eyes. "I do. And I love you, too. It's not hard to be there for you."

She smiled widely and squeezed my hands. "Oh!" She startled and grabbed my hand, pressing my palm to her round belly.

I smiled in wonder as the little one rolled beneath the surface. "You going to let me throw another baby shower?"

"As long as Harley helps. She cracks me up."

"She's some kind of wonderful, isn't she?"

"You're some kind of wonderful," she corrected.

I dipped my chin and leveled her with my mom stare. "I know you have news. Are you going to share?"

Leaning in, eyes twinkling, she whispered, "Your mom stare doesn't work on me, remember?"

I snorted out a laugh.

Tipping her head in Audrey's direction, she asked, "Audrey's doing well in school?"

"She is. She's doing well in all her classes, but in photography, she's excelling."

"She definitely has a gift," Nadine murmured. "Want to peek in on Thalia?"

"Is she sleeping?"

"Yes. All this fresh air has her conking out every day after lunch."

We eased the bedroom door open, and Nadine invited me to sit across the bottom of the bed while she took the chair. "She needs to get up soon. We can talk quietly in here so she slowly wakes up. She'll be so happy to see you."

Thalia lay on her side, curled into a ball around Hunter's teddy bear.

After that mammoth closet clean-up, I never put Hunter's bear or my Sage Ridge blanket away again. When Thalia was one, she latched onto Hunter's bear and claimed it for her own.

Audrey helped her name it.

She called him 'Bear.'

Ten minutes later, that precious baby stretched awake. Her bleary eyes blinked open as something akin to panic bloomed across her small face. "I'm right here, Tally," Nadine murmured.

Thalia's eyes sought out her mother for reassurance. When she sat up, she caught sight of my legs and followed them up the length of my body, her sweet squeal of happiness splitting my heart in two.

"G-ma!"

Never hesitating to accept the invitation of an open pair of arms, Thalia launched herself across the bed. Welcomed before she ever made her way into the world, she'd never questioned it since. If I had it my way, she never would.

Sitting in my lap, her little hands went immediately to play with the diamond pendant Max gave me for our second anniversary to match the diamond studs he bought me for our first.

God help me if she asked for it. I could deny her nothing.

Max was worse.

With Thalia's hand in mine, we went back out to the family room. As soon as she spied Max, she ditched me. "Mymax!"

Audrey rolled her eyes at the butchering of Max's name. I swear that girl didn't possess a single, nurturing, cell in her entire body.

But she adored her brother. And by extension, she loved 'Dean' and accepted Thalia who was admittedly quite loud.

"Boomer!" Max cheered while Nadine winced and shook her head.

Aaron laughed at her from across the room. "I told you to be careful with the name if you didn't want nicknames!"

Nadine rolled her pretty eyes.

Aaron continued, "Did you listen? No. You called my baby girl 'explosion.' I simply shortened it to Boomer."

Sitting around the table together after dinner, I could take it no longer. "Aaron Lewis. You said you have news. Tell me right this instant. I can't wait anymore."

Aaron looked at me, his face serious, and rested his folded hands on the table. "We've taken a lot of time, considered every angle, and weighed the pros and cons."

Nadine raised her hand to gently cover his.

I swallowed hard and pressed my lips together, preparing myself to be happy for them, whatever they'd decided.

"It wasn't easy, there are so many pros to being close by, especially taking Kian and Isaiah into consideration."

He sighed, and Nadine's hand tightened over his, her knuckles whitening.

With anxiety?

Chuckling, Aaron wrapped his other hand over hers. "Okay, Dini-baby, I'll cut the shit. We're moving to Sage Ridge."

I sat, unmoving, willing my brain to process what he said. "W-what?"

Nadine laughed.

Aaron's hazel eyes twinkled. "We're moving home to Sage Ridge."

"But...but...where will you work?" Tears sprang to my eyes. Confused and happy, I continued to babble. "Where will Dini work?"

"I'm going into private practice," Aaron's face softened as he nodded to Max. "With Max."

I sobbed. "What?"

Max's warm palm splayed across my back.

I spun to face him, and accused, "You knew?"

Flashing his dimple, he dipped his chin, "This is the first I'm hearing about it."

I rolled my eyes. "Oh my God, Max! You knew how worried I was about this!"

He shook his head. "I made the offer months ago. Aaron asked for time to think about it. Two weeks ago, he asked if the offer was still open. He told me he'd let me know this week. And he asked me not to tell you because he didn't want you to be disappointed if it didn't happen."

"Okay," I whispered, then flew to my feet, my chair flying back, and wagged my finger at Aaron. "You're a menace."

Grinning, he stood and opened his arms as I stumbled into them. "What about Dini?"

"She wants to be here as much as or even more than I do. I've never seen anyone so homesick in my life," he confessed. Grinning at his teary wife, he continued, "It was pathetic."

I tightened my hold on him. "I'm so happy."

Curling his body around mine, he pressed his face into my neck. "Good. I love you, Momma."

I hugged him back, reveling in his beautiful heart. Taking a deep breath, I released him and dropped a firm kiss to the crown of Nadine's head.

Later, curled up on the couch, my entire family filling almost every seat in the house, I watched them as they laughed and joked and played with Thalia, Audrey's dry comments spurring them on further.

My heart swelled with so much happiness I feared it would split clean open and spill out all the love stuffed inside it.

Brooklyn slowly pushed herself up off her bed and made her way over. Stepping up, she heaved her aging body up onto the couch beside me and flopped down, resting her chin in my lap.

Remembering the night I poured my heart out to Brooklyn, I figured she deserved an update. I ran my hand over her silky head.

"I'm so happy, Brooklyn. I'm so happy I could burst."

You did good.

The End.

Did you enjoy Max and Wren's love story? Want to see what went down to help Wren shed that good girl upbringing? Get it right here:
https://tinyurl.com/NoSweeterMadnessBonus
I would love it if you could take a moment to submit a review. Reviews help other readers to find my books. I appreciate you!
www.books2read.com/nosweetermadness

Acknowledgements

I wrote Wren's story from my heart of hearts.

For those of you who are parents, you know parenting stretches you, sometimes beyond your limits. Parenting special needs kids looks your limits in the face and laughs. It opens your heart in ways you can't imagine and draws on strength you never knew you had. Believe me when I tell you, there's nothing special or better about me as a special needs parent than any other parent. I'm just good enough, equally as flawed, and just as devoted. But one thing I struggled with was wanting more for myself, when my children needed so much, and I was missing the mark on a daily basis.

In a virtual world where the portrayal of perfect parenting has reached toxic levels, I've had to remind myself, constantly, that good enough is in fact good enough. I've had to forgive myself when my best meant I failed and validate my need to etch out a bit of space for the me I used to be.

That space is my writing.

I thank you, dear readers, for breathing life into my work. Your love and support mean the world to me.

I would like to thank all my street team members. You are the ones who get me in front of the readers I adore. Thank you from the bottom of my very tender heart. Some of you have stuck with me from the beginning: Amanda, Andrea, April, Ayana, Madeeha, Rachel, Carolann, Crystal, Jenn, Kristen, Michelle, Susie, and Tina. I can't appreciate you enough.

Thank you to my ARC readers. Your feedback is food for my soul and fuels me to keep going. Special mention to Amanda, Andrea, April, Ashley, Ayana, Bianca, Madeeha, Rachel, Carolann, Cheryl, Crystal, Jenn, Kristen, Simone, Michelle, Susie, Terri, and Yvette. Thank you for coming on this wild ride with me! I hope the HEA's have been worth the tears!

I also love our mini-brainstorming sessions! Thank you for coming up with 'Twitchy clit'(AMANDA), 'Bitchy Beaver', 'Cranky Kitty', and 'Crabby Clam', (RACHEL), and 'Blue Bean' (JENN), for the female equivalent of Blue Balls!

I must make special mention of @sionnatrenzauthor, @kelchickbooklover, @bookaddictblog, @jenner_reads, and @crystals_book_blab. Whether by beta reading, assisting, or giving me a loving kick in the pants, I thank you.

And, of course, my Super-Betas: @bookaddictblog and @kelchickbooklover.

Thank you to my kids for loving me and teaching me, sometimes in ways that have been painful for both of us. Raising you has been the privilege of my life, and my greatest, most epic, quest. If you forget everything else I've taught you, remember this: I love you. I've always loved you. I will always love you.

Last, and most, my husband. My Boo, it's been a wild ride. Honest to God, if we laid it all out there, no one would believe us. Our love is the thing of romance novels and family sagas. You are my husband, my muse, my lover, my best friend, the only father I'd ever want for my children, and my biggest fan. I love you with every beat of my heart.

Oh, and honey? I'm going to need some new material.

xo

Also by Devin Sloane

Nothing Truer Than This

About the Author

As a reader and a storyteller, I am irresistibly drawn to more mature characters. Though they often carry the fears, insecurities, and traumas from their younger years, they tend to do so with humor and panache!

They bumble along until life forces them to deal with their brokenness in the midst of parenting, building a career, looking after aging parents, and starting or mending a romantic relationship.

Here is where I write my stories.

Stories where physical intimacy reflects emotional intimacy and healing. Stories of sisterhood that celebrate family and chosen family. Soul-stirring stories that take you on an emotional journey, one where you might easily recognize yourself or someone you love.

As in the real world, there are no easy answers. But their hard-won HEAs will make your heart happy.

At home, I am outnumbered by one husband, four kids, a dog, a cat, and plumbing issues that never quit. You can most often find me curled up on my front porch, earbuds in, music cranked up, with my nose stuck in a book. Honestly, I'm most often hiding from my favorite people in the world who require far too many meals. When I'm really lucky, my husband, who is without a doubt the hero in my very own love story, is hiding with me.

Milton Keynes UK
Ingram Content Group UK Ltd.
UKHW041131030624
443552UK00001B/25

9 798223 806271